Darkness looms.

The Dark Queen's power grows stronger.

Armed with the magical dragon orbs
and the silver dragonlance,
the Companions refuse to surrender.
Betrayal and weakness threaten them all.

But through the darkness, one light
still flickers...

Hope's Flame

CHRONICLES

By Margaret Weis & Tracy Hickman

A Rumor Of Dragons

Night Of The Dragons

The Nightmare Lands

To The Gates Of Palanthas

Hope's Flame

A Dawn of Dragons
(Available March 2004)

CHRONICLES

PART 5

HOPE'S FLAME

MARGARET WEIS & TRACY HICKMAN

COVER ART
Glen Angus

INTERIOR ART
Vinod Rams

HOPE'S FLAME

Cover art by Glen Angus
First Printing: January 2004
Library of Congress Catalog Card Number: 2003111898

9 8 7 6 5 4 3 2 1

US ISBN: 0-7869-3099-3
UK ISBN: 0-7869-3100-0
620-86050-001-EN

U.S., CANADA,
ASIA, PACIFIC, & LATIN AMERICA
Wizards of the Coast, Inc.
P.O. Box 707
Renton, WA 98057-0707
+1-800-324-6496

EUROPEAN HEADQUARTERS
Wizards of the Coast, Belgium
T Hofveld 6d
1702 Groot-Bijgaarden
Belgium
+322 467 3350

Visit our website at **www.wizards.com**

To Angel and Curtis, my children, my hope, and my life
—Tracy Raye Hickman

To the Commons Bridge Group, University of Missouri,
1966-70: Nancy Olson, Bill Fisher, Nancy Burnett,
Ken Randolph, Ed Bristol, Herb the fry cook.
And in memory of Bob Campbell and John Steele,
who died in Vietnam.
And to the rest of that wonderful group of mismatched
friends—this book about friends is fondly dedicated
—Margaret Weis

continent of ansalon

1 palanthas
2 high clerist tower
3 kalaman
4 godshome
5 neraka
6 sanction
7 flotsam
8 solace
9 thorbardin
10 tarsis

northern ergoth
southern ergoth
solamnia
nordmaar
estwilde
khur
new sea
qualinesti
silvanesti
plains of dust
ice wall
blood sea of istar
goodlund
balifor
sirrion sea

TABLE OF CONTENTS

Kitiara, of all the days these days
are rocked in dark and waiting, in regret.
The clouds obscure the city as I write this,
delaying thought and sunlight, as the streets
hang between day and darkness. I have waited
past all decision, past the heart in shadows
to tell you this.

                      In absences you grew
more beautiful, more poisonous, you were
an attar of orchids in the swimming night,
where passion, like a shark drawn down a bloodstream,
murders four senses, only taste preserving,
buckling into itself, finding the blood its own,
a small wound first, but as the shark unravels
the belly tatters in the long throat's tunnel.
And knowing this, the night still seems a richness,
a gauntlet of desires ending in peace,
I would still be part of these allurements,
and to my arms I would take in the darkness,
blessed and renamed by pleasure;
                    but the light,
the light, my Kitiara, when the sun
spangles the rain-gorged sidewalks, and the oil
from doused lamps rises in the sunstruck water,
splintering the light to rainbows! I arise,
and though the storm resettles on the city,
I think of Sturm, Laurana, and the others,
but Sturm the foremost, who can see the sun
straight through the fog and cloudrack. How could I
abandon these?
                And so into the shadow,
and not your shadow but the eager grayness
expecting light, I ride the storm away.

THE EVERMAN

Why, look, Berem. Here's a path.... How strange. All the times we've been hunting in these woods and we've never seen it."

"It's not so strange. The fire burned off some of the brush, that's all. Probably just an animal trail."

"Let's follow it. If it is an animal trail, maybe we'll find a deer. We've been hunting all day with nothing to show for it. I hate to go home empty-handed."

Without waiting for my reply, she turns onto the trail. Shrugging, I follow her. It is pleasant being outdoors today, the first warm day after the bitter chill of winter. The sun is warm on my neck and shoulders. Walking through the fire-ravaged woods is easy. No vines to snag you. No brush to tear at your clothing. Lightning, probably that thunderstorm which struck late last fall.

But we walk for a long time and finally I begin to grow weary. She is wrong—this is no animal trail. It is a man-made path and an old one at that. We're not likely to find any game. Just the same as it's been all day. The fire, then the hard winter: The animals dead or gone. There'll be no fresh meat tonight.

More walking. The sun is high in the sky. I'm tired, hungry. There's been no sign of any living creature.

"Let's turn back, sister. There's nothing here...."

She stops, sighing. She is hot and tired and discouraged, I can tell. And too thin. She works too hard, doing women's work and men's as well. Out hunting when she should be home, receiving the pledges of suitors. She's pretty, I think. People say we look alike, but I know they are wrong. It is only that we are so close—closer than other brothers and their sisters. But we've had to be close. Our life has been so hard. . . .

"I suppose you're right, Berem. I've seen no sign . . . Wait, brother. . . Look ahead. What's that?"

I see a bright and shining glitter, a myriad colors dancing in the sunlight—as if all the jewels on Krynn were heaped together in a basket.

Her eyes widen. "Perhaps it's the gates of the rainbow!"

Ha! Stupid girlish notion. I laugh, but I find myself running forward. It is hard to catch up with her. Though I am bigger and stronger, she is fleet as a deer.

We come to a clearing in the forest. If lightning did strike this forest, this must have been where the bolt hit. The land around is scorched and blasted. There was a building here once, I notice. Ruined, broken columns jut up from the blackened ground like broken bones sticking through decaying flesh. An oppressive feeling hangs over the place. Nothing grows here, nor has anything grown here for many springs. I want to leave, but I cannot. . . .

Before me is the most beautiful, wonderful sight I have ever seen in my life, in my dreams. . . . A piece of a stone column, encrusted with jewels! I know nothing about gemstones, but I can tell these are valuable beyond belief! My body begins to shake. Hurrying forward, I kneel down beside the fire-blasted stone and brush away the dirt and filth.

She kneels beside me.

"Berem! How wonderful! Did you ever see anything like it? Such beautiful jewels in such a horrible place." She looks around and I feel her shivering. "I wonder what this used to be? There's such a solemn feeling about it, a holy feeling. But an evil feeling, too. It must have been a temple before the Cataclysm. A temple to the evil gods . . . Berem! What are you doing?"

I have taken out my hunting knife and I begin to chip away the stone around one of the jewels—a radiant green gemstone. It is as big as my fist and sparkles more brilliantly than the sun shining on green leaves. The rock around it comes away easily beneath my knife blade. "Stop it, Berem!" Her voice is shrill. "It—it's desecration! This place is sacred to some god! I know it!"

I can feel the gemstone's cold crystal, yet it burns with an inner green fire! I ignore her protests.

"Bah! You said before it was the rainbow's gates! You're right! We've found our fortune, as the old story says. If this place was sacred to the gods, they must have abandoned it years ago. Look round, it's nothing but rubble! If they wanted it, they should have taken care of it. The gods won't mind if I take a few of these jewels. . . ."

"Berem!"

An edge of fear in her voice! She's really frightened! Foolish girl. She's beginning to irritate me. The gemstone is almost free. I can wiggle it.

"Look, Jasla." I am shaking with excitement. I can barely talk. "We've nothing to live on, now—what with the fire and the hard winter. These jewels will bring money enough in the market at Gargath for us to move away from this wretched place. We'll go to a city, maybe Palanthas! You know you've wanted to see the wonders there. . . ."

"No! Berem, I forbid it! You are committing sacrilege!"

Her voice is stern. I have never seen her like this! For a moment I hesitate. I draw back, away from the broken stone column with its rainbow of jewels. I, too, am beginning to feel something frightening and evil about this place. But the jewels are so beautiful! Even as I stare at them, they glitter and sparkle in the sunshine. No god is here. No god cares about them. No god will miss them. Embedded in some old column that is crumbling and broken.

I reach down to pry the jewel out of stone with my knife. It is such a rich green, shining as brilliantly as the spring sun shines through the new leaves of the trees. . . .

"Berem! Stop!"

Her hand grasps my arm, her nails dig into my flesh. It hurts . . . I grow angry, and, as sometimes happens when I grow angry a haze

dims my vision and I feel a suffocating swelling inside of me. My head
pounds until it seems my eyes must burst from their sockets.

"Leave me be!" I hear a roaring voice—my own!

I shove her. . .

She falls . . .

It all happens so slowly. She is falling forever. I didn't mean to . . .
I want to catch her. . . But I cannot move.

She falls against the broken column.

Blood . . . blood . . .

"Jas!" I whisper, lifting her in my arms.

But she doesn't answer me. Blood covers the jewels. They don't
sparkle anymore. Just like her eyes. The light is gone. . . .

And then the ground splits apart! Columns rise from the blackened,
blasted soil, spiraling into the air! A great darkness comes forth and I
feel a horrible, burning pain in my chest. . . .

"Berem!"

Maquesta stood on the foredeck, glaring at her helmsman.

"Berem, I told you. A gale's brewing. I want the ship battened
down. What are you doing? Standing there, staring out to sea.
What are you practicing to be—a monument? Get moving, you
lubber! I don't pay good wages to statues!"

Berem started. His face paled and he cringed before Maquesta's irritation in such a pitiful manner that the captain of the
Perechon felt as if she were taking out her anger on a helpless
child.

That's all he is, she reminded herself wearily. Even though
he must be fifty or sixty years old, even though he was one of
the best helmsmen she had ever sailed with, mentally, he was
still a child.

"I'm sorry, Berem," Maq said, sighing. "I didn't mean to yell
at you. It's just the storm . . . it makes me nervous. There, there.
Don't look at me like that. How I wish you could talk! I wish I

knew what was going on in that head of yours—if there is anything! Well, never mind. Attend to your duties, then go below. Better get used to lying in your berth for a few days until the gale blows itself out."

Berem smiled at her—the simple, guileless smile of a child.

Maquesta smiled back, shaking her head. Then she hurried away, her thoughts busy with getting her beloved ship prepared to ride out the gale. Out of the corner of her eye, she saw Berem shuffle below, then promptly forgot about him when her first mate came aboard to report that he had found most of the crew and only about one-third of them were so drunk as to be useless. . . .

Berem lay in the hammock slung in the crew's quarters of the *Perechon*. The hammock swung back and forth violently as the first winds of the gale struck the *Perechon* as it rode at anchor in the harbor of Flotsam on the Blood Sea of Istar. Putting his hands—the hands that looked too young on the body of a fifty-year-old human—beneath his head, Berem stared up at the lamp swinging from the wooden planks above him.

"Why, look, Berem. Here's a path. . . . How strange. All the times we've been hunting in these woods and we've never seen it."

"It's not so strange. The fire burned off some of the brush, that's all. Probably just an animal trail."

"Let's follow it. If it is an animal trail, maybe we'll find a deer. We've been hunting all day with nothing to show for it. I hate to go home empty-handed."

Without waiting for my reply, she turns onto the trail. Shrugging, I follow her. It is pleasant being outdoors today—the first warm day after the bitter chill of winter. The sun is warm on my neck and shoulders. Walking through the fire-ravaged woods is easy. No vines to snag you. No brush to tear at your clothing. Lightning, probably that thunderstorm which struck late last fall. . . .

Flight from Darkness into Darkness.

1

The dragonarmy officer slowly descended the stairs from the second floor of the Saltbreeze Inn. It was past midnight. Most of the inn's patrons had long since gone to bed. The only sound the officer could hear was the crashing of waves of Blood Bay on the rocks below.

The officer paused a moment on the landing, casting a quick, sharp glance around the common room that lay spread out below him. It was empty, except for a draconian sprawled across a table, snoring loudly in a drunken stupor. The dragonman's wings shivered with each snort. The wooden table creaked and swayed beneath it.

The officer smiled bitterly, then continued down the stairs. He was dressed in the steel dragonscale armor copied from the real dragonscale armor of the Dragon Highlords. His helm covered his head and face, making it difficult to see his features. All that was visible beneath the shadow cast by the helm was a reddish brown beard that marked him—racially—as human.

At the bottom of the stairs, the officer came to a sudden halt, apparently nonplussed at the sight of the innkeeper, still awake and yawning over his account books. After a slight nod the dragon officer seemed about to go on out of the inn without speaking, but the innkeeper stopped him with a question.

"You expecting the Highlord tonight?"

The officer halted and half turned. Keeping his face averted, he pulled out a pair of gloves and began putting them on. The weather was bitterly chill. The sea city of Flotsam was in the grip of a winter storm the like of which it had not experienced in its three hundred years of existence on the shores of Blood Bay.

"In this weather?" The dragonarmy officer snorted. "Not likely! Not even dragons can outfly these gale winds!"

"True. It's not a fit night out for man or beast," the innkeeper agreed. He eyed the dragon officer shrewdly. "What business do you have, then, that takes you out in this storm?"

The dragonarmy officer regarded the innkeeper coldly. "I don't see that it's any of your business where I go or what I do."

"No offense," the innkeeper said quickly, raising his hands as if to ward off a blow. "It's just that if the Highlord comes back and happens to miss you, I'd be glad to tell her where you could be found."

"That won't be necessary," the officer muttered. "I—I've left her a—note . . . explaining my absence. Besides, I'll be back before morning. I—I just need a breath of air. That's all."

"I don't doubt that!" The innkeeper sniggered. "You haven't left her room for four days! Or should I say four nights! Now, don't get mad"—this on seeing the officer flush angrily beneath the helm, "I admire the man can keep *her* entertained that long! Where was she bound for?"

"The Highlord was called to deal with a problem in the west, somewhere near Solamnia," the officer replied, scowling. "I wouldn't inquire any further into her affairs if I were you."

"No, no," replied the innkeeper hastily. "Certainly not. Well, I bid you good evening. What was your name? She introduced us, but I failed to catch it."

"Tanis," the officer said, his voice muffled. "Tanis Half-Elven. And a good evening to you."

Nodding coldly, the officer gave his gloves a final sharp tug, then, pulling his cloak around him, he opened the door to the inn and stepped out into the storm. The bitter wind swept into the room, blowing out candles and swirling the innkeeper's papers around. For a moment, the officer struggled with the heavy door while the innkeeper cursed fluently and grabbed for his scattered accounts. Finally the officer succeeded in slamming the door shut behind him, leaving the inn peaceful, quiet, and warm once more.

Staring out after him, the innkeeper saw the officer walk past the front window, his head bent down against the wind, his cloak billowing out behind him.

One other figure watched the officer as well. The instant the door shut, the drunken draconian raised its head, its black, reptilian eyes glittering. Stealthily it rose from the table, its steps quick and certain. Padding lightly on its clawed feet, it crept to the window and peered outside. For a few moments, the draconian waited, then it too flung open the door and disappeared into the storm.

Through the window, the innkeeper saw the draconian head in the same direction as the dragonarmy officer. Walking over, the innkeeper peered out through the glass. It was wild and dark outside, the tall iron braziers of flaming pitch that lit the night streets sputtering and flickering in the wind and the driving rain. But the innkeeper thought he saw the dragonarmy officer turn down a street leading to the main part of town. Creeping along behind him, keeping to the shadows, came the draconian.

Shaking his head, the innkeeper woke the night clerk, who was dozing in a chair behind the desk. "I've a feeling the Highlord will be in tonight, storm or no storm," the innkeeper told the sleepy clerk. "Wake me if she comes."

Shivering, he glanced outside into the night once more, seeing in his mind's eye the dragonarmy officer walking the empty streets of Flotsam, the shadowy figure of the draconian slinking after him.

"On second thought," the innkeeper muttered, "let me sleep."

The storm shut down Flotsam tonight. The bars that normally stayed open until the dawn straggled through their grimy windows were locked up and shuttered against the gale. The streets were deserted, no one venturing out into the winds that could knock a man down and pierce even the warmest clothing with biting cold.

Tanis walked swiftly, his head bowed, keeping near the darkened buildings that broke the full force of the gale. His beard was soon rimed with ice. Sleet stung his face painfully. The half-elf shook with the cold, cursing the dragonarmor's cold metal against his skin. Glancing behind him occasionally, he watched to see if anyone had taken an unusual interest in his leaving the inn. But the visibility was reduced to almost nothing. Sleet and rain swirled around him so that he could barely see tall buildings looming up in the darkness, much less anything else. After a while, he realized he had better concentrate on finding his way through town. Soon he was so numb with cold that he didn't much care if anyone was following him or not.

He hadn't been in the town of Flotsam long—only four days to be precise. And most of those days had been spent with her.

Tanis blocked the thought from his mind as he stared through the rain at the street signs. He knew only vaguely where he was going. His friends were in an inn somewhere on the edge of town, away from the wharf, away from the bars and brothels. For a moment he wondered in despair what he would do if he got lost. He dared not ask about them. . . .

And then he found it. Stumbling through the deserted streets, slipping on the ice, he almost sobbed in relief when he saw the sign swinging wildly in the wind. He hadn't even been able to remember the name, but now he recognized it—the Jetties.

Stupid name for an inn, he thought, shaking so with the cold he could barely grasp the door handle. Pulling the door open, he was blown inside by the force of the wind, and it was with an effort that he managed to shove the door shut behind him.

There was no night clerk on duty, not at this shabby place. By the light of a smoking fire in the filthy grate, Tanis saw a stub of a candle sitting on the desk, apparently for the convenience of guests who staggered in after hours. His hands shook so he could barely strike the flint. After a moment he forced his cold-stiffened fingers to work, lit the candle, and made his way upstairs by its feeble light.

If he had turned around and glanced out the window, he would have seen a shadowy figure huddle in a doorway across the street. But Tanis did not look out the window behind him, his eyes were on the stairs.

"Caramon!"

The big warrior instantly sat bolt upright, his hand reaching reflexively for his sword, even before he turned to look questioningly at his brother.

"I heard a noise outside," Raistlin whispered. "The sound of a scabbard clanking against armor."

Caramon shook his head, trying to clear the sleep away, and climbed out of bed, sword in hand. He crept toward the door until he, too, could hear the noise that had wakened his light-sleeping brother. A man dressed in armor was walking stealthily down the hall outside their rooms. Then Caramon could see the faint glow of candlelight beneath the door. The sound of clanking armor came to a halt, right outside their room.

Gripping his sword, Caramon motioned to his brother. Raistlin nodded and melted back into the shadows. His eyes were abstracted. He was calling to mind a magic spell. The twin brothers worked well together, effectively combining magic and steel to defeat their foes.

The candlelight beneath the door wavered. The man must be shifting the candle to his other hand, freeing his sword hand. Reaching out, Caramon slowly and silently slid the bolt on the door. He waited a moment. Nothing happened. The man was hesitating, perhaps wondering if this was the right room. He'll find out soon enough, Caramon thought to himself.

Caramon flung open the door with a sudden jerk. Lunging around it, he grasped hold of the dark figure and dragged him inside. With all the strength of his brawny arms, the warrior flung the armor-clad man to the floor. The candle dropped, its flame extinguishing in melted wax. Raistlin began to chant a magic spell that would entrap their victim in a sticky web-like substance.

"Hold! Raistlin, stop!" the man shouted. Recognizing the voice, Caramon grabbed hold of his brother, shaking him to break the concentration of his spellcasting.

"Raist! It's Tanis!"

Shuddering, Raistlin came out of his trance, arms dropped limply to his sides. Then he began to cough, clutching his chest.

Caramon cast an anxious glance at his twin, but Raistlin warded him away with a wave of the hand. Turning, Caramon reached down to help the half-elf to his feet.

"Tanis!" he cried, nearly squeezing the breath out of him with an enthusiastic embrace. "Where have you been? We were sick with worry. By all the gods, you're freezing! Here, I'll poke up the fire. Raist"—Caramon turned to his brother—"are you sure you're all right?"

"Don't concern yourself with me!" Raistlin whispered. The mage sank back down on his bed, gasping for breath. His eyes glittered gold in the flaring firelight as he stared at the half-elf, who huddled thankfully beside the blaze. "You'd better get the others."

"Right." Caramon started out the door.

"I'd put some clothes on first," Raistlin remarked caustically.

Blushing, Caramon hurried back to his bed and grabbed a pair of leather breeches. Pulling these on, he slipped a shirt over his head, then went out into the hallway, softly closing the door behind him. Tanis and Raistlin could hear him knocking gently on the Plainsmen's door. They could hear Riverwind's stern reply and Caramon's hurried, excited explanation.

Tanis glanced at Raistlin, saw the mage's strange hourglass eyes focused on him with a piercing stare, and turned uncomfortably back to gaze into the fire.

"Where *have* you been, Half-Elf?" Raistlin asked in his soft, whispering voice.

Tanis swallowed nervously. "I was captured by a Dragon Highlord," he said, reciting the answer he had prepared. "The Highlord thought I was one of his officers, naturally, and asked me to escort him to his troops, who are stationed outside of town. Of course, I had to do as he asked or make him suspicious. Finally, tonight, I was able to get away."

"Interesting." Raistlin coughed the word.

Tanis glanced at him sharply. "What's interesting?"

"I've never heard you lie before, Half-Elf," Raistlin said softly. "I find it . . . quite . . . fascinating."

Tanis opened his mouth, but, before he could reply, Caramon returned, followed by Riverwind and Goldmoon and Tika, yawning sleepily.

Hurrying to him, Goldmoon embraced Tanis swiftly. "My friend!" she said brokenly, holding onto him tightly. "We've been so worried—"

Riverwind clasped Tanis by the hand, his usually stern face relaxed in a smile. Gently he took hold of his wife and removed her from Tanis's embrace, but it was only to take her place.

"My brother!" Riverwind said in Que-shu, the dialect of the Plains people, hugging the half-elf tightly. "We feared you were captured! Dead! We didn't know—"

"What happened? Where were you?" Tika asked eagerly, coming forward to hug Tanis.

Tanis looked over at Raistlin, but he was lying back on his hard pillow, his strange eyes fixed on the ceiling, seemingly uninterested in anything being said.

Clearing his throat self-consciously, intensely aware of Raistlin listening, Tanis repeated his story. The others followed it with expressions of interest and sympathy. Occasionally they asked questions. Who was this Highlord? How big was the army? Where was it located? What were the draconians doing in Flotsam? Were they really searching for them? How had Tanis escaped?

Tanis answered all their questions glibly. As for the Highlord, he hadn't seen much of him. He didn't know who he was. The army was not large. It was located outside of town. The draconians were searching for someone, but it was not them. They were looking for a human named Berem or something strange like that.

At this Tanis shot a quick look at Caramon, but the big man's face registered no recognition. Tanis breathed easier. Good, Caramon didn't remember the man they had seen patching the sail on the *Perechon*. He didn't remember or he hadn't caught the man's name. Either way was fine.

The others nodded, absorbed in his story. Tanis sighed in relief. As for Raistlin . . . well, it didn't really matter what the mage thought or said. The others would believe Tanis over Raistlin even if the half-elf claimed day was night. Undoubtedly Raistlin knew this, which was why he didn't cast any doubts on Tanis's story. Feeling wretched, hoping no one would ask him anything else and force him to mire himself deeper and deeper in lies, Tanis yawned and groaned as if exhausted past endurance.

Goldmoon immediately rose to her feet, her face soft with concern. "I'm sorry, Tanis," she said gently. "We've been selfish.

You are cold and weary and we've kept you up talking. And we must be up early in the morning to board the ship."

"Goldmoon, don't be a fool! We won't board any ship in this gale!" Tanis snarled.

Everyone stared at him in astonishment, even Raistlin sat up. Goldmoon's eyes were dark with pain, her face set in rigid lines, reminding the half-elf that no one spoke to her in that tone. Riverwind stood beside her, a troubled look on his face.

The silence grew uncomfortable. Finally Caramon cleared his throat with a rumble. "If we can't leave tomorrow, we'll try the next day," he said comfortably. "Don't worry about it, Tanis. The draconians won't be out in this weather. We're safe—"

"I know. I'm sorry," he muttered. "I didn't mean to snap at you, Goldmoon. It's been—nerve-racking these last few days. I'm so tired I can't think straight. I'll go to my room."

"The innkeeper gave it to someone else," Caramon said, then added hurriedly, "but you can sleep here, Tanis. Take my bed—"

"No, I'll just lie down on the floor." Avoiding Goldmoon's gaze, Tanis began unbuckling the dragonarmor, his eyes fixed firmly on his shaking fingers.

"Sleep well, my friend," Goldmoon said softly.

Hearing the concern in her voice, he could imagine her exchanging compassionate glances with Riverwind. There was the Plainsman's hand on his shoulder, giving him a sympathetic pat. Then they were gone. Tika left, too, closing the door behind her after a murmured goodnight.

"Here, let me help you," Caramon offered, knowing that Tanis, unaccustomed to wearing plate armor, found the intricate buckles and straps difficult to manage. "Can I get you something to eat? Drink? Some mulled wine?"

"No," Tanis said wearily, divesting himself thankfully of the armor, trying not to remember that in a few hours he would have to put it on again. "I just need sleep."

"Here—at least take my blanket," Caramon insisted, seeing that the half-elf was shivering with the cold.

Tanis accepted the blanket gratefully, although he was not certain whether he was shaking with the chill or the violence of his turbulent emotions. Lying down, he wrapped himself in both the blanket and his cloak. Then he closed his eyes and concentrated on making his breathing even and regular, knowing that the mother-hen, Caramon, would never sleep until he was certain Tanis was resting comfortably. Soon he heard Caramon get into bed. The fire burned low, darkness fell. After a moment, he heard Caramon's rumbling snore. In the other bed, he could hear Raistlin's fitful cough.

When he was certain both the twins were asleep, Tanis stretched out, putting his hands beneath his head. He lay awake, staring into the darkness.

It was near morning when the Dragon Highlord arrived back at the Saltbreeze Inn. The night clerk could see immediately that the Highlord was in a foul temper. Flinging open the door with more force than the gale winds, she glared angrily into the inn, as if its warmth and comfort were offensive. Indeed, she seemed to be at one with the storm outside. It was she who caused the candles to flicker, rather than the howling wind. It was she who brought the darkness indoors. The clerk stumbled fearfully to his feet, but the Highlord's eyes were not on him. Kitiara was staring at a draconian, who sat at a table and who signaled, by an almost imperceptible flicker in the dark reptilian eyes, that something was awry.

Behind the hideous dragonmask, the Highlord's eyes narrowed alarmingly, their expression grew cold. For a moment she stood in the doorway, ignoring the chill wind that blew through the inn, whipping her cloak around her.

"Come upstairs," she said finally, ungraciously, to the draconian.

The creature nodded and followed after her, its clawed feet clicking on the wooden floors.

"Is there anything—" the night clerk began, cringing as the door blew shut with a shattering crash.

"No!" Kitiara snarled. Hand on the hilt of her sword, she stalked past the quivering man without a glance and climbed the stairs to her suite of rooms, leaving the man to sink back, shaken, into his chair.

Fumbling with her key, Kitiara threw open the door. She gave the room a quick sweeping glance.

It was empty.

The draconian waited behind her, standing patiently and in silence.

Furious, Kitiara tugged viciously at the hinges on the dragonmask and yanked it off. Tossing it on the bed, she spoke over her shoulder.

"Come inside and shut the door!"

The draconian did as it was commanded, closing the door softly.

Kitiara did not turn to face the creature. Hands on her hips, she stared grimly at the rumpled bed.

"So, he's gone." It was a statement, not a question.

"Yes, Highlord," lisped the draconian in its hissing voice.

"You followed him, as I ordered?"

"Of course, Highlord." The draconian bowed.

"Where did he go?"

Kitiara ran a hand through her dark, curly hair. She still had not turned around. The draconian could not see her face and he had no idea what emotions, if any, she was keeping hidden.

"An inn, Highlord. Near the edge of town. Called the Jetties."

"Another woman?" The Highlord's voice was tense.

"I think not, Highlord." The draconian concealed a smile. "I believe he has friends there. We had reports of strangers staying in the inn, but since they did not match the description of the Green Gemstone Man, we did not investigate them."

"Someone is there now, watching him?"

"Certainly, Highlord. You will be informed immediately if he—or any inside—leaves the building."

The Highlord stood in silence for a moment, then she turned around. Her face was cold and calm, although extremely pale. But there were a number of factors which could have accounted for her pallor, the draconian thought. It was a long flight from the High Clerist's Tower, rumor had it her armies had been badly defeated there, the legendary Dragon-lance had reappeared, along with the dragon orbs. Then there was her failure to find the Green Gemstone Man, so desperately sought by the Queen of Darkness, and who was reported to have been seen in Flotsam. The Highlord had a great many things to worry about, the draconian thought with amusement. Why concern herself over one man? She had suitors aplenty, most of them much more charming, much more eager to please than that moody half-elf. Bakaris, for example . . .

"You have done well," Kitiara said finally, breaking in on the draconian's musings. Stripping off her armor with a careless lack of modesty, she waved a negligent hand. She almost seemed herself again. "You will be rewarded. Now leave me."

The draconian bowed again and left, eyes staring at the floor. The creature was not fooled. As it left, the dragonman saw the Highlord's gaze fall upon a scrap of parchment resting on the table. The draconian had seen that parchment upon entering. It was, the creature noted, covered with writing in a delicate elvish script. As the draconian shut the door, there came a crashing sound, the sound of a piece of dragonarmor being hurled full force against a wall.

PURSUIT.

2

The gale blew itself out toward morning. The sound of water dripping monotonously from the eaves thudded in Tanis's aching head, almost making him wish for a return of the shrieking wind. The sky was gray and lowering. Its leaden weight pressed down upon the half-elf.

"The seas will be running high," Caramon said sagely. Having listened eagerly to the sea stories told them by William, the innkeeper of the Pig and Whistle in Port Balifor, Caramon considered himself somewhat of an expert on nautical matters. None of the others disputed him, knowing nothing about the sea themselves. Only Raistlin regarded Caramon with a sneering smile when his brother, who had been on small boats only a few times in his life, began talking like an old seadog.

"Maybe we shouldn't even risk going out—" Tika began.

"We're going. Today," Tanis said grimly. "If we have to swim, we're leaving Flotsam."

The others glanced at each other, then looked back at Tanis. Standing, staring out the window, he did not see their raised eyebrows or their shrugging shoulders, though he was aware of them all the same.

The companions were gathered in the brothers' room. It would not be dawn for another hour, but Tanis had awakened them as soon as he heard the wind cease its savage howl.

He drew a deep breath, then turned to face them. "I'm sorry. I know I sound arbitrary," he said, "but there are dangers I know about that I can't explain right now. There isn't time. All I can tell you is this—we have never in our lives been in more dire peril than we are at this moment in this town. We must leave and we must leave now!" He heard an hysterical note creep into his voice and broke off.

There was silence, then, "Sure, Tanis," Caramon said uneasily.

"We're all packed," Goldmoon added. "We can leave whenever you're ready."

"Let's go then," Tanis said.

"I've got to get my things," Tika faltered.

"Go on. Be quick," Tanis told her.

"I—I'll help her," Caramon offered in a low voice.

The big man, dressed, like Tanis, in the stolen armor of a dragon-army officer, and Tika left quickly, probably hoping to snatch time enough for a last few minutes alone, Tanis thought, fuming in impatience. Goldmoon and Riverwind left to gather their things as well. Raistlin remained in the room, not moving. He had all he needed to carry with him—his pouches with his precious spell components, the Staff of Magius, and the precious marble of the dragon orb, tucked away inside its nondescript bag.

Tanis could feel Raistlin's strange eyes boring into him. It was as if Raistlin could penetrate the darkness of the half-elf's soul with the glittering light from those golden eyes. But still the mage said nothing. Why? Tanis thought angrily. He would almost have welcomed Raistlin's questioning, his accusations. He would almost welcome a chance to unburden himself and tell the truth, even though he knew what consequences would result.

But Raistlin was silent, except for his incessant cough.

Within a few minutes, the others came back inside the room.

"We're ready, Tanis," Goldmoon said in a subdued voice.

For a moment, Tanis couldn't speak. I'll tell them, he resolved. Taking a deep breath, he turned around. He saw their faces, he saw trust; a belief in him. They were following him without question. He couldn't let them down. He couldn't shake this faith. It was all they had to cling to. Sighing, he swallowed the words he had been about to speak.

"Right," he said gruffly and started toward the door.

Maquesta Kar-Thon was awakened from a sound sleep by a banging on her cabin door. Accustomed to having her sleep interrupted at all hours, she was almost immediately awake and reaching for her boots.

"What is it?" she called out.

Before the answer came, she was already getting the feel of the ship, assessing the situation. A glance through the porthole showed her the gale winds had died, but she could tell from the motion of the ship itself that the seas were running high.

"The passengers are here," called out a voice she recognized as that of her first mate.

Landlubbers, she thought bitterly, sighing and dropping the boot she had been dragging on.

"Send 'em back," she ordered, lying down again. "We're not sailing today."

There seemed to be some sort of altercation going on outside, for she heard her first mate's voice raised in anger and another voice shouting back. Wearily Maquesta struggled to her feet. Her first mate, Bas Ohn-Koraf, was a minotaur, a race not noted for its easy-going temper. He was exceptionally strong and was known to kill without provocation—one reason he had taken to the sea. On a ship like the *Perechon,* no one asked questions about the past.

Throwing open the door to her cabin, Maq hurried up onto deck.

"What's going on?" she demanded in her sternest voice as her eyes went from the bestial head of her first mate to the bearded face of what appeared to be a dragonarmy officer. But she recognized the slightly slanted brown eyes of the bearded man and fixed him with a cold stare. "I said we're not sailing today, Half-Elf, and I meant—"

"Maquesta," Tanis said quickly, "I've got to talk to you!" He started to push his way past the minotaur to reach her, but Koraf grabbed hold of him and yanked him backward. Behind Tanis, a larger dragonarmy officer growled and took a step forward. The minotaur's eyes glistened eagerly as he deftly slipped a dirk from the wide, bright-colored sash around his waist.

The crew above decks gathered around immediately, hoping for a fight.

"Caramon—" Tanis warned, holding out his hand restrainingly.

"Kof—!" Maquesta snapped with an angry look meant to remind her first mate that these were paying customers and were not to be handled roughly, at least while in sight of land.

The minotaur scowled, but the dirk disappeared as quickly as it had flashed into the open. Koraf turned and walked away disdainfully, the crew muttering in disappointment, but still cheerful. It promised already to be an interesting voyage.

Maquesta helped Tanis to his feet, studying the half-elf with the same intense scrutiny she fixed on a man wanting to sign on as a crew member. She saw at once that the half-elf had changed drastically since she had seen him only four days before, when he and the big man behind him closed the bargain for passage aboard the *Perechon.*

He looks like he's been through the Abyss and back. Probably in some sort of trouble, she decided ruefully. Well, I'm not getting him out of it! Not at the risk of my ship. Still, he and his friends had paid for half their passage. And she needed the money. It was hard these days for a pirate to compete with the Highlords. . . .

"Come to my cabin," Maq said ungraciously, leading the way below.

"Stay with the others, Caramon," the half-elf told his companion. The big man nodded. Glancing darkly at the minotaur, Caramon went back over to stand with the rest of the companions, who stood silently, huddled around their meager belongings.

Tanis followed Maq down to her cabin and squeezed inside. Even two people in the small cabin were a tight fit. The *Perechon* was a trim vessel, designed for swift sailing and quick maneuvers. Ideal for Maquesta's trade, for which it was necessary to slip in and out of harbors quickly, unloading or picking up cargo that wasn't necessarily hers either to pick up or deliver. On occasion, she might enhance her income by catching a fat merchant ship sailing out of Palanthas or Tarsis and slip up on it before it knew what was happening. Then board it quickly, loot it, and make good her escape.

She was adept at outrunning the massive ships of the Dragon Highlords, too, although she made it a point to leave them strictly alone. Too often now, though, the Highlords' ships were seen "escorting" the merchant vessels. Maquesta had lost money on her last two voyages, one reason why she had deigned to carry passengers—something she would never do under normal circumstances.

Removing his helm, the half-elf sat down at the table, or rather fell down, since he was unaccustomed to the motion of the rocking ship. Maquesta remained standing, balancing easily.

"Well, what is it you want?" she demanded, yawning. "I told you we can't sail. The seas are—"

"We have to," Tanis said abruptly.

"Look," Maquesta said patiently (reminding herself he was a paying customer), "if you're in some kind of trouble, it's not my concern! I'm not risking my ship or my crew—"

"Not me," Tanis interrupted, looking at Maquesta intently, "you."

"Me?" Maquesta said, drawing back, amazed.

Tanis folded his hands on the table and gazed down at them. The pitching and tossing of the vessel at anchor, combined with his exhaustion from the past few days, made him nauseous. Seeing the faint green tinge of his skin beneath his beard and the dark shadows under his hollow eyes, Maquesta thought she'd seen corpses that looked better than this half-elf.

"What do you mean?" she asked tightly.

"I—I was captured by a Dragon Highlord . . . three days ago," Tanis began, speaking in a low voice, staring at his hands. "No, I guess 'captured' is the wrong word. H-He saw me dressed like this and assumed I was one of his men. I had to accompany h-him back to his camp. I've been there, in camp, the last few days, and I—I found out something. I know why the Highlord and the draconians are searching Flotsam. I know what—who—they're looking for."

"Yes?" Maquesta prompted, feeling his fear creep over her like a contagious disease. "Not the *Perechon*—"

"Your helmsman." Tanis finally looked up at her. "Berem."

"Berem!" Maquesta repeated, stunned. "What for? The man's a mute! A half-wit! A good helmsman, maybe, but nothing more. What could he have done that the Dragon Highlords are looking for him?"

"I don't know," Tanis said wearily, fighting his nausea. "I wasn't able to find out. I'm not sure they know! But they're under orders to find him at all costs and bring him alive to"—

he closed his eyes to shut out the swaying lamps—"the Dark Queen. . . ."

The breaking light of dawn threw slanted red beams across the sea's rough surface. For an instant it shone on Maq's glistening black skin, a flash like fire came from her golden earrings that dangled nearly to her shoulders. Nervously she ran her fingers through her closely cropped black hair.

Maquesta felt her throat close. "We'll get rid of him!" she muttered tightly, pushing herself up from the table. "We'll put him ashore. I can find another helmsman—"

"Listen!" Catching hold of Maquesta's arm, Tanis gripped her tightly, forcing her to stop. "They may already know he's here! Even if they don't and they catch him, it won't make any difference. Once they find out he was here, on this vessel, and they *will* find out, believe me; there are ways of making even a mute talk—they'll arrest you and everyone on this ship. Arrest you or get rid of you."

He dropped his hand from her arm, realizing he hadn't the strength to hold her. "It's what they've done in the past. I know. The Highlord told me. Whole villages destroyed. People tortured, murdered. Anyone this man comes in contact with is doomed. They fear whatever deadly secret he carries will be passed on, and they can't allow that."

Maquesta sat down. "Berem?" she whispered softly, unbelievingly.

"They couldn't do anything because of the storm," Tanis said wearily, "and the Highlord was called away to Solamnia, some battle there. But sh—the Highlord will be back today. And then," He couldn't go on. His head sank into his hands as a shudder racked his body.

Maquesta eyed him warily. Could this be true? Or was he making all this up to force her to take him away from some danger? Watching him slump miserably over the table, Maquesta swore softly. The ship's captain was a shrewd judge of men. She needed to be, in order to control her rough-and-ready crew. And she knew the half-elf wasn't lying. At least, not much. She suspected there were things he wasn't telling, but this story about Berem, as strange as it seemed, had the ring of truth.

It all made sense, she thought uneasily, cursing herself. She prided herself on her judgment, her good sense. Yet she had turned a blind eye to Berem's strangeness. Why? Her lip curled in derision. She liked him—admit it. He was like a child, cheerful, guileless. And so she had overlooked his unwillingness to go ashore, his fear of strangers, his eagerness to work for a pirate when he refused to share in the loot they captured. Maquesta sat a moment, getting the feel of her ship. Glancing outside, she watched the golden sun glint off the white caps, then the sun vanished, swallowed by the lowering gray clouds. It would be dangerous, taking the ship out, but if the wind was right . . .

"I'd rather be out on the open sea," she murmured, more to herself than to Tanis, "than trapped like a rat on shore."

Making up her mind, Maq rose quickly and started for the door. Then she heard Tanis groan. Turning around, she regarded him pityingly.

"Come on, Half-Elf," Maquesta said, not unkindly. She put her arms around him and helped him stand. "You'll feel better above deck in the fresh air. Besides, you'll need to tell your friends that this isn't going to be what you might call a 'relaxing ocean voyage.' Do you know the risk you're taking?"

Tanis nodded. Leaning heavily on Maquesta, he walked across the heaving deck.

"You're not telling me everything, that's for certain," Maquesta said under her breath as she kicked open the cabin door and helped Tanis struggle up the stairs to the main deck. "I'll wager Berem's not the only one the Highlord's looking for. But I have a feeling this isn't the first bad weather you and your crew have ridden out. I just hope your luck holds!"

The Perechon wallowed in the high seas. Riding under short sail, the ship seemed to make little headway, fighting for every inch it gained. Fortunately, the wind backed. Blowing steadily from the southwest, it was taking them straight into the Blood Sea of Istar. Since they were heading for Kalaman, northwest of Flotsam, around the cape of Nordmaar, this was a little out of their way. But Maquesta didn't mind. She wanted to avoid land as much as possible.

There was even the possibility, she told Tanis, that they could sail northeast and arrive in Mithras, homeland of the minotaurs. Although a few minotaurs fought in the armies of the Highlords, the minotaurs in general had not yet sworn allegiance to the Dark Queen. According to Koraf, the minotaurs wanted control of eastern Ansalon in return for their services. And control of the east had just been handed over to a new Dragon Highlord, a hobgoblin called Toede. The minotaurs had no love for humans or elves, but, at this point in time, neither had they any use for the Highlords. Maq and her crew had sheltered in Mithras before. They would be safe there again, at least for a little while.

Tanis was not happy at this delay, but his fate was no longer in his hands. Thinking of this, the half-elf glanced over at the man who stood alone at the center of a whirlwind of blood and flame. Berem was at the helm, guiding the wheel with firm, sure hands, his vacant face unconcerned, unworried.

Tanis, staring hard at the helmsman's shirt front, thought perhaps he could detect a faint glimmer of green. What dark secret beat in the chest where, months ago at Pax Tharkas, he had seen the green glowing jewel embedded in the man's flesh? Why were hundreds of draconians wasting their time, searching for this one man when the war still hung in balance? Why was Kitiara so desperate to find Berem that she had given up command of her forces in Solamnia to supervise the search of Flotsam on just a rumor that he had been seen there?

"He is the key!" Tanis remembered Kitiara's words. "If we capture him, Krynn will fall to the might of the Dark Queen. There will be no force in the land able to defeat us then!"

Shivering, his stomach heaving, Tanis stared at the man in awe. Berem seemed so, so apart from everything, beyond everything, as if the problems of the world affected him not at all. Was he half-witted, as Maquesta said? Tanis wondered. He remembered Berem as he had seen him for those few brief seconds in the midst of the horror of Pax Tharkas. He remembered the look on the man's face as he allowed the traitor Eben to lead him away in a desperate attempt to escape. The look on his face had not been fearful or dull or uncaring. It had been, what? Resigned! That was it! As if he knew the fate that awaited him and went ahead anyway. Sure enough, just as Berem and Eben reached the gates, hundreds of tons of rocks had cascaded down from the gate-blocking mechanism, burying them beneath boulders it would take a dragon to lift. Both bodies were lost, of course.

Or at least Eben's body was lost. Only weeks later, during the celebration of the wedding of Goldmoon and Riverwind, Tanis and Sturm had seen Berem again—alive! Before they could catch him, the man had vanished into the crowd. And they had not seen him again. Not until Tanis found him three, no, four, days ago, calmly sewing a sail on this ship.

Berem steered the ship on its course, his face filled with peace. Tanis leaned over the ship's side and retched.

Maquesta said nothing to the crew about Berem. In explanation of their sudden departure, she said only that she had received word that the Dragon Highlord was a bit too interested in their ship, it would be wise to head for the open seas. None of the crew questioned her. They had no love for the Highlords, and most had been in Flotsam long enough to lose all their money anyway.

Nor did Tanis reveal to his friends the reason for their haste. The companions had all heard the story of the man with the green gemstone and, though they were too polite to say so (with the exception of Caramon), Tanis knew they thought he and Sturm had drunk one too many toasts at the wedding. They did not ask for reasons why they were risking their lives in the rough seas. Their faith in him was complete.

Suffering from bouts of seasickness and torn by gnawing guilt, Tanis hunched miserably upon the deck, staring out to sea. Goldmoon's healing powers had helped him recover somewhat, though there was apparently little even clerics could do for the turmoil in his stomach. But the turmoil in his soul was beyond her help.

He sat upon the deck, staring out to sea, fearing always to see the sails of a ship on the horizon. The others, perhaps because they were better rested, were little affected by the erratic motion of the ship as it swooped through the choppy water, except that all were wet to the skin from an occasional high wave breaking over the side.

Even Raistlin, Caramon was astonished to see, appeared quite comfortable. The mage sat apart from the others, crouched beneath a sail one of the sailors had rigged to help keep the passengers as dry as possible. The mage was not sick. He did not even cough much. He just seemed lost in thought, his golden eyes glittering brighter than the morning sun that flickered in and out of view behind the racing storm clouds.

Maquesta shrugged when Tanis mentioned his fears of pursuit. The *Perechon* was faster than the Highlords' massive ships. They'd been able to sneak out of the harbor safely, the only other ships aware of their going were pirate ships like themselves. In that brotherhood, no one asked questions.

The seas grew calmer, flattening out beneath the steady breeze. All day, the storm clouds lowered threateningly, only to be finally blown to shreds by the freshening wind. The night was clear and starlit. Maquesta was able to add more sail. The ship flew over the water. By morning, the companions awakened to one of the most dreadful sights in all of Krynn.

They were on the outer edge of the Blood Sea of Istar.

The sun was a huge, golden ball balanced upon the eastern horizon when the *Perechon* first sailed into the water that was red as the robes the mage wore, red as the blood that flecked his lips when he coughed.

"It is well-named," Tanis said to Riverwind as they stood on deck, staring out into the red, murky water. They could not see far ahead. A perpetual storm hung from the sky, shrouding the water in a curtain of leaden gray.

"I did not believe it," Riverwind said solemnly, shaking his head. "I heard William tell of it and I listened as I listened to his tales of sea dragons that swallow ships and women with the tails of fish instead of legs. But this—" The barbarian Plainsman shook his head, eyeing the blood-colored water uneasily.

"Do you suppose it's true that this is the blood of all those who died in Istar when the fiery mountain struck the Kingpriest's temple?" Goldmoon asked softly, coming to stand beside her husband.

"What nonsense!" Maquesta snorted. Walking across the deck to join them, her eyes flicked constantly around to make certain that she was getting the most out of her ship and her crew.

"You've been listening to Pig-faced William again!" She laughed. "He loves to frighten lubbers. The water gets its color from soil washed up from the bottom. Remember, this is not sand we're sailing over, like the bottom of the ocean. This used to be dry land—the capital city of Istar and the rich countryside around it. When the fiery mountain fell, it split the land apart. The waters from the ocean rushed in, creating a new sea. Now the wealth of Istar lies far beneath the waves."

Maquesta stared over the railing with dreamy eyes, as if she could penetrate the choppy water and see the rumored wealth of the glittering lost city below. She sighed longingly. Goldmoon glanced at the swarthy ship's captain in disgust, her own eyes filled with sadness and horror at the thought of the terrible destruction and loss of life.

"What keeps the soil stirred up?" Riverwind asked, frowning down at the blood-red water. "Even with the motion of the waves and the tides, the heavy soil should settle more than it appears to have."

"Truly spoken, barbarian." Maquesta looked at the tall, handsome Plainsman with admiration. "But then, your people are farmers, or so I've heard, and know a lot about soil. If you put your hand into the water, you can feel the grit of the dirt. Supposedly there is a maelstrom in the center of the Blood Sea that whirls with such force it drags the soil up from the bottom. But whether that is true or another one of Pigface's stories, I cannot say. I have never seen it, nor have any I've sailed with and I've sailed these waters since I was a child, learning my craft from my father. No one I ever knew was foolish enough to sail into the storm that hangs over the center of the sea."

"How do we get to Mithras, then?" Tanis growled. "It lies on the other side of the Blood Sea, if your charts are correct."

"We can reach Mithras by sailing south, if we are pursued. If not, we can circle the western edge of the sea and sail up the coast north to Nordmaar. Don't worry, Half-Elven." Maq waved her hand grandly. "At least you can say you've seen the Blood Sea. One of the wonders of Krynn."

Turning to walk aft, Maquesta was hailed from the crow's nest.

"Deck ho! Sail to the west!" the lookout called.

Instantly Maquesta and Koraf both pulled out spyglasses and trained them upon the western horizon. The companions exchanged worried glances and drew together. Even Raistlin left his place beneath the shielding sail and walked across the deck, peering westward with his golden eyes.

"A ship?" Maquesta muttered to Koraf.

"No," the minotaur grunted in his corrupt form of Common.

"A cloud, mebbe. But it go fast, very fast. Faster any cloud I ever see."

Now they all could make out the specks of darkness on the horizon, specks that grew larger even as they watched.

Then Tanis felt a wrenching pain inside of him, as if he'd been pierced by a sword. The pain was so swift and so real he gasped, clutching hold of Caramon to keep from falling. The rest stared at him in concern, Caramon wrapping his big arm around his friend to support him.

Tanis knew what flew toward them.

And he knew who led them.

GATHERING DARKNESS.

3

"A flight of dragons," said Raistlin, coming to stand beside his brother. "Five, I believe."

"Dragons!" Maquesta breathed. For a moment, she clutched the rail with trembling hands, then she whirled around. "Set all sail!" she commanded.

The crew stared westward, their eyes and minds locked onto the approaching terror. Maquesta raised her voice and shouted her order again, her only thoughts on her beloved ship. The strength and calmness in her voice penetrated the first faint feelings of dragonfear creeping over the crew. Instinctively a few sprang to carry out their orders, then more followed. Koraf with his whip helped as well, striking briskly at any man who didn't move quickly enough to suit him. Within moments, the great sails billowed out. Lines creaked ominously, the rigging sang a whining tune.

"Keep her near the edge of the storm!" Maq yelled to Berem. The man nodded slowly, but it was hard to tell from the vacant expression on his face if he heard or not.

Apparently he did, for the *Perechon* hovered close to the perpetual storm that shrouded the Blood Sea, skimming along on the surface of the waves, propelled by the storm's fog-gray wind.

It was reckless sailing, and Maq knew it. Let a spar be blown away, a sail split, a line break, and they would be helpless. But she had to take the risk.

"Useless," Raistlin remarked coolly. "You cannot outsail dragons. Look, see how fast they gain on us. You were followed, Half-Elf." He turned to Tanis. "You were followed when you left the camp . . . either that"—the mage's voice hissed—"or you led them to us!"

"No! I swear—" Tanis stopped.

The drunken draconian! . . . Tanis shut his eyes, cursing himself. Of course, Kit would have had him watched! She didn't trust him any more than she trusted the other men who shared her bed. What a damn egotistical fool he was! Believing he was something special to her, believing she loved him! She loved no one. She was incapable of loving—

"I was followed!" Tanis said through clenched teeth. "You must believe me. I—I may have been a fool. I didn't think they'd follow me in that storm. But I didn't betray you! I swear!"

"We believe you, Tanis," Goldmoon said, coming to stand beside him, glancing at Raistlin angrily out of the corner of her eyes.

Raistlin said nothing, but his lip curled in a sneer. Tanis avoided his gaze, turning instead to watch the dragons. They could see the creatures clearly now. They could see the enormous wingspans, the long tails snaking out behind, the cruel taloned feet hanging beneath the huge blue bodies.

"One has a rider," Maquesta reported grimly, the spyglass to her eye. "A rider with a horned mask."

"A Dragon Highlord," Caramon stated unnecessarily, all of them knowing well enough what that description meant. The big man turned a somber gaze to Tanis. "You better tell us what's going on, Tanis. If this Highlord thought you were a soldier under his own command, why has he taken the trouble to have you followed and come out after you?"

Tanis started to speak, but his faltering words were submerged in an agonized, inarticulate roar; a roar of mingled fear and terror and rage that was so beastlike, it wrenched everyone's thoughts from the dragons. It came from near the ship's helm. Hands on their weapons, the companions turned. The crew members halted their frantic labors, Koraf came to a dead stop, his bestial face twisted in amazement as the roaring sound grew louder and more fearful.

Only Maq kept her senses. "Berem," she called, starting to run across the deck, her fear giving her sudden horrifying insight into his mind. She leaped across the deck, but it was too late.

A look of insane terror on his face, Berem fell silent, staring at the approaching dragons. Then he roared again, a garbled howl of fear that chilled even the minotaur's blood. Above him, the sails were tight in the wind, the rigging stretched taut. The ship, under all the sail it could bear, seemed to leap over the waves, leaving a trail of white foam behind. But still the dragons gained.

Maq had nearly reached him when, shaking his head like a wounded animal, Berem spun the wheel.

"No! Berem!" Maquesta shrieked.

Berem's sudden move brought the small ship around so fast he nearly sent it under. The mizzenmast snapped with the strain as the ship heeled. Rigging, shrouds, sails, and men plummeted to the deck or fell into the Blood Sea.

Grabbing hold of Maq, Koraf dragged her clear of the falling mast. Caramon caught his brother in his arms and hurled him to the deck, covering Raistlin's frail body with his own as the tangle of rope and splintered wood crashed over them. Sailors tumbled to the deck or slammed up against the bulkheads. From down below, they could hear the sound of cargo breaking free. The companions clung to the ropes or whatever they could grab, hanging on desperately as it seemed Berem would run the ship under. Sails flapped horribly, like dead bird's wings, the rigging went slack, the ship floundered helplessly.

But the skilled helmsman, though seemingly mad with panic, was a sailor still. Instinctively, he held the wheel in a firm grip when it would have spun free. Slowly, he nursed the ship back into the wind with the care of a mother hovering over a deathly sick child. Slowly the *Perechon* righted herself. Sails that had been limp and lifeless caught the wind and filled. The *Perechon* came about and headed on her new course.

It was only then that everyone on board realized that sinking into the sea might have been a quicker and easier death as a gray shroud of wind-swept mist engulfed the ship.

"He's mad! He's steering us into the storm over the Blood Sea!" Maquesta said in a cracked, nearly inaudible voice as she pulled herself to her feet. Koraf started toward Berem, his face twisted in a snarl, a belaying pin in his hand.

"No! Koraf!" Maquesta gasped, grabbing hold of him. "Maybe Berem's right! This could be our only chance! The dragons won't dare follow us into the storm. Berem got us into this, he's the only helmsman we've got with a chance of getting us out! If we can just keep on the outskirts—"

A jagged flash of lightning tore through the gray curtain. The mists parted, revealing a gruesome sight. Black clouds swirled in the roaring wind, green lightning cracked, charging the air with the acrid smell of sulphur. The red water heaved and tossed. Whitecaps bubbled on the surface, like froth on the mouth of a dying man. No one could move for an instant. They could only stare, feeling petty and small against the awesome forces of nature. Then the wind hit them. The ship pitched and tossed, dragged over by the trailing, broken mast. Sudden rain slashed down, hail clattered on the wooden deck, the gray curtain closed around them once more.

Under Maquesta's orders, men scrambled aloft to reef the remaining sails. Another party worked desperately to clear the broken mast that was swinging around wildly. The sailors attacked it with axes, cutting away the ropes, letting it fall into the blood-red water. Free of the mast's dragging weight, the ship slowly righted itself. Though still tossed by the wind, under shortened sail, the *Perechon* seemed capable of riding out the storm, even with one mast gone.

The immediate peril had nearly driven all thoughts of dragons from their minds. Now that it seemed they might live a few moments longer, the companions turned to stare through the driving, leaden gray rain.

"Do you think we've lost them?" Caramon asked. The big warrior was bleeding from a savage cut on his head. His eyes showed the pain. But his concern was all for his brother. Raistlin staggered beside him, uninjured, but coughing so he could barely stand.

Tanis shook his head grimly. Glancing around quickly to see if anyone was hurt, he motioned the group to keep together. One by one, they stumbled through the rain, clinging to the ropes until they were gathered around the half-elf. All of them stared back out over the tossing seas.

At first they saw nothing; it was hard to see the bow of the ship through the rain and wind-tossed seas. Some of the sailors even raised a ragged cheer, thinking they had lost them.

But Tanis, his eyes looking to the west, knew that nothing short of death itself would stop the Highlord's pursuit. Sure enough, the sailor's cheers changed to cries of shock when the head of a blue dragon suddenly cleaved the gray clouds, its fiery eyes blazing red with hatred, its fanged mouth gaping open.

The dragon flew closer still, its great wings holding steady even though buffeted by gusts of wind and rain and hail. A Dragon Highlord sat upon the blue dragon's back. The Highlord held no weapon, Tanis saw bitterly. She needed no weapon. She would take Berem, then her dragon would destroy the rest of them. Tanis bowed his head, sick with the knowledge of what would come, sick with the knowledge that *he* was responsible.

Then he looked up. There was a chance, he thought frantically. Maybe she won't recognize Berem . . . and she wouldn't dare destroy them all for fear of harming him. Turning to look at the helmsman, Tanis's wild hope died at birth. It seemed the gods were conspiring against them.

The wind had blown Berem's shirt open. Even through the gray curtain of rain, Tanis could see the green jewel embedded in the man's chest glow more brilliantly than the green lightning, a terrible beacon shining through the storm. Berem did not notice. He did not even see the dragon. His eyes stared with fixed intensity into the storm as he steered the ship farther and farther into the Blood Sea of Istar.

Only two people saw that glittering jewel. Everyone else was held in thrall by the dragonfear, unable to look away from the huge blue creature soaring above them. Tanis saw the gemstone, as he had seen it before, months ago. And the Dragon Highlord saw it. The eyes behind the metal mask were drawn to the glowing jewel, then the Highlord's eyes met Tanis's eyes as the half-elf stood upon the storm-tossed deck.

A sudden gust of wind caught the blue dragon. It veered slightly, but the Highlord's gaze never wavered. Tanis saw the horrifying future in those brown eyes. The dragon would swoop down upon them and snatch Berem up in its claws. The Highlord would exult in her victory for a long agonizing moment, then she would order the dragon to destroy them all. . . .

Tanis saw this in her eyes as clearly as he had seen the passion in them only days before when he held her in his arms.

Never taking her eyes from him, the Dragon Highlord raised a gloved hand. It might have been a signal to the dragon to dive down upon them; it might have been a farewell to Tanis. He never knew, because at that moment a shattered voice shouted above the roar of the storm with unbelievable power.

"Kitiara!" Raistlin cried.

Shoving Caramon aside, the mage ran toward the dragon.

Slipping on the wet deck, his red robes whipped about him in the wind that was blowing stronger every moment. A sudden gust tore the hood from his head. Rain glistened on his metallic-colored skin, his hourglass eyes gleamed golden through the gathering darkness of the storm.

The Dragon Highlord grabbed her mount by the spiky mane along his blue neck, pulling the dragon up so sharply that Skie roared in protest. She stiffened in shock, her brown eyes grew wide behind the dragonhelm as she stared down at the frail half-brother she had raised from a baby. Her gaze shifted slightly as Caramon came to stand beside his twin.

"Kitiara?" Caramon whispered in a strangled voice, his face pale with horror as he watched the dragon hovering above them, riding the winds of the storm.

The Highlord turned the masked head once more to look at Tanis, then her eyes went to Berem. Tanis caught his breath. He saw the turmoil in her soul reflected in those eyes.

To get Berem, she would have to kill the little brother who had learned all of what he knew about swordsmanship from her. She would have to kill his frail twin. She would have to kill a man she had, once—loved. Then Tanis saw her eyes grow cold, and he shook his head in despair. It didn't matter. She would kill her brothers, she would kill him. Tanis remembered her words: "Capture Berem and we will have all Krynn at our feet. The Dark Queen will reward us beyond anything we ever dreamed!"

Kitiara pointed at Berem and loosed her hold upon the dragon. With a cruel shriek, Skie prepared to dive. But Kitiara's moment of hesitation proved disastrous. Steadfastly ignoring her, Berem had steered the ship deeper and deeper into the heart of the storm. The wind howled, snapping the rigging. Waves crashed over the bows. The rain slashed down like knives, and hailstones began to pile up on the deck, coating it with ice.

Suddenly the dragon was in trouble. A gust of wind hit him, then another. Skie's wings beat frantically as gust after gust pummeled him. The hail drummed upon his head and threatened to tear through the leathery wings. Only the supreme will of his master kept Skie from fleeing this perilous storm and flying to the safety of calmer skies.

Tanis saw Kitiara gesture furiously toward Berem. He saw Skie make a valiant effort to fly closer to the helmsman.

Then a gust of wind hit the ship. A wave broke over them. Water cascaded around them, foaming white, knocking men off their feet and sending them skidding across the deck. The ship listed. Everyone grabbed what they could—ropes, netting, anything—to keep from being washed overboard.

Berem fought the wheel, which was like a living thing, leaping in his hands. Sails split in two, men disappeared into the Blood Sea with terrifying screams. Then, slowly, the ship righted itself again, the wood creaking with the strain. Tanis looked up quickly.

The dragon—and Kitiara—were gone.

Freed from the dragonfear, Maquesta sprang into action, determined once more to save her dying ship. Shouting orders, she ran forward and stumbled into Tika.

"Get below, you lubbers!" Maquesta shouted furiously to Tanis above the storm wind. "Take your friends and get below! You're in our way! Use my cabin."

Numbly, Tanis nodded. Acting by instinct, feeling as if he were in a senseless dream filled with howling darkness, he led everyone below.

The haunted look in Caramon's eyes pierced his heart as the big man staggered past him, carrying his brother. Raistlin's golden eyes swept over him like flame, burning his soul. Then they were past him, stumbling with the others into the small cabin that shivered and rocked, tossing them about like rag dolls.

Tanis waited until everyone was safely inside the tiny cabin, then he slumped against the wooden door, unable to turn around, unable to face them. He had seen the haunted look in Caramon's eyes as the big man staggered past, he had seen the exultant gleam in Raistlin's eyes. He heard Goldmoon weeping quietly and he wished he might die on this spot before he had to face her.

But that was not to be. Slowly he turned around. Riverwind stood next to Goldmoon, his face dark and brooding as he braced himself between ceiling and deck. Tika bit her lip, tears sliding down her cheeks. Tanis stayed by the door, his back against it, staring at his friends mutely. For long moments, no one said a word. All that could be heard was the storm, the waves crashing onto the deck. Water trickled down on them. They were wet and cold and shaking with fear and sorrow and shock.

"I—I'm sorry," Tanis began, licking his salt-coated lips. His throat hurt, he could barely speak. "I—I wanted to tell you—"

"So *that's* where you were these four days," Caramon said in a soft, low voice. "With our *sister.* Our sister, the Dragon Highlord!"

Tanis hung his head. The ship listed beneath his feet, sending him staggering into Maquesta's desk, which was bolted to the floor. He caught himself and slowly pushed himself back to face them. The half-elf had endured much pain in his life, pain of prejudice, pain of loss, pain of knives, arrows, swords. But he did not think he could endure this pain. The look of betrayal in their eyes ran straight through his soul.

"Please, you must believe me . . ." What a stupid thing to say! he thought savagely. Why *should* they believe me! I've done nothing but lie to them ever since I returned. "All right," he began again, "I know you don't have any reason to believe me, but at least listen to me! I was walking through Flotsam when an elf attacked me. Seeing me in this get-up"—Tanis gestured at his dragonarmor—"he thought I was a dragon officer. Kitiara saved my life, then she recognized me. She thought I had joined the dragonarmy! What could I say? She"—Tanis swallowed and wiped his hand across his face, "she took me back to the inn and . . . and . . ." He choked, unable to continue.

"And you spent four days and nights in the loving embrace of a Dragon Highlord!" Caramon said, his voice rising in fury. Lurching to his feet, he stabbed an accusing finger at Tanis. "Then after four days, you needed a little rest! So you remembered us and you came calling to make certain we were still waiting for you! And we were! Just like the bunch of trusting lame-brains—"

"All right, so I was with Kitiara!" Tanis shouted, suddenly angry. "Yes, I loved her! I don't expect you to understand, any of you! But I never betrayed you! I swear by the gods! When she left for Solamnia, it was the first chance I had to escape and I took it. A draconian followed me, apparently under Kit's orders. I may be a fool. But I'm not a traitor!"

"Pah!" Raistlin spit on the floor.

"Listen, mage!" Tanis snarled. "If I had betrayed you, why was she so shocked to see you two, her brothers! If I had betrayed you, why didn't I just send a few draconians to the inn to pick you up? I could have, any time. I could have sent them to pick up Berem, too. *He's* the one she wants. *He's* the one the draconians are searching for in Flotsam! I knew he was on this ship. Kitiara offered me the rulership of Krynn if I'd tell her. That's how important he is. All I would've had to do was lead Kit to him and the Queen of Darkness herself would have rewarded me!"

"Don't tell us you didn't consider it!" Raistlin hissed.

Tanis opened his mouth, then fell silent. He knew his guilt was as plain on his face as the beard no true elf could grow. He choked, then put his hand over his eyes to block out their faces. "I—I loved her," he said brokenly. "All these years. I refused to see what she was. And even when I knew, couldn't help myself. You love"—his eyes went to Riverwind—"and you"—turning to Caramon. The boat pitched again. Tanis gripped the side of the desk as he felt the deck cant away beneath his feet. "What would you have done? For five years, she's been in my dreams!" He stopped. They were quiet. Caramon's face was unusually thoughtful. Riverwind's eyes were on Goldmoon.

"When she was gone," Tanis continued, his voice soft and filled with pain, "I lay in her bed and I *hated* myself. You may hate me now, but you cannot hate me as much as I loathe and despise what I have become! I thought of Laurana and—"

Tanis fell silent, raising his head. Even as he talked, he had become aware of the motion of the ship changing. The rest glanced around, too. It did not take an experienced seaman to notice that they were no longer pitching around wildly. Now they were running in a smooth forward motion, a motion somehow more ominous because it was so unnatural. Before anyone could wonder what it meant, a crashing knock nearly split the cabin door.

"Maquesta she say get up here!" shouted Koraf hoarsely.

Tanis cast one swift glance around at his friends. Riverwind's face was dark; his eyes met Tanis's and held them, but there was no light in them. The Plainsman had long distrusted all who were not human. Only after weeks of danger faced together had he come to love and trust Tanis as a brother. Had all that been shattered? Tanis looked at him steadily. Riverwind lowered his gaze and, without a word, started to walk past Tanis, then he stopped.

"You are right, my friend," he said, glancing at Goldmoon who was rising to her feet. "I have loved." Without another word, he turned abruptly and went up on deck.

Goldmoon gazed mutely as Tanis as she followed her husband, and he saw compassion and understanding in that silent look. He wished he understood, that he could be so forgiving.

Caramon hesitated, then walked past him without speaking or looking at him. Raistlin followed silently, his head turning, keeping his golden eyes on Tanis every step of the way. Was there a hint of glee in those golden eyes? Long mistrusted by the others, was Raistlin happy to have company in ignominy at last? The half-elf had no idea what the mage might be thinking. Then Tika went past him, giving him a gentle pat on the arm. She knew what it was to love. . . .

Tanis stood a moment alone in the cabin, lost in his own darkness. Then, with a sigh, he followed his friends.

As soon as he set foot on the deck, Tanis realized what had happened. The others were staring over the side, their faces pale and strained. Maquesta paced the foredeck, shaking her head and swearing fluently in her own language.

Hearing Tanis approach, she looked up, hatred in her black flashing eyes.

"You have destroyed us," she said venomously. "You and the god-cursed helmsman!"

Maquesta's words seemed redundant, a repetition of words resounding in his own mind. Tanis began to wonder if she had even spoken, or if it was himself he was hearing.

"We are caught in the maelstrom."

My brother . . .

4

The *Perechon* hurtled forward, skimming along on top of the water as lightly as a bird. But it was a bird with its wings clipped, riding the swirling tide of a watery cyclone into a blood-red darkness.

The terrible force pulled the sea waters smooth, until they looked like painted glass. A hollow, eternal roar swelled from the black depths. Even the storm clouds circled endlessly above it, as if all nature were caught in the maelstrom, hurtling to its own destruction.

Tanis gripped the rail with hands that ached from the tension. Staring into the dark heart of the whirlpool, he felt no fear, no terror, only a strange numb sensation. It didn't matter anymore. Death would be swift and welcome.

Everyone on board the doomed ship stood silently, their eyes wide with the horror of what they saw. They were still some distance from the center; the whirlpool was miles and miles in diameter. Smoothly and swiftly, the water flowed. Above them and around them the winds still howled, the rain still beat upon their faces. But it didn't matter. They didn't notice it anymore. All they saw was that they were being carried relentlessly into the center of the darkness.

This fearsome sight was enough to wake Berem from his

lethargy. After the first shock, Maquesta began shouting frantic orders. Dazedly, the men carried them out, but their efforts were useless. Sails rigged against the whirling wind tore apart; ropes snapped, flinging men screaming into the water. Try as he might, Berem could not turn the ship or break it free of the water's fearsome grip. Koraf added his strength to the handling of the wheel, but they might as well have been trying to stop the world from revolving.

Then Berem quit. His shoulders sagged. He stood staring out into the swirling depths, ignoring Maquesta, ignoring Koraf. His face was calm, Tanis saw; the same calm Tanis remembered seeing on Berem's face at Pax Tharkas when he took Eben's hand and ran with him into that deadly wall of cascading boulders. The green jewel in his chest glowed with an eerie light, reflecting the blood red of the water.

Tanis felt a strong hand clutch his shoulder, shaking him out of his rapt horror.

"Tanis! Where's Raistlin?"

Tanis turned. For a moment he stared at Caramon without recognition, then he shrugged.

"What does it matter?" he muttered bitterly. "Let him die where he chooses—"

"Tanis!" Caramon took him by the shoulders and shook him. "Tanis! The dragon orb! His magic! Maybe it can help—"

Tanis came awake. "By all the gods! You're right, Caramon!"

The half-elf looked around swiftly, but he saw no sign of the mage. A cold chill crept over him. Raistlin was capable either of helping them or of helping himself! Dimly Tanis remembered the elven princess, Alhana, saying the dragon orbs had been imbued by their magical creators with a strong sense of self-preservation.

"Below!" Tanis yelled. Leaping for the hatch, he heard Caramon pounding along behind.

"What is it?" called Riverwind from the rail.

Tanis shouted over his shoulder. "Raistlin. The dragon orb. Don't come. Let Caramon and I handle this. You stay here, with them."

"Caramon—" Tika yelled, starting to run after until Riverwind caught her and held her. Giving the warrior an anguished look, she fell silent, slumping back against the rail.

Caramon did not notice. He plunged ahead of Tanis, his huge body moving remarkably fast. Tumbling down the stairway below decks after him, Tanis saw the door to Maquesta's cabin open, swinging on its hinges with the motion of the ship. The half-elf dashed in and came to a sudden stop, just inside the door, as if he had run headlong into a wall.

Raistlin stood in the center of the small cabin. He had lit a candle in a lamp clamped to the bulkhead. The flame made the mage's face glisten like a metal mask, his eyes flared with golden fire. In his hands, Raistlin held the dragon orb, their prize from Silvanesti. It had grown, Tanis saw. It was now the size of child's ball. A myriad colors swirled within it. Tanis grew dizzy watching and wrenched his gaze away.

In front of Raistlin stood Caramon, the big warrior's face as white as Tanis had seen his corpse in the Silvanesti dream when the warrior lay dead at his feet.

Raistlin coughed, clutching at his chest with one hand. Tanis started forward, but the mage looked up quickly.

"Don't come near me, Tanis!" Raistlin gasped through bloodstained lips.

"What are you doing?"

"I am fleeing certain death, Half-Elf!" The mage laughed unpleasantly, the strange laughter Tanis had heard only twice before. "What do you think I am doing?"

"How?" Tanis asked, feeling a strange fear creep over him as he looked into the mage's golden eyes and saw them reflect the swirling light of the orb.

"Using my magic. And the magic of the dragon orb. It is quite simple, though probably beyond your weak mind. I now have the power to harness the energy of my corporeal body and the energy of my spirit into one. I will become pure energy—light, if you want to think of it that way. And, becoming light, I can travel through the heavens like the rays of the sun, returning to this physical world whenever and wherever I choose!"

Tanis shook his head. Raistlin was right—the thought was beyond him. He could not grasp it, but hope sprang into his heart.

"Can the orb do this for all of us?" he demanded.

"Possibly," Raistlin answered, coughing, "but I am not certain. I will not chance it. I know I can escape. The others are not my concern. You led *them* into this blood-red death, Half-Elf. You get them out!"

Anger surged through Tanis, replacing his fear. "At least, your brother—" he began hotly.

"No one," Raistlin said, his eyes narrowing. "Stand back."

Insane, desperate rage twisted Tanis's mind. Somehow he'd make Raistlin listen to reason! Somehow they would all use this strange magic to escape! Tanis knew enough about magic to realize that Raistlin dared not cast a spell now. He would need all his strength to control the dragon orb. Tanis started forward, then saw silver flash in the mage's hand. From nowhere, seemingly, had come a small silver dagger, long concealed on the mage's wrist by a cunningly designed leather thong. Tanis stopped, his eyes meeting Raistlin's.

"All right," Tanis said, breathing heavily. "You'd kill me without a second thought. But you won't harm your brother. Caramon, stop him!"

Caramon took a step toward his twin. Raistlin raised the silver dagger warningly.

"Don't do it, my brother," he said softly. "Come no closer."

Caramon hesitated.

"Go ahead, Caramon!" Tanis said firmly. "He won't hurt you."

"Tell him, Caramon," Raistlin whispered. The mage's eyes never left his brother's. Their hourglass pupils dilated, the golden light flickered dangerously. "Tell Tanis what I am capable of doing. You remember. So do I. It is in our thoughts every time we look at one another, isn't it, my dear brother?"

"What's he talking about?" Tanis demanded, only half listening. If he could distract Raistlin . . . jump him . . .

Caramon blanched. "The Towers of High Sorcery . . ." he faltered. "But we are forbidden to speak of it! Par-Salian said—"

"That doesn't matter now," Raistlin interrupted in his shattered voice. "There is nothing Par-Salian can do to me. Once I have what has been promised me, not even the great Par-Salian will have the power to face me! But that's none of your concern. This is."

Raistlin drew a deep breath, then began to speak, his strange eyes still on his twin. Only half-listening, Tanis crept closer, his heart pounding in his throat. One swift movement and the frail mage would crumble. . . . Then Tanis found himself caught and held by Raistlin's voice, compelled to stop for a moment and listen, almost as if Raistlin was weaving a spell around him.

"The last test in the Tower of High Sorcery, Tanis, was against myself. And I failed. I killed him, Tanis. I killed my brother"—Raistlin's voice was calm—"or at least I thought it was Caramon." The mage shrugged. "As it turned out, it was an illusion created to teach me the depths of my hatred and jealousy. Thus they thought to purge my soul of darkness. What I truly learned was that I lacked self-control. Still, since it was not part of the true Test, my failure did not count against me—except with one person."

"I watched him kill me!" Caramon cried wretchedly. "They made me watch so that I would understand him!" The big man's head dropped in his hands, his body convulsed with a shudder.

"I do understand!" he sobbed. "I understood then! I'm sorry! Just don't go without me, Raist! You're so weak! You need me—"

"No longer, Caramon," Raistlin whispered with a soft sigh. "I need you no longer!"

Tanis stared at them both, sick with horror. He couldn't believe this! Not even of Raistlin! "Caramon, go ahead!" he commanded hoarsely.

"Don't make him come near me, Tanis," Raistlin said, his voice gentle, as if he read the half-elf's thoughts. "I assure you, I am capable of this. What I have sought all my life is within my grasp. I will let nothing stop me. Look at Caramon's face, Tanis. He knows! I killed him once. I can do it again. Farewell, my brother."

The mage put both hands upon the dragon orb and held it up to the light of the flaming candle. The colors swirled madly in the orb, flaring brilliantly. A powerful magical aura surrounded the mage.

Fighting his fear, Tanis tensed his body to make a last desperate attempt to stop Raistlin. But he could not move. He heard Raistlin chanting strange words. The glaring, whirling light grew so bright it pierced his head. He covered his eyes with his hands, but the light burned right through his flesh, searing his brain. The pain was intolerable. He stumbled back against the door frame, hearing Caramon cry out in agony beside him. He heard the big man's body fall to the floor with a thud.

Then all was still, the cabin plunged into darkness. Trembling, Tanis opened his eyes. For a moment he could see nothing but the afterimage of a giant red globe imprinted on his brain. Then his eyes became accustomed to the chill dark. The candle guttered, hot wax dripping onto the wooden floor of the cabin to form a white puddle near where Caramon lay, cold and unmoving. The warrior's eyes were wide open, staring blankly into nothingness.

Raistlin was gone.

MARGARET WEIS & TRACY HICKMAN

Tika Waylan stood on the deck of the *Perechon* staring into the blood-red sea and trying very hard to keep from crying. You must be brave, she told herself over and over. You've learned to fight bravely in battle. Caramon said so. Now you must be brave about this. We'll be together, at least, at the end. He mustn't see me cry.

But the last four days had been unnerving for all of them. Fearful of discovery by the draconians swarming over Flotsam, the companions had remained hidden in the filthy inn. Tanis's strange disappearance had been terrifying. They were helpless, they dared do nothing, not even inquire about him. So for long days they had been forced to stay in their rooms and Tika had been forced to be around Caramon. The tension of their strong attraction to each other, an attraction they were not able to express, was torture. She wanted to put her arms around Caramon, to feel his arms around her, his strong, muscular body pressed against hers.

Caramon wanted the same thing, she was certain. He looked at her, sometimes, with so much tenderness in his eyes that she longed to nestle close to him and share the love that she knew was in the big man's heart.

It could never be, not as long as Raistlin hovered near his twin brother, clinging to Caramon like a frail shadow. Over and over she repeated Caramon's words, spoken to her before they reached Flotsam.

"My commitment is to my brother. They told me, in the Tower of High Sorcery, that his strength would help save the world. I am his strength, his physical strength. He needs me. My first duty is to him, and until that changes, I can't make any other commitments. You deserve someone who puts you first, Tika. And so I'll leave you free to find someone like that."

But I don't *want* anyone else, Tika thought sadly. And then the tears did start to fall. Turning quickly, she tried to hide them from Goldmoon and Riverwind. They would misunderstand, think she was crying from fear. No, fear of dying was something she had conquered long ago. Her biggest fear was fear of dying *alone*.

What are they doing? she wondered frantically, wiping her eyes with the back of her hand. The ship was being carried closer and closer into that dreadful dark eye. Where was Caramon? I'll go find them, she decided. Tanis or no Tanis.

Then she saw Tanis come slowly up out of the hatchway, half-dragging, half-supporting Caramon. One look at the big warrior's pale face and Tika's heart stopped beating.

She tried to call out, but she couldn't speak. At her inarticulate scream, however, Goldmoon and Riverwind both turned around from where they had been watching the awesome maelstrom. Seeing Tanis stagger beneath his burden, Riverwind ran forward to help. Caramon walked like a man in drunken stupor, his eyes glazed and sightless. Riverwind caught hold of Caramon just as Tanis's legs gave way completely.

"I'm all right," Tanis said softly in answer to Riverwind's look of concern. "Goldmoon, Caramon needs your help."

"What is it, Tanis?" Tika's fear gave her a voice. "What's the matter? Where's Raistlin? Is he—" She stopped. The half-elf's eyes were dark with the memory of what he had seen and heard below.

"Raistlin's gone," Tanis said briefly.

"Gone? Where?" Tika asked, staring wildly around as if expecting to see his body in the swirling blood-colored water.

"He lied to us," Tanis answered, helping Riverwind ease Caramon down onto a mass of coiled rope. The big warrior said nothing. He didn't seem to see them, or anything for that matter; he just stared sightlessly out over the blood-red sea. "Remember how he kept insisting we had to go to Palanthas, to *learn how* to use the dragon orb? He *knows how* to use the orb already. And now he's gone—to Palanthas, perhaps. I don't suppose it matters." Looking at Caramon, he shook his head in sorrow, then turned away abruptly and walked to the rail.

Goldmoon laid her gentle hands upon the big man, murmuring his name so softly the others could not hear it above the rush of the wind. At her touch, however, Caramon shivered, then began to shake violently. Tika knelt beside him, holding his hand in hers. Still staring straight ahead, Caramon began to cry silently, tears spilling down his cheeks from wide open, staring eyes. Goldmoon's eyes glimmered with her own tears, but she stroked his forehead and kept calling to him as a mother calls a lost child.

Riverwind, his face stern and dark with anger, joined Tanis.

"What happened?" the Plainsman asked grimly.

"Raistlin said he—I can't talk about it. Not now!" Tanis shook his head, shuddering. Leaning over the rail, he stared into the murky water below. Swearing softly in elven—a language the half-elf rarely used—he clutched his head with his hands.

Saddened by his friend's anguish, Riverwind laid his hand comfortingly on the half-elf's slumped shoulders.

"So at the end it comes to this," the Plainsman said. "As we foresaw in the dream, the mage has gone, leaving his brother to die."

"And as we saw in the dream, I have failed you," Tanis mumbled, his voice low and trembling. "What have I done? This is my fault! I have brought this horror upon us!"

"My friend," Riverwind said, moved by the sight of Tanis's suffering. "It is not ours to question the ways of the gods—"

"Damn the gods!" Tanis cried viciously. Lifting his head to stare at his friend, he struck his clenched fist on the ship's rail. "It was *me! My choosing!* How often during those nights when she and I were together and I held her in my arms, how often did I tell myself it would be so easy to stay there, with her, forever! I can't condemn Raistlin! We're very much alike, he and I. Both destroyed by an all-consuming passion!"

"You *haven't* been destroyed, Tanis," Riverwind said. Gripping the half-elf's shoulders in his strong hands, the stern-faced Plainsman forced Tanis to face him. "You did not fall victim to your passion, as did the mage. If you had, you would have stayed with Kitiara. You left her, Tanis—"

"I left her," Tanis said bitterly. "I sneaked out like a thief! I should have confronted her. I should have told her the truth about myself! She would have killed me then, but you would have been safe. You and the others could have escaped. How much easier my death would have been—But I didn't have the courage. Now I've brought us to this," the half-elf said, wrenching himself free of Riverwind's grip. "I have failed—not only myself, but all of you."

He glanced around the deck. Berem still stood at the helm, gripping the useless wheel in his hands, that strange look of resignation on his face. Maquesta still fought to save her ship, shrieking commands above the wind's howl and the deep-throated roaring that issued from the depths of the maelstrom. But her crew, stunned by terror, no longer obeyed. Some wept. Some cursed. Most made no sound but stared in horrid fascination at the gigantic swirl that was pulling them inexorably into the vast darkness of the deep. Tanis felt Riverwind's hand once again touch his shoulder. Almost angrily, he tried to withdraw, but the Plainsman was firm.

"Tanis, my brother, you made your choice to walk this road in the Inn of the Last Home in Solace, when you came to Goldmoon's aid. In my pride, I would have refused your help, and both she and I would have died. Because you could not turn from us in our need, we brought the knowledge of the ancient gods into the world. We brought healing. We brought hope. Remember what the Forestmaster told us? We do not grieve for those who fulfill their purpose in life. We *have* fulfilled our purpose, my friend. Who knows how many lives we have touched? Who knows but that this hope will lead to a great victory? For us, it seems, the battle has ended. So be it. We lay down our swords, only that others may pick them up and fight on."

"Your words are pretty, Plainsman," Tanis snapped, "but tell me truthfully. Can you look on death and not feel bitterness? You have everything to live for, Goldmoon, the children not yet born to you—"

A swift spasm of pain crossed Riverwind's face. He turned his head to hide it, but Tanis, watching him closely, saw the pain and suddenly understood. So he was destroying that, too! The half-elf shut his eyes in despair.

"Goldmoon and I weren't going to tell you. You had enough to worry about." Riverwind sighed. "Our baby would have been born in the autumn," he murmured, "in the time when the leaves on the vallenwoods turn red and golden as they were when Goldmoon and I came into Solace that day, carrying the blue crystal staff. That day the knight, Sturm Brightblade, found us and brought us to the Inn of the Last Home—"

Tanis began to sob, deep racking sobs that tore through his body like knives. Riverwind put his arms around his friend and held him tightly.

"The vallenwoods we know are dead now, Tanis," he continued in a hushed voice. "We could have shown the child only burned and rotted stumps. But now the child will see the vallenwoods as the gods meant them to be, in a land where the trees live forever. Do not grieve, my friend, my brother. You helped bring knowledge of the gods back to the people. You must have faith in those gods."

Gently Tanis pushed Riverwind away. He could not meet the Plainsman's eyes. Looking into his own soul, Tanis saw it twist and writhe like the tortured trees of Silvanesti. Faith? He had no faith. What were the gods to him? *He* had made the decisions. *He* had thrown away everything he ever had of value in his life—his elven homeland, Laurana's love. He had come close to throwing away friendship, too. Only Riverwind's strong loyalty—a loyalty that was badly misplaced—kept the Plainsman from denouncing him.

Suicide is forbidden to the elves. They consider it blasphemy, the gift of life being the most precious of all gifts. But Tanis stared into the blood-red sea with anticipation and longing.

Let death come swiftly, he prayed. Let these blood-stained waters close over my head. Let me hide in their depths. And if there *are* gods, if you *are* listening to me, I ask only one thing: keep the knowledge of my shame from Laurana. I have brought pain to too many. . . .

But even as his soul breathed this prayer he hoped would be his last upon Krynn, a shadow darker than the storm clouds fell across him. Tanis heard Riverwind cry out and Goldmoon scream, but their voices were lost in the roar of the water as the ship began to sink into the heart of the maelstrom. Dully, Tanis looked up to see the fiery red eyes of a blue dragon shining through the black swirling clouds. Upon the dragon's back was Kitiara.

Unwilling to give up the prize that would win them glorious victory, Kit and Skie had fought their way through the storm, and now the dragon, wicked talons extended, dove straight for Berem. The man's feet might have been nailed to the deck. In dreamlike helplessness he stared at the diving dragon.

Jolted to action, Tanis flung himself across the heaving deck as the blood-red water swirled around him. He hit Berem full in the stomach, knocking the man backward just as a wave broke over them. Tanis grabbed hold of something, he wasn't sure what, and clung to the deck as it canted away beneath him. Then the ship righted itself. When he looked up, Berem was gone. Above him, he heard the dragon shriek in anger.

And then Kitiara was shouting above the storm, pointing at Tanis. Skie's fiery gaze turned on him. Raising his arm as if he could ward off the dragon, Tanis looked up into the enraged eyes of the beast who was fighting madly to control his flight in the whipping winds.

This is life, the half-elf found himself thinking, seeing the dragon's claws above him. This is life! To live, to be carried out of this horror! For an instant Tanis felt himself suspended in mid-air as the bottom dropped out of his world. He was conscious only of shaking his head wildly, screaming incoherently. The dragon and the water hit him at the same time. All he could see was blood. . . .

Tika crouched beside Caramon, her fear of death lost in her concern for him. But Caramon wasn't even aware of her presence. He stared out into the darkness, tears coursing down his face, his hands clenched into fists, repeating two words over and over in a silent litany.

In agonizing dreamlike slowness, the ship balanced on the edge of the swirling water, as if the very wood of the vessel itself hesitated in fear. Maquesta joined her frail ship in its final desperate struggle for life, lending her own inner strength, trying to change the laws of nature by force of will alone. But it was useless. With a final, heart-breaking shudder, the *Perechon* slipped over the edge into the swirling, roaring darkness.

Timber cracked. Masts fell. Men were flung, screaming, from the listing decks as the blood-red blackness sucked the *Perechon* down into its gaping maw.

After all was gone, two words lingered like a benediction.

"My brother . . ."

The Chronicler and the Mage.

5

Astinus of Palanthas sat in his study. His hand guided the quill pen he held in firm, even strokes. The bold, crisp writing flowing from that pen could be read clearly, even at a distance. Astinus filled a sheet of parchment quickly, rarely pausing to think. Watching him, one had the impression that his thoughts flowed from his head straight into the pen and out onto the paper, so rapidly did he write. The flow was interrupted only when he dipped the quill in ink, but this, too, had become such an automatic motion to Astinus that it interrupted him as little as the dotting of an "i" or the crossing of a "t."

The door to his study creaked opened. Astinus did not look up from his writing, though the door did not often open while he was engaged in his work. The historian could count the number of times on his fingers. One of those times had been during the Cataclysm. That had disturbed his writing, he recalled, remembering with disgust the spilled ink that had ruined a page.

The door opened and a shadow fell across his desk. But there came no sound, though the body belonging to the shadow drew in a breath as though about to speak. The shadow wavered, the sheer enormity of its offense causing the body to tremble.

It is Bertrem, Astinus noted, as he noted everything, filing the information for future reference in one of the many compartments of his mind.

This day, as above Afterwatch Hour falling 29, Bertrem entered my study.

The pen continued its steady advance over the paper. Reaching the end of a page, Astinus lifted it smoothly and placed it on top of similar pieces of parchment stacked neatly at the end of his desk. Later that night, when the historian had finished his work and retired, the Aesthetics would enter the study reverently, as clerics enter a shrine, and gather up the stacks of paper. Carefully they would take them into the great library. Here the pieces of parchment covered with the bold, firm handwriting, were sorted, categorized, and filed in the giant books labeled *Chronicles, A History of Krynn* by Astinus of Palanthas.

"Master . . ." spoke Bertrem in a shivering voice.

This day, as above Afterwatch Hour falling 30, Bertrem spoke, Astinus noted in the text.

"I regret disturbing you, Master," said Bertrem faintly, "but a young man is dying on your doorstep."

This day, as above Restful Hour climbing 29, a young man died on our doorstep.

"Get his name," Astinus said without looking up or pausing in his writing, "so that I may record it. Be certain as to the spelling. And find out where he's from and his age, if he's not too far gone."

"I have his name, Master," Bertrem replied. "It is Raistlin. He comes from Solace township in the land of Abanasinia."

This day, as above Restful Hour climbing 28, Raistlin of Solace died—

Astinus stopped writing. He looked up.

"Raistlin . . . of Solace?"

"Yes, Master," Bertrem replied, bowing at this great honor. It was the first time Astinus had ever looked directly at him, though Bertrem had been with the Order of Aesthetics who lived in the great library for over a decade. "Do you know him, Master? That was why I took the liberty of disturbing your work. He has asked to see you."

"Raistlin . . ."

A drop of ink fell from Astinus's pen onto the paper.

"Where is he?"

"On the steps, Master, where we found him. We thought, perhaps, one of these new healers we have heard about, the ones who worship the Goddess Mishakal, might aid him. . . ."

The historian glared at the blot of ink in annoyance. Taking a pinch of fine, white sand, he carefully sprinkled it over the ink to dry it so that it would not stain other sheets that would later be set upon it. Then, lowering his gaze, Astinus returned to his work.

"No healer can cure this young man's malady," the historian remarked in a voice that might have come from the depths of time. "But bring him inside. Give him a room."

"Bring him inside the library?" Bertrem repeated in profound astonishment. "Master, no one has ever been admitted except those of our order—"

"I will see him, if I have time at the end of the day," Astinus continued as if he had not heard the Aesthetic's words. "If he is still alive, that is."

The pen moved rapidly across the paper.

"Yes, Master," Bertrem murmured and backed out of the room.

Shutting the door to the study, the Aesthetic hurried through the cool and silent marble halls of the ancient library, his eyes wide with the wonder of this occurrence. His thick, heavy robes swept the floor behind him, his shaved head glistened with sweat as he ran, unaccustomed to such strenuous exertion. The others of his order gazed at him in astonishment as he swept into the library's front entryway. Glancing quickly through the glass pane set in the door, he could see the young man's body upon the stairs.

"We are commanded to bring him inside," Bertrem told the others. "Astinus will see the young man tonight, if the mage is still alive."

One by one, the Aesthetics regarded each other in shocked silence, wondering what doom this portended.

I am dying.

The knowledge was bitter to the mage. Lying in the bed in the cold, white cell where the Aesthetics had placed him, Raistlin cursed his frail and fragile body, he cursed the Tests that shattered it, he cursed the gods who had inflicted it upon him. He cursed until he had no more words to hurl, until he was too exhausted even to think. And then he lay beneath the white linen sheets that were like winding cloths and felt his heart flutter inside his breast like a trapped bird.

For the second time in his life, Raistlin was alone and frightened. He had been alone only once before, and that had been during those three torturous days of Testing in the Tower of High Sorcery. Even then, had he been alone? He didn't think so, although he couldn't remember clearly. The voice . . . the voice that spoke to him sometimes, the voice he could never identify, yet seemed to know . . . He always connected the voice with the Tower. It had helped him there, as it had helped him since. Because of that voice he had survived the ordeal.

But he wouldn't survive this, he knew. The magical transformation he had undergone had placed too great a strain on his frail body. He had succeeded, but at what a cost!

The Aesthetics found him huddled in his red robes, vomiting blood upon their stairs. He managed to gasp out the name of Astinus and his own name when they asked. Then he lost consciousness. When he awoke, he was here, in this cold, narrow monk's cell. And with waking came the knowledge that he was dying. He had asked more of his body than it was capable of giving. The dragon orb might save him, but he had no more strength to work his magic. The words to draw upon its enchantment were gone from his mind.

I am too weak to control its tremendous power anyway, he realized. Let it once know I have lost my strength and it would devour me.

No, there was only one chance remaining to him, the books inside the great library. The dragon orb had promised him that these books held the secrets of the ancient ones, great and powerful mages whose like would never be seen again on Krynn. Perhaps there he could find the means to extend his life. He had to talk to Astinus! He had to gain admittance to the great library, he had shrieked at the complacent Aesthetics. But they only nodded.

"Astinus will see you," they said, "this evening, if he has time."

If *he* has time! Raistlin swore viciously. If *I* have time! He could feel the sands of his life running through his fingers and, grasp at them as he might, he could not stop them.

Gazing at him with pitying eyes, not knowing what to do for him, the Aesthetics brought Raistlin food, but he could not eat. He could not even swallow the bitter herbal medicine that eased his cough. Furious, he sent the idiots away from him. Then he lay back on his hard pillow, watching the sun's light creep across his cell. Exerting all his effort to cling to life, Raistlin forced himself to relax, knowing that this feverish anger would burn him up. His thoughts went to his brother.

Closing his eyes wearily, Raistlin imagined Caramon sitting beside him. He could almost feel Caramon's arms around him, lifting him up so that he could breathe more easily. He could smell his brother's familiar scent of sweat and leather and steel. Caramon would take care of him. Caramon would not let him die. . . .

No, Raistlin thought dreamily. Caramon is dead now. They are all dead, the fools. I must look after myself. Suddenly he realized he was losing consciousness again. Desperately he fought, but it was a losing battle. Making a final, supreme effort, he thrust his shaking hand into a pocket in his robe. His fingers closed around the dragon orb, shrunk to the size of a child's marble, even as he sank into darkness.

He woke to the sound of voices and the knowledge that someone was in the cell with him. Fighting through layers of blackness, Raistlin struggled to the surface of his consciousness and opened his eyes.

It was evening. Lunitari's red light glanced through his window, a shimmering blood-stain upon the wall. A candle burned beside his bed and, by its light, he saw two men standing over him. One he recognized as the Aesthetic who had discovered him. The other? He seemed familiar. . . .

"He wakes, Master," said the Aesthetic.

"So he does," remarked the man imperturbably. Bending down, he studied the young mage's face, then smiled and nodded to himself, almost as if someone he had long expected had finally arrived. It was a peculiar look, and it did not go unnoticed by either Raistlin or the Aesthetic.

"I am Astinus," the man spoke. "You are Raistlin of Solace."

"I am." Raistlin's mouth formed the words, his voice was little more than a croak. Gazing up at Astinus, Raistlin's anger returned as he remembered the man's callous remark that he would see him *if he had time.* As Raistlin stared at the man, he felt suddenly chilled. He had never seen a face so cold and unfeeling, totally devoid of human emotion and human passion. A face untouched by time—

Raistlin gasped. Struggling to sit up—with the Aesthetic's help—he stared at Astinus.

Noticing Raistlin's reaction, Astinus remarked, "You look at me strangely, young mage. What do you see with those hourglass eyes of yours?"

"I see . . . a man . . . who is *not* dying. . . ." Raistlin could speak only through painful struggles to draw breath.

"Of course, what did you expect?" the Aesthetic chided, gently propping the dying man against the pillows of his bed. "The Master was here to chronicle the birth of the first upon Krynn and so he will be here to chronicle the death of the last. So we are taught by Gilean, God of the Book."

"Is that true?" Raistlin whispered.

Astinus shrugged slightly.

"My personal history is of no consequence compared to the history of the world. Now speak, Raistlin of Solace. What do you want of me? Whole volumes are passing as I waste my time in idle talk with you."

"I ask . . . I beg . . . a favor!" The words were torn from Raistlin's chest and came out stained with blood. "My life . . . is measured . . . in hours. Let me . . . spend them . . . in study . . . in the great library!"

Bertrem's tongue clicked against the roof of his mouth in shock at this young mage's temerity. Glancing at Astinus fearfully, the Aesthetic waited for the scathing refusal which, he felt certain, must flail this rash young man's skin from his bones.

Long moments of silenced passed, broken only by Raistlin's labored breathing. The expression on Astinus's face did not change. Finally he answered coldly. "Do what you will."

Ignoring Bertrem's shocked look, Astinus turned and began to walk toward the door.

"Wait!" Raistlin's voice rasped. The mage reached out a trembling hand as Astinus slowly came to a halt. "You asked me what I saw when I looked at you. Now I ask you the same thing. I saw that look upon your face when you bent over me. You recognized me! You know me! Who am I? What do you see?"

Astinus looked back, his face cold, blank, and impenetrable as marble.

"You said you saw a man who was not dying," the historian told the mage softly. Hesitating a moment, he shrugged and once again turned away. "I see a man who is."

And, with that, he walked out the door.

"Yes, yes," muttered Raistlin, hurriedly scanning the runes that crawled like spiders across the page. Reading impatiently through the list of spells, he finally reached the conclusion.

With a shriek of inarticulate rage, Raistlin shoved the spellbook with its night-blue binding and silver runes aside. His hand shaking, he reached for the next night-blue bound book in the huge pile he had amassed at his side. A fit of coughing forced him to stop. Fighting for breath, he feared for a moment that he could not go on.

The pain was unbearable. Sometimes he longed to sink into oblivion, end this torture he must live with daily. Weak and dizzy, he let his head sink to the desk, cradled in his arms. Rest, sweet, painless rest. An image of his brother came to his mind. There was Caramon in the afterlife, waiting for his little brother. Raistlin could see his twin's sad, doglike eyes, he could feel his pity. . . .

Raistlin drew a breath with a gasp, then forced himself to sit up. Meeting Caramon! I'm getting light-headed, he sneered at himself. What nonsense!

Moistening his blood-caked lips with water, Raistlin took hold of the next night-blue spellbook and pulled it over to him. Its silver runes flashed in the candlelight, its cover—icy cold to the touch—was the same as the covers of all the other spellbooks stacked around him. Its cover was the same as the spellbook in his possession already, the spellbook he knew by heart and by soul, the spellbook of the greatest mage who ever lived, Fistandantilus.

With trembling hands, Raistlin opened the cover. His feverish eyes devoured the page, reading the same requirements—only mages high in the Order had the skill and control necessary to study the spells recorded inside. Those without it who tried to read the spells saw nothing on the pages but gibberish.

Raistlin fulfilled all the requirements. He was probably the only White or Red-Robed mage on Krynn, with the possible exception of the great Par-Salian himself, who could say that. Yet, when Raistlin looked at the writing inside the book, it was nothing more than a meaningless scrawl.

Thus, with the Key, You unlock our Mysteries—

Raistlin screamed, a thin, wailing sound cut off by a choking sob. In bitter anger and frustration, he flung himself upon the table, scattering the books to the floor. Frantically his hands clawed the air and he screamed again. The magic that he had been too weak to summon came now in his anger.

The Aesthetics, passing outside the doors of the great library, exchanged fearful glances as they heard those terrible cries. Then they heard another sound. A crackling sound followed by a booming explosion of thunder. They stared at the door in alarm. One put his hand upon the handle and turned it, but the door was locked fast. Then one pointed and they all backed up as a ghastly light flared beneath the closed door. The smell of sulphur drifted out of the library, only to be blown away by a great gust of wind that hit the door with such force it seemed it might split in two. Again the Aesthetics heard that bubbling wail of rage, and then they fled down the marble hallway, calling wildly for Astinus.

The historian arrived to find the door to the great library held spellbound. He was not much surprised. With a sigh of resignation, he took a small book from the pocket of his robes and then sat down in a chair, beginning to write in his quick, flowing script. The Aesthetics huddled together near him, alarmed at the strange sounds emanating from within the locked room.

Thunder boomed and rolled, shaking the library's very foundation. Light flared around the closed door so constantly it might have been day within the room instead of the darkest hour of the night. The howling and shrieking of a windstorm blended with the mage's shrill screams. There were thuds and thumps, the rustling sounds of sheaves of paper swirling about in a storm. Tongues of flame flicked from beneath the door.

"Master!" one of the Aesthetics cried in terror, pointing to the flames. "He is destroying the books!"

Astinus shook his head and did not cease his writing.

Then, suddenly, all was silent. The light seen beneath the library door went out as if swallowed by darkness. Hesitantly the Aesthetics approached the door, cocking their heads to listen. Nothing could be heard from within, except a faint rustling sound. Bertrem placed his hand upon the door. It yielded to his gentle pressure.

"The door opens, Master," he said.

Astinus stood up. "Return to your studies," he commanded the Aesthetics. "There is nothing you can do here."

Bowing silently, the monks gave the door a final, scared glance, then walked hurriedly down the echoing corridor, leaving Astinus alone. He waited a few moments to make certain they were gone, then the historian slowly opened the door to the great library.

Silver and red moonlight streamed through the small windows. The orderly rows of shelves that held thousands of bound books stretched into the darkness. Recessed holes containing thousands of scrolls lined the walls. The moonlight shone upon a table, buried under a pile of paper. A guttered candle stood in the center of the table, a night-blue spellbook lay open beside it, the moonlight shining on its bone-white pages. Other spellbooks lay scattered on the floor.

Looking around, Astinus frowned. Black streaks marked the walls. The smell of sulphur and of fire was strong inside the room. Sheets of paper swirled in the still air, falling like leaves after an autumn storm upon a body lying on the floor.

Entering the room, Astinus carefully shut and locked the door behind him. Then he approached the body, wading through the mass of parchment scattered on the floor. He said nothing, nor did he bend down to help the young mage. Standing beside Raistlin, he regarded him thoughtfully.

But, as he drew near, Astinus's robes brushed the metallic-colored, outstretched hand. At that touch, the mage lifted his head. Raistlin stared at Astinus with eyes already darkening with the shadows of death.

"You did not find what you sought?" Astinus asked, staring down at the young man with cold eyes.

"The Key!" Raistlin gasped through white lips flecked with blood. "Lost . . . in time! . . . Fools!" His clawlike hand clenched, anger the only fire that burned in him. "So simple! Everyone knew it. . . no one recorded it! The Key . . . all I need . . . lost!"

"So this ends your journey, my old friend," Astinus said without compassion.

Raistlin raised his head, his golden eyes glittering feverishly. "You *do* know me! *Who am I?*" he demanded.

"It is no longer important," Astinus said. Turning, he started to walk out of the library.

There was a piercing shriek behind him, a hand grasped his robe, dragging him to a halt.

"Don't turn your back on me as you have turned it on the world!" Raistlin snarled.

"Turn my back on the world . . ." the historian repeated softly and slowly, his head moving to face the mage. "Turn my back on the world!" Emotion rarely marred the surface of Astinus's cold voice, but now anger struck the placid calm of his soul like a rock hurled into still water.

"I? Turn my back on the world?" Astinus's voice rolled around the library as the thunder had rolled previously. "I *am* the world, as you well know, old friend! Countless times I have been born! Countless deaths I have died! Every tear shed—mine have flowed! Every drop of blood spilled—mine has drained! Every agony, every joy ever felt has been mine to share!

"I sit with my hand on the Sphere of Time, the sphere *you* made for me, old friend, and I travel the length and breadth of this world chronicling its history. I have committed the blackest deeds! I have made the noblest sacrifices. I am human, elf, and ogre. I am male and female. I have borne children. I have murdered children. I saw you as you were. I see you as you are. If I seem cold and unfeeling, it is because that is how I survive without losing my sanity! My passion goes into my words. Those who read my books *know* what it is to have lived in any time, in any body that ever walked this world!"

Raistlin's hand loosed its grip on the historian's robes and he fell weakly to the floor. His strength was fading fast. But the mage clung to Astinus's words, even as he felt the coldness of death clutch his heart. I must live, just a moment longer. Lunitari, give me just a moment more, he prayed, calling upon the spirit of the moon from which Red-Robed mages draw their magic. Some word was coming, he knew. Some word that would save him. If only he could hold on!

Astinus's eyes flared as he gazed upon the dying man. The words he hurled at him had been pent up inside the chronicler for countless centuries.

"On the last, perfect day," Astinus said, his voice shaking, "the three gods will come together: Paladine in his Radiance, Queen Takhisis in her Darkness, and lastly Gilean, Lord of Neutrality. In their hands, each bears the Key of Knowledge. They will place these Keys upon the great Altar, and upon the Altar will also be placed my books—the story of every being who has lived upon Krynn throughout time! And then, at last, the world will be complete —"

Astinus stopped, appalled, realizing what he had said, what he had done.

But Raistlin's eyes no longer saw him. The hourglass pupils were dilated, the golden color surrounding them gleamed like flame.

"The Key . . ." Raistlin whispered in exultation. "The Key! I know . . . I know!"

So weak he could scarcely move, Raistlin reached into the small, nondescript pouch that hung from his belt and brought forth the marble-sized dragon orb. Holding it in his trembling hand, the mage stared into it with eyes that were fast growing dim.

"I know who you are," Raistlin murmured with his dying breath. "I know you now and I beseech you—come to my aid as you came to my aid in the Tower and in Silvanesti! Our bargain is struck! Save me, and you save yourself!"

The mage collapsed. His head with its sparse white wispy hair lolled back onto the floor, his eyes with their cursed vision closed. The hand that held the orb went limp, but its fingers did not relax. It held the orb fast in a grip stronger than death.

Little more than a heap of bones garbed in blood-red robes, Raistlin lay unmoving amid the papers that littered the spell-blasted library.

Astinus stared at the body for long moments, bathed in the garish purplish light of the two moons. Then, his head bowed, the historian left the silent library, closing and locking the door behind him with hands that shook.

Returning to his study, the historian sat for hours, gazing unseeing into the darkness.

PALANTHAS.

6

"I tell you, it was Raistlin!"

"And I tell you, one more of your furry-elephant, teleporting-ring, plants-living-off-air stories and I'll twist that hoopak around your neck!" Flint snapped angrily.

"It was *too* Raistlin," Tasslehoff retorted, but he said it under his breath as the two walked along the wide, gleaming streets of the beautiful city of Palanthas. The kender knew by long association just how far he could push the dwarf, and Flint's threshold for irritation was very low these days.

"And don't go bothering Laurana with your wild tales, either," Flint ordered, correctly guessing Tas's intentions. "She has enough problems."

"But—"

The dwarf stopped and gazed grimly at the kender from beneath bushy white eyebrows.

"Promise?"

Tas sighed. "Oh, all right."

It wouldn't have been so bad if he didn't feel quite certain he had seen Raistlin! He and Flint were walking past the steps of the great library of Palanthas when the kender's sharp eyes caught sight of a group of monks clustered around something lying on the steps. When Flint stopped for a moment to admire some particularly fine piece of dwarven-crafted stonework in a building opposite, Tas took advantage of the opportunity to creep silently up the stairs to see what was going on.

To his amazement, he saw a man that looked just like Raistlin, golden-colored metallic skin, red robes, and all, being lifted up off the stairs and carried inside the library. But by the time the excited kender ran across the street, grabbed Flint, and hauled the grumbling dwarf back again, the group was gone.

Tasslehoff even ran up to the door, banging on it and demanding entrance. But the Aesthetic who answered appeared so horrified at the thought of a kender coming into the great library that the scandalized dwarf hustled Tas off before the monk could open his mouth.

Promises being very nebulous things to kenders, Tas considered telling Laurana anyway, but then he thought of the elfmaid's face as it had appeared lately, wan and drawn from grief, worry, and lack of sleep, and the soft-hearted kender decided maybe Flint was right. If it was Raistlin, he was probably here on some secret business of his own and wouldn't thank them for dropping in on him uninvited. Still . . .

Heaving a sigh, the kender walked on, kicking stones with his feet and looking around the city once more. Palanthas was well worth the look. The city had been fabled even during the Age of Might for its beauty and grace. There was no other city on Krynn that could compare to it, at least to human thought. Built on a circular pattern like a wheel, the center was, literally, the hub of the city. All the major official buildings were located here, and the great sweeping staircases and graceful columns were breathtaking in their grandeur. From this central circle, wide avenues led off in the directions of the eight major compass points. Paved with fitted stone (dwarven work, of course) and lined with trees whose leaves were like golden lace year-round, these avenues led to the seaport on the north and to the seven gates of the Old City Wall.

Even these gates were masterpieces of architecture, each one guarded by twin minarets whose graceful towers rose over three hundred feet into the air. The Old Wall itself was carved with intricate designs, telling the story of Palanthas during the Age of Dreams. Beyond Old City Wall lay New City. Carefully planned to conform to the original design, New City extended from Old City Wall in the same circular pattern with the same wide, tree-lined avenues. There were, however, no walls around New City. The Palanthians didn't particularly like walls (walls ruined the over-all design), and nothing in either Old or New City was ever built these days without first consulting the overall design, both within and without. Palanthas's silhouette upon the horizon in the evening was as lovely to the eye as the city itself, with one exception.

Tas's thoughts were rudely interrupted by a poke in the back from Flint.

"What is the matter with you?" the kender demanded, facing the dwarf.

"Where are we?" Flint asked surlily, hands on his hips.

"Well, we're . . ." Tas looked around. "Uh . . . that is, I think we're . . . then again, perhaps we're not." He fixed Flint with a cold stare. "How did you get us lost?"

"ME!" The dwarf exploded. "*You're* the guide! *You're* the map reader. *You're* the kender who knows this city like he knows his own house!"

"But *I* was thinking," Tas said loftily.

"What with?" Flint roared.

"I was thinking deep thoughts," Tas said in wounded tones.

"I—oh, never mind," Flint grumbled and began to peer up and down the street. He didn't quite like the looks of things.

"This certainly does seem strange," Tas said cheerfully, echoing the dwarf's thoughts. "It's so empty, not at all like the other streets of Palanthas." He stared longingly down the rows of silent empty buildings. "I wonder—"

"No," said Flint.

"Absolutely not. We're going back the way we came—"

"Oh, come on!" Tas said, heading down the deserted street. "Just a little way, to see what's down here. You know Laurana told us to look around, inspect the forti—forta—the whatch-ma-call-its."

"Fortifications," muttered Flint, stumping reluctantly along after the kender. "And there aren't any around here, you door-knob. This is the center of the city! She meant the walls around the outside of the city."

"There aren't any walls around the outside of the city," Tas said triumphantly. "Not around New City, anyway. And if it's the center, why is it deserted? I think we should find out."

Flint snorted. The kender was beginning to make sense, a fact that caused the dwarf to shake his head and wonder if maybe he shouldn't lie down somewhere out of the sun.

The two walked for several minutes in silence, traveling deeper and deeper into the heart of the city. To one side, only a few blocks away, rose the palatial mansion of the Lord of Palanthas. They could see its towering spires from here. But ahead of them, nothing was visible. It was all lost in shadow. . . .

Tas glanced into windows and stuck his nose into doorways of the buildings they passed. He and Flint proceeded clear to the end of the block before the kender spoke.

"You know, Flint," Tas said uneasily, "these buildings are all empty."

"Abandoned," said Flint in hushed tones. The dwarf laid his hand on his battle-axe, starting nervously at the sound of Tas's shrill voice.

"There's a queer feeling about this place," Tas said, edging closer to the dwarf. "I'm not afraid, mind you—"

"I am," said Flint emphatically. "Let's get out of here!"

Tas looked up at the tall buildings on either side of them. They were well-kept. Apparently the Palanthians were so proud of their city that they even spent money keeping up vacant buildings. There were shops and dwellings of all kinds, obviously structurally sound. The streets were clean and free from litter and garbage. But it was all deserted. This had once been a prosperous area, the kender thought. Right in the heart of the city. Why wasn't it now? Why had everyone left? It gave him an "eerie" feeling and there were not many things in Krynn that gave kender "eerie" feelings.

"There aren't even any rats!" Flint muttered. Taking hold of Tas's arm, he tugged at the kender. "We've seen enough."

"Oh, come on," Tas said. Pulling his arm away, he fought down the strange eerie sensation and, straightening his small shoulders, started off down the sidewalk once more. He hadn't gone three feet when he realized he was alone. Stopping in exasperation, he looked back. The dwarf was standing on the sidewalk, glowering at him.

"I only want to go as far as that grove of trees at the end of the street," Tas said, pointing. "Look—it's just an ordinary grove of ordinary oak trees. Probably a park or something. Maybe we could have lunch—"

"I don't like this place!" Flint said stubbornly. "It reminds me of . . . of . . . Darken Wood—that place where Raistlin spoke to the spooks."

"Oh, you're the only spook here!" Tas said irritably, determined to ignore the fact that it reminded him of the same thing. "It's broad daylight. We're in the center of a city, for the love of Reorx—"

"Then why is it freezing cold?"

"It's winter!" the kender shouted, waving his arms. He hushed immediately, staring around in alarm at the weird way his words echoed through the silent streets. "Are you coming?" he asked in a loud whisper.

Flint drew a deep breath. Scowling, he gripped his battle-axe and marched down the street toward the kender, casting a wary eye at the buildings as though at any moment a spectre might leap out at him.

"'Tisn't winter," the dwarf muttered out of the corner of his mouth. "Except around here."

"It won't be spring for weeks," Tas returned, glad to have something to argue about and keep his mind off the strange things his stomach was doing—twisting into knots and the like.

But Flint refused to quarrel—a bad sign. Silently, the two crept down the empty street until they reached the end of the block. Here the buildings ended abruptly in a grove of trees. As Tas had said, it seemed just an ordinary grove of oak trees, although they were certainly the tallest oaks either the dwarf or the kender had seen in long years of exploring Krynn.

But as the two approached, they felt the strange chilling sensation become stronger until it was worse than any cold they had ever experienced, even the cold of the glacier in Ice Wall. It was worse because it came from within and it made no sense! Why should it be so cold in just this part of the city? The sun was shining. There wasn't a cloud in the sky. But soon their fingers were numb and stiff. Flint could no longer hold his battle-axe and was forced to put it back in its holder with shaking hands. Tas's teeth chattered, he had lost all feeling in his pointed ears, and he shivered violently.

"L-let's g-get out-t of h-here . . ." stammered the dwarf through blue lips.

"W-we're j-just s-standing in a sh-shadow of a building." Tas nearly bit his tongue. "W-when we g-get in the s-s-sunshine, it'll war-warm up."

"No f-fire on K-K-Krynn will w-warm th-this!" Flint snapped viciously, stomping on the ground to get the circulation started in his feet.

"J-just a f-few m-more f-feet . . ." Tas kept going along gamely, even though his knees knocked together. But he went alone.

Turning around, he saw that Flint seemed paralyzed, unable to move. His head was bowed, his beard quivered.

I should go back, Tas thought, but he couldn't. The curiosity that did more than anything in the world to reduce the kender population kept drawing him forward.

Tas came to the edge of the grove of oak trees and—here—his heart almost failed him. Kender are normally immune to the sensation of fear, so only a kender could have come even this far. But now Tas found himself a prey to the most unreasoning terror he had ever experienced. And whatever was causing it was located within that grove of oak trees.

They're ordinary trees, Tas said to himself, shivering. I've talked to spectres in Darken Wood. I've faced three or four dragons. I broke a dragon orb. Just an ordinary grove of trees. I was prisoner in a wizard's castle. I saw a demon from the Abyss. Just a grove of ordinary trees.

Slowly, talking to himself, Tasslehoff inched his way through the oak trees. He didn't go far, not even past the row of trees that formed the outer perimeter of the grove. Because now he could see into the heart of the grove.

Tasslehoff gulped, turned, and ran.

At the sight of the kender running back toward him, Flint knew it was All Over. Something Awful was going to crash out of that grove of trees. The dwarf whirled so rapidly he tripped over his feet and fell sprawling to the pavement. Running up to him, Tas grabbed Flint's belt and pulled him up. Then the two dashed madly down the street, the dwarf running for his very life. He could almost hear gigantic footsteps thudding along behind him. He did not dare turn around. Visions of a slobbering monster drove him on until his heart seemed about to burst from his body. Finally they reached the end of the street.

It was warm. The sun shone.

They could hear the voices of real live people drifting from the crowded streets beyond. Flint stopped, exhausted, gasping for breath. Glancing fearfully back down the street, he was surprised to see it was still empty.

"What was it?" he managed to ask when he could speak past the thudding of his heart.

The kender's face was pale as death. "A-a t-tower . . ." Tas gulped, puffing.

Flint's eyes opened wide. "A tower?" the dwarf repeated. "I *ran* all that way, nearly killing myself, and I was running from a *tower!* I don't suppose"—Flint's bushy eyebrows came together alarmingly—"that the tower was chasing you?"

"N-no," Tas admitted. "It, it just stood there. But it was the most horrible thing I've ever seen in my life," the kender avowed solemnly, shuddering.

"That would be the Tower of High Sorcery," the Lord of Palanthas told Laurana that evening as they entered the map room of the beautiful palace on the hill overlooking the city. "No wonder your little friend was terrified. I'm surprised he got as far as the Shoikan Oak Grove."

"He's a kender," Laurana replied, smiling.

"Ah, yes. Well, that explains it. Now that's something I hadn't considered, you know. Hiring kender to do the work around the Tower. We have to pay the most outrageous prices to get men to go into those buildings once a year and keep them in good repair. But then"—the Lord appeared downcast—"I don't suppose the townspeople would be at all pleased to see a sizeable number of kender in the city."

Amothus, Lord of Palanthas, padded across the polished marble floor of the map room, his hands clasped behind his robes of state. Laurana walked next to him, trying to keep from tripping over the hem of the long, flowing gown the Palanthians had insisted she wear. They had been quite charming about the dress, offering it as a gift. But she knew they were horrified to see a Princess of the Qualinesti parading around in blood-stained, battle-scarred armor. Laurana had no choice but to accept it; she could not afford to offend the Palanthians whom she was counting on for help. But she felt naked and fragile and defenseless without her sword at her side and the steel around her body.

And she knew that the generals of the Palanthian army, the temporary commanders of the Solamnic Knights, and the other nobles, advisors from the City Senate, were the ones making her feel fragile and defenseless. All of them reminded her with every look that she was, to them, a woman playing at being a soldier. All right, she had done well. She had fought her little war and she had won. Now, back to the kitchen. . . .

"What *is* the Tower of High Sorcery?" Laurana asked abruptly. She had learned after a week of negotiating with the Lord of Palanthas that, although an intelligent man, his thoughts tended to wander into unexplored regions and he needed constant guidance to keep to the central topic.

"Oh, yes. Well, you can see it from the window here, if you really want to . . ." The Lord seemed reluctant.

"I would like to see it," Laurana said coolly.

Shrugging, Lord Amothus veered from his course and led Laurana to a window she had already noticed because it was covered with thick curtains. The curtains over the other windows of the room were open, revealing a breathtaking view of the city in whatever direction one looked.

"Yes, this is the reason I keep these shut," the Lord said with a sigh in answer to Laurana's question. "A pity, too. This was once the most magnificent view in the city, according to the old records. But that was before the Tower was cursed—"

The Lord drew the curtains aside with a trembling hand, his face dark with sorrow. Startled at such emotion, Laurana looked out curiously, then drew in a breath. The sun was sinking behind the snow-capped mountains, streaking the sky with red and purple. The vibrant colors shimmered on the pure white buildings of Palanthas as the rare, translucent marble from which they were built caught the dying light. Laurana had never imagined such beauty could exist in the world of humans. It rivaled her beloved homeland of Qualinesti.

Then her eyes were drawn to a darkness within the shimmering pearl radiance. A single tower rose up to the sky. It was tall; even though the palace was perched on a hill, the top of the Tower was only slightly below her line of sight. Made of black marble, it stood out in distinct contrast to the white marble of the city around it. Minarets must have once graced its gleaming surface, she saw, though these were now crumbling and broken. Dark windows, like empty eyesockets, stared sightlessly into the world. A fence surrounded it. The fence, too, was black and, on the gate of the fence, Laurana saw something fluttering. For a moment she thought it was a huge bird, trapped there, for it seemed alive. But just as she was about to call the Lord's attention to it, he shut the curtains with a shiver.

"I'm sorry," he apologized. "I can't stand it. Shocking. And to think we've lived with that for centuries. . . ."

"I don't think it's so terrible," Laurana said earnestly, her mind's eye remembering the view of the Tower and the city around it. "The Tower . . . seems right somehow. Your city is very beautiful, but sometimes it's such a cold, perfect beauty that I don't notice it anymore." Looking out the other windows, Laurana was once more as enchanted with the view as she had been when she first entered Palanthas. "But after seeing that, that flaw in your city, it makes the beauty stand out in my mind . . . if you understand. . . ."

It was obvious from the bemused expression on the Lord's face that he did not understand. Laurana sighed, though she caught herself glancing at the drawn curtains with a strange fascination. "How did the Tower come to be cursed?" she asked instead.

"It was during the—oh, I say, here's someone who can tell the story far better than I," Lord Amothus said, looking up in relief as the door opened. "It isn't a story I enjoy relating, to be perfectly honest."

"Astinus of the Library of Palanthas," announced the herald.

To Laurana's astonishment, every man in the room rose respectfully to his feet, even the great generals and noblemen. All this, she thought, for a librarian? Then, to her even greater astonishment, the Lord of Palanthas and all his generals and all the nobles bowed as the historian entered. Laurana bowed, too, out of confused courtesy. As a member of the royal house of Qualinesti, she was not supposed to bow before anyone on Krynn unless it be her own father, Speaker of the Suns. But when she straightened and studied this man, she felt suddenly that bowing to him had been most fitting and proper.

Astinus entered with an ease and assurance that led her to believe he would stand unabashed in the presence of all the royalty on Krynn and the heavens as well. He seemed middle-aged, but there was an ageless quality about him. His face might have been chiseled out of the marble of Palanthas itself and, at first, Laurana was repelled by the cold, passionless quality of that face. Then she saw that the man's dark eyes literally blazed with life, as though lit from within by the fire of a thousand souls.

"You are late, Astinus," Lord Amothus said pleasantly, though with a marked respect. He and his generals all remained standing until the historian had seated himself, Laurana noticed, as did even the Knights of Solamnia. Almost overcome with an unaccustomed awe, she sank into her seat at the huge, round table covered with maps which stood in the center of the great room.

"I had business to attend to," Astinus replied in a voice that might have sounded from a bottomless well.

"I heard you were troubled by a strange occurrence." The Lord of Palanthas flushed in embarrassment. "I really must apologize. We have no idea how the young man came to be found in such an appalling condition upon your stairs. If only you had let us know! We could have removed the body without fuss—"

"It was no trouble," Astinus said abruptly, glancing at Laurana. "The matter has been properly dealt with. All is now at an end."

"But . . . uh . . . what about the. . . uh . . . remains?" Lord Amothus asked hesitantly. "I know how painful this must be, but there are certain health proclamations that the Senate has passed and I'd like to be sure all has been attended to. . . ."

"Perhaps I should leave," Laurana said coldly, rising to her feet, "until this conversation has ended."

"What? Leave?" The Lord of Palanthas stared at her vaguely. "You've only just come—"

"I believe our conversation is distressing to the elven princess," Astinus remarked. "The elves, as you remember, my lord, have a great reverence for life. Death is not discussed in this callous fashion among them."

"Oh, my heavens!" Lord Amothus flushed deeply, rising and taking her hand. "I do beg your pardon, my dear. Absolutely abominable of me. Please forgive me and be seated again. Some wine for the princess—" Amothus hailed a servant, who filled Laurana's glass.

"You were discussing the Towers of High Sorcery as I entered. What do you know of the Towers?" Astinus asked, his eyes staring into Laurana's soul.

Shivering at that penetrating gaze, she gulped a sip of wine, sorry now that she had mentioned it. "Really," she said faintly, "perhaps we should turn to business. I'm certain the generals are anxious to return to their troops and I—"

"What do you know of the Towers?" Astinus repeated.

"I—uh—not much," Laurana faltered, feeling as if she were back in school being confronted by her tutor. "I had a friend, that is, an acquaintance, who took the Tests at the Tower of High Sorcery in Wayreth, but he is—"

"Raistlin of Solace, I believe," Astinus said imperturbably.

"Why, yes!" Laurana answered, startled. "How—"

"I am a historian, young woman. It is my business to know," Astinus replied. "I will tell you the history of the Tower of Palanthas. Do not consider it a waste of time, Lauralanthalasa, for its history is bound up in your destiny." Ignoring her shocked look, he gestured to one of the generals. "You, there, open that curtain. You are shutting out the best view in the city, as I believe the princess remarked before I entered. This, then, is the story of the Tower of High Sorcery of Palanthas.

"My tale must begin with what became known, in hindsight, as the Lost Battles. During the Age of Might, when the Kingpriest of Istar began jumping at shadows, he gave his fears a name—magic-users! He feared them, he feared their vast power. He did not understand it, and so it became a threat to him.

"It was easy to arouse the populace against the magic-users. Although widely respected, they were never trusted, primarily because they allowed among their ranks representatives of all three powers in the universe, the White Robes of Good, the Red Robes of Neutrality, and the Black Robes of Evil. For they understood—as the Kingpriest did not—that the universe swings in balance among these three and that to disturb the balance is to invite destruction.

"And so the people rose against the magic-users. The five Towers of High Sorcery were prime targets, naturally, for it was in these Towers that the powers of the Order were most concentrated. And it was in these Towers that the young mages came to take the Tests—those who dared. For the Trials are arduous and, worse, hazardous. Indeed, failure means one thing: death!"

"Death?" repeated Laurana, incredulously. "Then Raistlin—"

"Risked his life to take the Test. And he nearly paid the price. That is neither here nor there, however. Because of this deadly penalty for failure, dark rumors were spread about the Towers of High Sorcery. In vain the magic-users sought to explain that these were only centers of learning and that each young mage risking his life did so willingly, understanding the purpose behind it. Here, too, in the Towers, the mages kept their spell-books and their scrolls, their implements of magic. But no one believed them. Stories of strange rites and rituals and sacrifices spread among the people, fostered by the Kingpriest and his clerics for their own ends.

"And the day came when the populace rose against the magic-users. And for only the second time in the history of the Order, the Robes came together. The first time was during the creation of the dragon orbs which contained the essences of good and evil, bound together by neutrality. After that, they went their separate ways. Now, allied by a common threat, they came together once more to protect their own.

"The magicians themselves destroyed two of the Towers, rather than let the mobs invade them and meddle with that which was beyond their understanding. The destruction of these two Towers laid waste to the countryside around them and frightened the Kingpriest, for there was a Tower of High Sorcery located in Istar and one in Palanthas. As for the third, in the Forest of Wayreth, few cared what became of it, for it was far from any center of civilization.

"And so the Kingpriest approached the magic-users with a show of piety. If they would leave the two Towers standing, he would let them withdraw in peace, removing their books and scrolls and magical implements to the Tower of High Sorcery in Wayreth. Sorrowfully the magic-users accepted his offer."

"But why didn't they fight?" Laurana interrupted. "I've seen Raistlin and . . . and Fizban when they're angry! I can't imagine what truly powerful wizards must be like!"

"Ah, but stop and consider this, Laurana. Your young friend, Raistlin, grew exhausted casting even a few relatively minor spells. And once a spell is cast, it is gone from his memory forever unless he reads his spellbook and studies it once more. This is true of even the highest level mages. It is how the gods protect us from those who might otherwise become too powerful and aspire to godhood itself. Wizards must sleep, they must be able to concentrate, they must spend time in daily study. How could they withstand besieging mobs? And, too, how could they destroy their own people?

"No, they felt they had to accept the Kingpriest's offer. Even the Black Robes, who cared little for the populace, saw that they must be defeated and that magic itself might be lost from the world. They withdrew from the Tower of High Sorcery at Istar, and almost immediately the Kingpriest moved in to occupy it. Then they abandoned the Tower here, in Palanthas. And the story of this Tower is a terrible one."

Astinus, who had been relating this without expression in his voice, suddenly grew solemn, his face darkening.

"Well I remember that day," he said, speaking more to himself than to those around the table. "They brought their books and scrolls to me, to be kept in my library. For there were many, many books and scrolls in the Tower, more than the magic-users could carry to Wayreth. They knew I would guard them and treasure them. Many of the spellbooks were ancient and could no longer be read, since they had been bound with spells of protection, spells to which the Key . . . had been lost. The Key . . ."

Astinus fell silent, pondering. Then, with a sigh, as if brushing away dark thoughts, he continued.

"The people of Palanthas gathered around the Tower as the highest of the Order—the Wizard of the White Robes—closed the Tower's slender gates of gold and locked them with a silver key. The Lord of Palanthas watched him eagerly. All knew the

Lord intended to move into the Tower, as his mentor, the King-priest of Istar, had done. His eyes lingered greedily on the Tower, for legends of the wonders within, both fair and evil, had spread throughout the land."

"Of all the beautiful buildings in Palanthas," murmured Lord Amothus, "the Tower of High Sorcery was said to be the most splendid. And now . . ."

"What happened?" asked Laurana, feeling chilled as the darkness of night crept through the room, wishing someone would summon the servants to light the candles.

"The Wizard started to hand the silver key to the Lord," continued Astinus in a deep, sad voice. "Suddenly, one of the Black Robes appeared in a window in the upper stories. As the people stared at him in horror, he shouted, 'The gates will remain closed and the halls empty until the day comes when the master of both the past and the present returns with power!' Then the evil mage leaped out, hurling himself down upon the gates. And as the barbs of silver and of gold pierced the black robes, he cast a curse upon the Tower. His blood stained the ground, the silver and golden gates withered and twisted and turned to black. The shimmering tower of white and red faded to ice-gray stone, its black minarets crumbled.

"The Lord and the people fled in terror and, to this day, no one dares approach the Tower of Palanthas. Not even kender"— Astinus smiled briefly—"who fear nothing in this world. The curse is so powerful it keeps away *all* mortals—"

"Until the master of past and present returns," Laurana murmured.

"Bah! The man was mad." Lord Amothus sniffed. "No man is master of past and present, unless it be you, Astinus."

"I am not master!" Astinus said in such hollow, ringing tones that everyone in the room stared at him. "I remember the past, I record the present. I do not seek to dominate either!"

"Mad, like I said." The Lord shrugged. "And now we are forced to endure an eyesore like the Tower because no one can stand to live around it or get close enough to tear it down."

"I think to tear it down would be a shame," Laurana said softly, gazing at the Tower through the window. "It belongs here. . . ."

"Indeed it does, young woman," Astinus replied, regarding her strangely.

Night's shadows had deepened as Astinus talked. Soon the Tower was shrouded in darkness while lights sparkled in the rest of the city. Palanthas seemed to be trying to out-glitter the stars, thought Laurana, but a round patch of blackness will remain always in its center.

"How sad and how tragic," she murmured, feeling that she must say something, since Astinus was staring straight at her. "And that, that dark thing I saw fluttering, pinned to the fence. . . ." She stopped in horror.

"Mad, mad," repeated Lord Amothus gloomily. "Yes, that is what's left of the body, so we suppose. No one has been able to get close enough to find out."

Laurana shuddered. Putting her hands to her aching head, she knew that this grim story would haunt her for nights, and she wished she'd never heard it. *Bound up in her destiny!* Angrily she put the thought out of her mind. It didn't matter. She didn't have time for this. Her destiny looked bleak enough without adding nightmarish nursery tales.

As if reading her thoughts, Astinus suddenly rose to his feet and called for more light.

"For," he said coldly, staring at Laurana, "the past is lost. Your future is your own. And we have a great deal of work to do before morning."

7

"First, I must read a communique I received from Lord Gunthar only a few hours ago." The Lord of Palanthas withdrew a scroll from the folds of his finely woven, woolen robes and spread it on the table, smoothing it carefully with his hands. Leaning his head back, he peered at it, obviously trying to bring it into focus.

Laurana, feeling certain that this must be in reply to a message of her own she had prompted Lord Amothus to send to Lord Gunthar two days earlier, bit her lip in impatience.

"It's creased," Lord Amothus said in apology. "The griffons the elven lords have so kindly loaned us"—he bowed to Laurana, who bowed back, suppressing the urge to rip the message from his hand—"cannot be taught to carry these scrolls without rumpling them. Ah, now I can make it out. 'Lord Gunthar to Amothus, Lord of Palanthas. Greetings.' Charming man, Lord Gunthar." The Lord looked up. "He was here only last year, during Spring Dawning festival, which, by the way, takes place in three weeks, my dear. Perhaps you would grace our festivities—"

"I would be pleased to, lord, if any of us are here in three weeks," Laurana said, clenching her hands tightly beneath the table in an effort to remain calm.

Lord Amothus blinked, then smiled indulgently. "Certainly.

The dragonarmies. Well, to continue reading. 'I am truly grieved to hear of the loss of so many of our Knighthood. Let us find comfort in the knowledge that they died victorious, fighting this great evil that darkens our lands. I feel an even greater personal grief in the loss of three of our finest leaders: Derek Crownguard, Knight of the Rose, Alfred MarKenin, Knight of the Sword, and Sturm Brightblade, Knight of the Crown.' " The Lord turned to Laurana. "Brightblade. He was your close friend, I believe, my dear?"

"Yes, my lord," Laurana murmured, lowering her head, letting her golden hair fall forward to hide the anguish in her eyes. It had been only a short time since they had buried Sturm in the Chamber of Paladine beneath the ruins of the High Clerist's Tower. The pain of his loss still ached.

"Continue reading, Amothus," Astinus commanded coldly. "I cannot afford to take too much time from my studies."

"Certainly, Astinus," the Lord said, flushing. He began to read again hurriedly. " 'This tragedy leaves the Knights in unusual circumstances. First, the Knighthood is now made up of, as I understand, primarily Knights of the Crown, the lowest order of Knights. This means that, while all have passed their tests and won their shields, they are, however, young and inexperienced. For most, this was their first battle. It also leaves us without any suitable commanders since—according to the Measure—there must be a representative from each of the three Orders of Knights in command.' "

Laurana could hear the faint jingle of armor and the rattle of swords as the knights present shifted uncomfortably. They were temporary leaders until this question of command could be settled. Closing her eyes, Laurana sighed. Please, Gunthar, she thought, let your choice be a wise one. So many have died because of political manuevering. Let this be an end to it!

" 'Therefore I appoint to fill the position of leadership of the Knights of Solamnia, Lauralanthalasa of the royal house of

Qualinesti . . .' " The Lord paused a moment, as if uncertain he had read correctly. Laurana's eyes opened wide as she stared at him in shocked disbelief. But she was not more shocked than the knights themselves.

Lord Amothus peered vaguely at the scroll, rereading it. Then, hearing a murmur of impatience from Astinus, he hurried on, " 'who is the most experienced person currently in the field and the only one with knowledge of how to use the dragonlances. I attest to the validity of this Writ by my seal. Lord Gunthar Uth Wistan, Grand Master of the Knights of Solamnia, and so forth.' " The Lord looked up. "Congratulations, my dear, or perhaps I should say 'general.' "

Laurana sat very still. For a moment she was so filled with anger she thought she might stalk out of the room. Visions swam before her eyes, Lord Alfred's headless corpse, poor Derek dying in his madness, Sturm's peace-filled, lifeless eyes, the bodies of the knights who had died in the Tower laid out in a row. . . .

And now *she* was in command. An elfmaid from the royal household. Not even old enough, by elven standards, to be free of her father's house. A spoiled little girl who had run away from her home to "chase after" her childhood sweetheart, Tanis Half-Elven. That spoiled little girl had grown up. Fear, pain, great loss, great sorrow, she knew that, in some ways, she was older than her father now.

Turning her head, she saw Sir Markham and Sir Patrick exchange glances. Of all the Knights of the Crown, these two had served longest. She knew both men to be valiant soldiers and honorable men. They had both fought bravely at the High Clerist's Tower. Why hadn't Gunthar picked one of them, as she herself had recommended?

Sir Patrick stood up, his face dark. "I cannot accept this," he said in a low voice. "Lady Laurana is a valiant warrior, certainly, but she has never commanded men in the field."

"Have you, young knight?" Astinus asked imperturbably.

Patrick flushed. "No, but that's different. She's a wom—"

"Oh, really, Patrick!" Sir Markham laughed. He was a carefree, easy-going young man, a startling contrast to the stern and serious Patrick. "Hair on your chest doesn't make you a general. Relax! It's politics. Gunthar has made a wise move."

Laurana flushed, knowing he was right. She was a safe choice until Gunthar had time to rebuild the Knighthood and entrench himself firmly as leader.

"But there is no precedent for this!" Patrick continued to argue, avoiding Laurana's eyes.

"I'm certain that, according to the Measure, women are not permitted in the Knighthood—"

"You are wrong," Astinus stated flatly. "And there is precedent. In the Third Dragonwar, a young woman was accepted into the Knighthood following the deaths of her father and her brothers. She rose to Knight of the Sword and died honorably in battle, mourned by her brethren."

No one spoke. Lord Amothus appeared extremely embarrassed, he had almost sunk beneath the table at Sir Markham's reference to hairy chests. Astinus stared coldly at Sir Patrick. Sir Markham toyed with his wine glass, glancing once at Laurana and smiling. After a brief, internal struggle, visible in his face, Sir Patrick sat back down, scowling.

Sir Markham raised his glass. "To our commander."

Laurana did not respond. She was in command. Command of what? she asked herself bitterly. The tattered remnants of the Knights of Solamnia who had been sent to Palanthas; of the hundreds that had sailed, no more than fifty survived. They had won a victory . . . but at what terrible cost? A dragon orb destroyed, the High Clerist's Tower in ruins. . . .

"Yes, Laurana," said Astinus, "they have left you to pick up the pieces."

She looked up startled, frightened of this strange man who spoke her thoughts.

"I didn't want this," she murmured through lips that felt numb.

"I don't believe any of us were sitting around praying for a war," Astinus remarked caustically. "But war has come, and now you must do what you can to win it." He rose to his feet. The Lord of Palanthas, the generals, and the Knights stood up respectfully.

Laurana remained seated, her eyes on her hands. She felt Astinus staring at her, and she stubbornly refused to look at him.

"Must you go, Astinus?" Lord Amothus asked plaintively.

"I must. My studies wait. Already I have been gone too long. You have a great deal to do now, much of it mundane and boring. You do not need me. You have your leader." He made a motion with his hand.

"What?" Laurana said, catching his gesture out of the corner of her eye. Now she looked at him, then her eyes went to the Lord of Palanthas. "Me? You can't mean that! I'm only in command of the Knights—"

"Which makes you commander of the armies of the city of Palanthas, if we so choose," the Lord said. "And if Astinus recommends you—"

"I don't," Astinus said bluntly. "I cannot recommend anyone. I do not shape history," He stopped suddenly, and Laurana was surprised to see the mask slip from his face, revealing grief and sorrow. "That is, I have endeavored not to shape history. Sometimes, even I fail. . . ." He sighed, then regained control of himself, replacing the mask. "I have done what I came to do, given you a knowledge of the past. It may or may not be relevant to your future."

He turned to leave.

"Wait!" Laurana cried, rising. She started to take a step toward him, then faltered as the cold, stern eyes met hers, forbidding as solid stone. "You—you see—everything that is happening, as it occurs?"

"I do."

"Then you could tell us, where the dragonarmies are, what they are doing—"

"Bah! You know that as well as I do." Astinus turned away again.

Laurana cast a quick glance around the room. She saw the lord and the generals watching her with amusement. She knew she was acting like that spoiled little girl again, but she must have answers! Astinus was near the door, the servants were opening it. Casting a defiant look at the others, Laurana left the table and walked quickly across the polished marble floor, stumbling over the hem of her dress in her haste. Astinus, hearing her, stopped within the doorway.

"I have two questions," she said softly, coming near him.

"Yes," he answered, staring into her green eyes, "one in your head and one in your heart. Ask the first."

"Is there a dragon orb still in existence?"

Astinus was silent a moment. Once more Laurana saw pain in his eyes as his ageless face appeared suddenly old. "Yes," he said finally. "I can tell you that much. One still exists. But it is beyond your ability to use or to find. Put it out of your thoughts."

"Tanis had it," Laurana persisted. "Does this mean he has lost it? Where"—she hesitated, this was the question in her heart—"where is he?"

"Put it out of your thoughts."

"What do you mean?" Laurana felt chilled by the man's frost-rimed voice.

"I do not predict the future. I see only the present as it becomes the past. Thus I have seen it since time began. I have seen love that, through its willingness to sacrifice everything, brought hope to the world. I have seen love that tried to overcome pride and a lust for power, but failed. The world is darker for its failure, but it is only as a cloud dims the sun. The sun—

the love, still remains. Finally I have seen love lost in darkness. Love misplaced, misunderstood, because the lover did not know his—or her—own heart."

"You speak in riddles," Laurana said angrily.

"Do I?" Astinus asked. He bowed. "Farewell, Lauralanthalasa. My advice to you is: concentrate on your duty."

The historian walked out the door.

Laurana stood staring after him, repeating his words: "love lost in darkness." Was it a riddle or did she know the answer and simply refuse to admit it to herself, as Astinus implied?

" 'I left Tanis in Flotsam to handle matters in my absence.'" Kitiara had said those words. Kitiara, the Dragon Highlord. Kitiara, the human woman Tanis loved.

Suddenly the pain in Laurana's heart, the pain that had been there since she heard Kitiara speak those words, vanished, leaving a cold emptiness, a void of darkness like the missing constellations in the night sky. "Love lost in darkness." Tanis was lost. That is what Astinus was trying to tell her. Concentrate on your duties. Yes, she would concentrate on her duties, since that was all she had left.

Turning around to face the Lord of Palanthas and his generals, Laurana threw back her head, her golden hair glinting in the light of the candles. "I will take the leadership of the armies," she said in a voice nearly as cold as the void in her soul.

"Now *this* is stonework!" stated Flint in satisfaction, stamping on the battlements of the Old City Wall beneath his feet. "Dwarves built this, no doubt about it. Look how each stone is cut with careful precision to fit perfectly within the wall, no two quite alike."

"Fascinating," said Tasslehoff, yawning. "Did dwarves build that Tower we—"

"Don't remind me!" Flint snapped. "And dwarves did *not*

build the Towers of High Sorcery. They were built by the wizards themselves, who created them from the very bones of the world, raising the rocks up out of the soil with their magic."

"That's wonderful!" breathed Tas, waking up. "I wish I could have been there. How—"

"It's nothing," continued the dwarf loudly, glaring at Tas, "compared to the work of the dwarven rockmasons, who spent centuries perfecting their art. Now look at this stone. See the texture of the chisel marks—"

"Here comes Laurana," Tas said thankfully, glad to end his lesson in dwarven architecture.

Flint quit peering at the rock wall to watch Laurana walk toward them from a great dark hallway which opened onto the battlement. She was dressed once more in the armor she had worn at the High Clerist's Tower; the blood had been cleaned off the gold-decorated steel breastplate, the dents repaired. Her long, honey-colored hair flowed from beneath her red-plumed helm, gleaming in Solinari's light. She walked slowly, her eyes on the eastern horizon where the mountains were dark shadows against the starry sky. The moonlight touched her face as well. Looking at her, Flint sighed.

"She's changed," he said to Tasslehoff softly. "And elves never change. Do you remember when we met her in Qualinesti? In the fall, only six months ago. Yet it could be years—"

"She's still not over Sturm's death. It's only been a week," Tas said, his impish kender face unusually serious and thoughtful.

"It's not just that." The old dwarf shook his head. "It had something to do with that meeting she had with Kitiara, up on the wall of the High Clerist's Tower. It was something Kitiara did or said. Blast her!" the dwarf snapped viciously. "I never did trust her! Even in the old days. It didn't surprise me to see her in the get-up of a Dragon Highlord! I'd give a mountain of steel coins to know what she said to Laurana that snuffed the light right out of her. She was like a ghost when we brought her down from the wall, after Kitiara and her blue dragon left. I'll bet my beard," muttered the dwarf, "that it had something to do with Tanis."

"I can't believe Kitiara's a Dragon Highlord. She was always . . . always . . ." Tas groped for words. "Well, fun!"

"Fun?" said Flint, his brows contracting. "Maybe. But cold and selfish, too. Oh, she was charming enough when she wanted to be." Flint's voice sank to a whisper. Laurana was getting close enough to hear. "Tanis never did see it. He always believed there was more to Kitiara beneath the surface. He thought he alone knew her, that she covered herself with a hard shell to conceal her tender heart. Hah! She had as much heart as these stones."

"What's the news, Laurana?" Tas asked cheerfully as the elfmaid came up to them.

Laurana smiled down at her old friends, but, as Flint said, it was no longer the innocent, gay smile of the elfmaid who had walked beneath the aspen trees of Qualinesti. Now her smile was like the bleakness of the sun in a cold winter sky. It gave light but no warmth, perhaps because there was no matching warmth in her eyes.

"I am commander of the armies," she said flatly.

"Congratu—" began Tas, but his voice died at the sight of her face.

"There is nothing to congratulate me about," Laurana said bitterly. "What do I command? A handful of knights, stuck in a ruined bastion miles away in the Vingaard Mountains, and a thousand men who stand upon the walls of this city." She clenched her gloved fist, her eyes on the eastern sky that was beginning to show the faintest glimmer of morning light. "We should be out there! Now! While the dragonarmy is still scattered and trying to regroup! We could defeat them easily. But, no, we dare not go out onto the Plains, not even with the dragonlances. For what good are they against dragons in flight? If we had a dragon orb—"

She fell silent for a moment, then drew a deep breath. Her face hardened. "Well, we don't. It's no use thinking about it. So we'll stand here, on the battlements of Palanthas, and wait for death."

"Now, Laurana," Flint remonstrated, clearing his throat gruffly, "perhaps things aren't that dark. There are good solid walls around this city. A thousand men can hold it easily. The gnomes with their catapults guard the harbor. The knights guard the only pass through the Vingaard Mountains and we've sent men to reinforce them. And we do have the dragonlances, a few at any rate, and Gunthar sent word more are on the way. So we can't attack dragons in flight? They'll think twice about flying over the walls—"

"That isn't enough, Flint!" Laurana sighed. "Oh, sure, we may hold the dragonarmies off for a week or two weeks or maybe even a month. But then what? What happens to us when they control the land around us? All we can do against the dragons is shut ourselves up in safe little havens. Soon this world will be nothing but tiny islands of light surrounded by vast oceans of darkness. And then, one by one, the darkness will engulf us all."

Laurana laid her head down upon her hand, resting against the wall.

"How long has it been since you've slept?" Flint asked sternly.

"I don't know," she answered. "My waking and sleeping seem mixed together. I'm walking in a dream half the time, and sleeping through reality the other half."

"Get some sleep now," the dwarf said in what Tas referred to as his Grandfather Voice. "We're turning in. Our watch is almost up."

"I can't," Laurana said, rubbing her eyes. The thought of sleep suddenly made her realize how exhausted she was. "I came to tell you, we received reports that dragons were seen, flying westward over the city of Kalaman."

"They're heading this direction then," Tas said, visualizing a map in his head.

"Whose reports?" asked the dwarf suspiciously.

"The griffons. Now don't scowl like that." Laurana smiled slightly at the sight of the dwarf's disgust. "The griffons have been a vast help to us. If the elves contribute nothing more to this war than their griffons, they will have already done a great deal."

"Griffons are dumb animals," Flint stated. "And I trust them about as far as I trust kender. Besides," the dwarf continued, ignoring Tas's indignant glare, "it doesn't make sense. The Highlords don't send dragons to attack without the armies backing them up. . . ."

"Maybe the armies aren't as disorganized as we heard." Laurana sighed wearily. "Or maybe the dragons are simply being sent to wreak what havoc they can. Demoralize the city, lay waste to the surrounding countryside. I don't know. Look, word's spread."

Flint glanced around. Those soldiers that were off duty were still in their places, staring eastward at the mountains whose snow-capped peaks were turning a delicate pink in the brightening dawn. Talking in low voices they were joined by others, just waking and hearing the news.

"I feared as much." Laurana sighed. "This will start a panic! I warned Lord Amothus to keep the news quiet, but the Palanthians aren't used to keeping anything quiet! There, what did I tell you?"

Looking down from the wall, the friends could see the streets starting to fill with people—half-dressed, sleepy, frightened. Watching them run from house to house, Laurana could imagine the rumors being spread.

She bit her lip, her green eyes flared in anger. "Now I'll have to pull men off the walls to get these people back into their homes.

I can't have them in the streets when the dragons attack! You men, come with me!" Gesturing to a group of soldiers standing nearby, Laurana hurried away. Flint and Tas watched her disappear down the stairs, heading for the Lord's palace. Soon they saw armed patrols fanning out into the streets, trying to herd people back into their homes and quell the rising tide of panic.

"Fine lot of good that's doing!" Flint snorted. The streets were getting more crowded by the moment.

But Tas, standing on a block of stone staring out over the wall, shook his head. "It doesn't matter!" he whispered in despair "Flint, look—"

The dwarf climbed hurriedly up to stand beside his friend. Already men were pointing and shouting, grabbing bows and spears. Here and there, the barbed silver point of a dragonlance could be seen, glinting in the torchlight.

"How many?" Flint asked, squinting.

"Ten," Tas answered slowly. "Two flights. Big dragons, too. Maybe the red ones, like we saw in Tarsis. I can't see their color against the dawn's light, but I can see riders on them. Maybe a Highlord. Maybe Kitiara . . . Gee," Tas said, struck by a sudden thought, "I hope I get to talk to her this time. It must be interesting being a Highlord—"

His words were lost in the sound of bells ringing from towers all over the city. The people in the streets stared up at the walls where the soldiers were pointing and exclaiming. Far below them, Tas could see Laurana emerge from the Lord's palace, followed by the Lord himself and two of his generals. The kender could tell from the set of her shoulders that Laurana was furious. She gestured at the bells, apparently wanting them silenced. But it was too late. The people of Palanthas went wild with terror. And most of the inexperienced soldiers were in nearly as bad a state as the civilians. The sound of shrieks and wails and hoarse calls rose up into the air. Grim memories of Tarsis came back to Tas, people trampled to death in the streets, houses exploding in flames.

The kender turned slowly around. "I guess I don't want to talk to Kitiara," he said softly, brushing his hand across his eyes as he watched the dragons fly closer and closer. "I don't want to know what it's like being a Highlord, because it must be sad and dark and horrible. . . . Wait—"

Tas stared eastward. He couldn't believe his eyes, so he leaned far out, perilously close to falling over the edge of the wall.

"Flint!" he shouted, waving his arms.

"What is it?" Flint snapped. Catching hold of Tas by the belt of his blue leggings, the dwarf hauled the excited kender back in with jerk.

"It's like in Pax Tharkas!" Tas babbled incoherently. "Like Huma's Tomb. Like Fizban said! They're here! They've come!"

"Who's here!" Flint roared in exasperation.

Jumping up and down in excitement, his pouches bouncing around wildly, Tas turned without answering and dashed off, leaving the dwarf fuming on the stairs, calling out, "Who's here, you rattlebrain?"

"Laurana!" shouted Tas's shrill voice, splitting the early morning air like a slightly off-key trumpet. "Laurana, they've come! They're here! Like Fizban said! Laurana!"

Cursing the kender beneath his breath, Flint stared back out to the east. Then, glancing around swiftly, the dwarf slipped a hand inside a vest pocket. Hurriedly he drew out a pair of glasses and, looking around again to make certain no one was watching him, he slipped them on.

Now he could make out what had been nothing more than a haze of pink light broken by the darker, pointed masses of the mountain range. The dwarf drew a deep, trembling breath. His eyes dimmed with tears. Quickly he snatched the glasses off his nose and put them back into their case, slipping them back into his pocket. But he'd worn the glasses just long enough to see the dawn touch the wings of dragons with a pink light, pink glinting off silver.

"Put your weapons down, lads," Flint said to the men around him, mopping his eyes with one of the kender's handkerchiefs. "Praise be to Reorx. Now we have a chance. Now we have a chance. . . ."

The Oath of the Dragons.

8

As the silver dragons settled to the ground on the outskirts of the great city of Palanthas, their wings filled the morning sky with a blinding radiance. The people crowded the walls to stare out uneasily at the beautiful, magnificent creatures.

At first the people had been so terrified of the huge beasts that they were intent on driving them away, even when Laurana assured them that these dragons were not evil. Finally Astinus himself emerged from his library and coldly informed Lord Amothus that these dragons would not harm them. Reluctantly the people of Palanthas laid down their weapons.

Laurana knew, however, that the people would have believed Astinus if he told them the sun would rise at midnight. They did *not* believe in the dragons.

It wasn't until Laurana herself walked out of the city gates and straight into the arms of a man who had been riding one of the beautiful silver dragons that the people begin to think there might be something to this children's story after all.

"Who is that man? Who has brought the dragons to us? Why have the dragons come?"

Jostling and shoving, the people leaned over the wall, asking questions and listening to the wrong answers. Out in the valley, the dragons slowly fanned their wings to keep their circulation going in the chill morning.

As Laurana embraced the man, another person climbed down off one of the dragons, a woman whose hair gleamed as silver as the dragon's wings. Laurana embraced this woman, too. Then, to the wonder of the people, Astinus led the three of them to the great library, where they were admitted by the Aesthetics. The huge doors shut behind them.

The people were left to mill about, buzzing with questions and casting dubious glances at the dragons sitting before their city walls.

Then the bells rang out once more. Lord Amothus was calling a meeting. Hurriedly the people left the walls to fill the city square before the Lord's palace as he came out onto a balcony to answer their questions.

"These are silver dragons," he shouted, "good dragons who have joined us in our battle against the evil dragons as in the legend of Huma. The dragons have been brought to our city by—"

Whatever else the Lord intended to say was lost in cheering. The bells rang out again, this time in celebration. People flooded the streets, singing and dancing. Finally, after a futile attempt to continue, the Lord simply declared the day a holiday and returned to his palace.

The following is an excerpt from the Chronicles, A History of Krynn, as recorded by Astinus of Palanthas. It can be found under the heading: "The Oath of the Dragons."

As I, Astinus, write these words, I look on the face of the elflord, Gilthanas, younger son of Solostaran, Speaker of the Suns, lord of the Qualinesti. Gilthanas's face is very much like his sister Laurana's face, and not just in family resemblance. Both have the delicate features and ageless quality of all elves.

But these two are different. Both faces are marked with a sorrow not to be seen on the faces of elves living on Krynn. Although I fear that before this war is ended, many elves will have this same look. And perhaps this is not a bad thing, for it seems that, finally, the elves are learning that they are part of this world, not above it.

To one side of Gilthanas sits his sister. To the other sits one of the most beautiful women I have seen walk on Krynn. She appears to be an elfmaid, a Wilder elf. But she does not deceive my eyes with her magic arts. She was never born of woman, elf or no. She is a dragon, a silver dragon, sister of the Silver Dragon who was beloved of Huma, Knight of Solamnia. It has been Silvara's fate to fall in love with a mortal, as did her sister. But, unlike Huma, this mortal, Gilthanas, cannot accept his fate. He looks at her . . . she looks at him. Instead of love, I see a smoldering anger within him that is slowly poisoning both their souls.

Silvara speaks. Her voice is sweet and musical. The light of my candle gleams in her beautiful silver hair and in her deep night-blue eyes.

"After I gave Theros Ironfeld the power to forge the dragon-lances within the heart of the Monument of the Silver Dragon," Silvara tells me, "I spent much time with the companions before they took the lances to the Council of Whitestone. I showed them through the Monument, I showed them the paintings of the Dragon War, which picture good dragons, silver and gold and bronze, fighting the evil dragons.

" 'Where are your people?' the companions asked me. 'Where are the good dragons? Why aren't they helping us in our time of need?'

"I held out against their questions, as long as I could. . . ."

Here Silvara stops speaking and looks at Gilthanas with her heart in her eyes. He does not meet her gaze but stares at the floor. Silvara sighs and resumes her story.

"Finally, I could resist his—their—pressure no longer. I told them about the Oath.

"When Takhisis, the Queen of Darkness, and her evil dragons were banished, the good dragons left the land to maintain the balance between good and evil. Made of the world, we returned to the world, sleeping an ageless sleep. We would have remained asleep, in a world of dreams, but then came the Cataclysm and Takhisis found her way back into the world again.

"Long had she planned for this return, should fate give it to her, and she was prepared. Before Paladine was aware of her, Takhisis woke the evil dragons from their sleep and ordered them to slip into the deep and secret places of the world and steal the eggs of the good dragons, who slept on, unaware. . . .

"The evil dragons brought the eggs of their brethren to the city of Sanction where the dragonarmies were forming. Here, in the volcanoes known as the Lords of Doom, the eggs of good dragons were hidden.

"Great was the grief of the good dragons when Paladine woke them from their sleep and they discovered what had occurred. They went to Takhisis to find out what price they would have to pay for the return of their unborn children. It was a terrible price. Takhisis demanded an oath. Each of the good dragons must swear that they would not participate in the war she was about to wage on Krynn. It was the good dragons who had helped bring about her defeat in the last war. This time she meant to insure that they would not become involved."

Here Silvara looks at me pleadingly, as if I were to judge them. I shake my head sternly. Far be it from me to judge anyone. I am a historian.

She continues:

"What could we do? Takhisis told us they would murder our children as they slept in their eggs unless we took the Oath. Paladine could not help us. The choice was ours. . . ."

Silvara's head droops, her hair hiding her face. I can hear tears choke her voice. Her words are barely audible to me.

"We took the Oath."

She cannot continue, that is obvious. After staring at her for a moment, Gilthanas clears his throat and begins to speak, his voice harsh.

"I, that is, Theros and my sister and I, finally persuaded Silvara that this Oath was wrong. There must be a way, we said, to rescue the eggs of the good dragons. Perhaps a small force of men might be able to steal the eggs back. Silvara was not convinced that I was right, but she did agree, after much talking, to take me to Sanction so that I could see for myself if such a plan might work.

"Our journey was long and difficult. Someday I may relate the dangers we faced, but I cannot now. I am too weary and we do not have time. The dragonarmies are reorganizing. We can catch them offguard, if we attack soon. I can see Laurana burning with impatience, eager to pursue them, even as we are speaking. So I will make our tale short.

"Silvara, in her 'elven form' as you see her now"—the bitterness in the elflord's voice cannot be expressed—"and I were captured outside of Sanction and made prisoners of the Dragon Highlord, Ariakas."

Gilthanas's fist clenches, his face is pale with anger and fear.

"Lord Verminaard was nothing, nothing compared to Lord Ariakas. This man's evil power is immense! And he is as intelligent as he is cruel, for it is his strategy that controls the dragonarmies and has led them to victory after victory.

"The suffering we endured at his hands, I cannot describe. I do not believe I can ever relate what they did to us!"

The young elflord trembles violently. Silvara starts to reach out a hand to comfort him, but he draws away from her and continues his story.

"Finally, with help, we escaped. We were in Sanction itself, a hideous town, built in the valley formed by the volcanoes, the Lords of Doom. These mountains tower over all, their foul smoke corrupts the air. The buildings are all new and modern, constructed with the blood of slaves. Built into the sides of the mountains is a temple to Takhisis, the Dark Queen. The dragon eggs are held deep within the heart of the volcanoes. It was here, into the temple of the Dark Queen, that Silvara and I made our way.

"Can I describe the temple, except to say it is a building of darkness and of flame? Tall pillars, carved out of the burning rock, soar into the sulphurous caverns. By secret ways known only to the priests of Takhisis themselves, we traveled, descending lower and lower. You ask who helped us? I cannot say, for her life would be forfeit. I will add only that some god must have been watching over us."

Here Silvara interrupts to murmur, "Paladine," but Gilthanas brushes that aside with a gesture.

"We came to the very bottom chambers and here we found the eggs of the good dragons. At first it seemed all was well. I had . . . a plan. It matters little now, but I saw how we might have been able to rescue the eggs. As I said, it matters little. Chamber after chamber we passed, and the shining eggs, the eggs tinged with silver, gold, and bronze lay gleaming in the fire's light. And then . . ."

The elflord pauses. His face, already paler than death, grows more pallid still. Fearing he might faint, I beckon to one of the Aesthetics to bring him wine. On taking a sip, he rallies and keeps on talking. But I can tell by the far-off look in his eyes that he sees the remembered horror of what he witnessed. As for Silvara, I will write of her in its place.

Gilthanas continues:

"We came to a chamber and found there . . . not eggs . . . nothing but the shells . . . shattered, broken. Silvara cried out in

109

anger, and I feared we might be discovered. Neither of us knew what this portended, but we both felt a chill in our blood that not even the heat of the volcano could warm."

Gilthanas pauses. Silvara begins to sob, very softly. He looks at her and I see, for the first time, love and compassion in his eyes.

"Take her out," he tells one of the Aesthetics. "She must rest."

The Aesthetics lead her gently from the room. Gilthanas licks lips that are cracked and dry, then speaks softly.

"What happened next will haunt me, even after death. Nightly I dream of it. I have not slept since but that I waken, screaming.

"Silvara and I stood before the chamber with the shattered eggs, staring at it, wondering . . . when we heard the sound of chanting coming from the flame-lit corridor.

" 'The words of magic!' Silvara said.

"Cautiously we crept nearer, both of us frightened, yet drawn by some horrid fascination. Closer and closer we came, and then we could see . . . "

He shuts his eyes, he sobs. Laurana lays her hand on his arm, her eyes soft with mute sympathy. Gilthanas regains control and goes on.

"Inside a cavern room, at the bottom of the volcano, stands an altar to Takhisis. What it may have been carved to represent, I could not tell, for it was so covered with green blood and black slime that it seemed a horrid growth springing from the rock. Around the altar were robed figures—dark clerics of Takhisis and magic-users wearing the Black Robes. Silvara and I watched in awe as a dark-robed cleric brought forth a shining golden dragon egg and placed it upon that foul altar. Joining hands, the Black Robed magic-users and the dark clerics began a chant. The words burned the mind. Silvara and I clung to each other, fearing we would be driven mad by the evil we could feel but could not understand.

"And then . . . then the golden egg upon the altar began to darken. As we watched, it turned to a hideous green and then to black. Silvara began to tremble.

"The blackened egg upon the altar cracked open . . . and a larva-like creature emerged from the shell. It was loathsome and corrupt to look upon, and I retched at the sight. My only thought was to flee this horror, but Silvara realized what was happening and she refused to leave. Together we watched as the larva split its slime-covered skin and from its body came the evil forms of . . . draconians."

There is a gasp of shock at this statement. Gilthanas's head sinks into his hands. He cannot continue. Laurana puts her arms around him, comforting him, and he holds onto her hands. Finally he draws a shuddering breath.

"Silvara and I . . . were nearly discovered. We escaped Sanction, with help once again, and, more dead than alive, we traveled paths unknown to man or elf to the ancient haven of the good dragons."

Gilthanas sighs. A look of peace comes to his face.

"Compared to the horrors we had endured, this was like sweet rest after a night of feverish nightmares. It was difficult to imagine, amid the beauty of the place, that what we had seen really occurred. And when Silvara told the dragons what was happening to their eggs, they refused at first to believe it. Some even accused Silvara of making it up to try to win their aid. But, deep within their hearts, all knew she spoke truly, and so, at last, they admitted that they had been deceived and that the Oath was no longer binding.

"The good dragons have come to aid us now. They are flying to all parts of the land, offering their help. They have returned to the Monument of the Dragon, to aid in forging the dragonlances just as they came to Huma's aid long ago. And they have brought with them the Greater Lances that can be mounted on the dragons themselves, as we saw in the paintings. Now we may ride the dragons into battle and challenge the Dragon Highlords in the sky."

Gilthanas adds more, a few minor details that I need not record here. Then his sister leads him from the library to the palace, where he and Silvara may find what rest they can. I fear it will be long before the terror fades for them, if it ever does. Like so much that is beautiful in the world, it may be that their love will fall beneath the darkness that spreads its foul wings over Krynn.

Thus ends the writing of Astinus of Palanthas on the Oath of the Dragons. A footnote reveals that further details of the journey of Giltha-nas and Silvara into Sanction, their adventures there, and the tragic history of their love were recorded by Astinus at a later date and may be found in subsequent volumes of his Chronicles.

Laurana sat late at night, writing up her orders for the morrow. Only a day had passed since the arrival of Gilthanas and the silver dragons, but already her plans for pressing the beleaguered enemy were taking shape. Within a few days more, she would lead flights of dragons with mounted riders, wielding the new dragonlances, into battle.

She hoped to secure Vingaard Keep first, freeing the prisoners and slaves held there. Then she planned to push on south and east, driving the dragonarmies before her. Finally she would catch them between the hammer of her troops and the anvil of the Dargaard Mountains that divided Solamnia from Estwilde. If she could retake Kalaman and its harbor, she could cut the supply lines the dragonarmy depended on for its survival on this part of the continent.

So intent was Laurana on her plans that she ignored the ringing challenge of the guard outside her door, nor did she hear the answer. The door opened, but, assuming it was one of her aides, she did not look up from her work until she had completed detailing her orders.

Only when the person who entered took the liberty of sitting down in a chair across from her did Laurana glance up, startled.

"Oh," she said, flushing, "Gilthanas, forgive me. I was so involved. . . . I thought you were . . . but, never mind. How are you feeling? I was worried—"

"I'm all right, Laurana," Gilthanas said abruptly. "I was just more tired than I realized and I—I haven't slept very well since Sanction." Falling silent, he sat staring at the maps she had spread on her table. Absently he picked up a freshly sharpened quill pen and began to smooth the feather with his fingers.

"What is it, Gilthanas?" Laurana asked softly.

Her brother looked up at her and smiled sadly. "You know me too well," he said. "I never could hide anything from you, not even when we were children."

"Is it Father?" Laurana asked fearfully. "Have you heard something—"

"No, I've heard nothing about our people," Gilthanas said, "except what I told you, that they have allied with the humans and are working together to drive the dragonarmies from the Ergoth Isles and from Sancrist."

"It was all because of Alhana," Laurana murmured. "She convinced them that they could no longer live apart from the world. She even convinced Porthios. . . ."

"I gather she has convinced him of more than that?" Gilthanas asked without looking at his sister. He began to poke holes in the parchment with the point of the quill.

"There has been talk of a marriage," Laurana said slowly. "If so, I am certain it would be a marriage of convenience only, to unite our people. I cannot imagine Porthios has it in his heart to love anyone, even a woman as beautiful as Alhana. As for the elven princess herself—"

Gilthanas sighed. "Her heart is buried in the High Clerist's Tower with Sturm."

"How did you know?" Laurana looked at him, astonished.

"I saw them together in Tarsis," Gilthanas said. "I saw his face, and I saw hers. I knew about the Starjewel, too. Since he obviously wanted to keep it secret, I did not betray him. He was a fine man," Gilthanas added gently. "I am proud to have known him, and I never thought I would say that of a human."

Laurana swallowed, brushing her hand across her eyes. "Yes," she whispered huskily, "but that wasn't what you came to tell me."

"No," Gilthanas said, "although perhaps it leads into it." For a moment he sat in silence, as if making up his mind. Then he drew a breath. "Laurana, something happened in Sanction that I did not tell Astinus. I won't tell anyone else, ever, if you ask me not to—"

"Why me?" Laurana said, turning pale. Her hand trembling, she laid down her pen.

Gilthanas seemed not to have heard her. He stared fixedly at the map as he spoke. "When—when we were escaping from Sanction, we had to go back to the palace of Lord Ariakas. I cannot tell you more than that, for to do so would betray the one who saved our lives many times and who lives in danger there still, doing what she can to save as many of her people as possible.

"The night we were there, in hiding, waiting to escape, we overheard a conversation between Lord Ariakas and one of his Highlords. It was a woman, Laurana"—Gilthanas looked up at her now—"a human woman named Kitiara."

Laurana said nothing. Her face was deathly white, her eyes large and colorless in the lamplight.

Gilthanas sighed, then leaned near her and placed his hand on hers. Her flesh was so cold, she might have been a corpse, and he saw, then, that she knew what he was about to say.

"I remembered what you told me before we left Qualinesti, that this was the human woman Tanis Half-Elven loved, sister to Caramon and Raistlin. I recognized her from what I had heard the brothers say about her. I would have recognized her anyway, she and Raistlin, particularly, bear a family resemblance. She, she was talking of Tanis, Laurana." Gilthanas stopped, wondering whether or not he could go on. Laurana sat perfectly still, her face a mask of ice.

"Forgive me for causing you pain, Laurana, but you must know," Gilthanas said at last. "Kitiara laughed about Tanis with this Lord Ariakas and said"—Gilthanas flushed—"I cannot repeat what she said. But they are together, Laurana, that much I can tell you. She made it graphically clear. She asked Ariakas's permission to have Tanis promoted to the rank of general in the dragonarmy . . . in return for some sort of information he was going to provide, something about a Green Gemstone Man—"

"Stop," Laurana said without a voice.

"I'm sorry, Laurana!" Gilthanas squeezed her hand, his face filled with sorrow. "I know how much you love him. I—I understand now what it is like to, to love someone that much." He closed his eyes, his head bowed. "I understand what it is like to have that love betrayed. . . ."

"Leave me, Gilthanas," Laurana whispered.

Patting her hand in silent sympathy, the elflord rose and walked softly from the room, shutting the door behind him.

Laurana sat without moving for long moments. Then, pressing her lips firmly together, she picked up her pen and continued writing where she had left off when her brother entered.

VICTORY.

9

"L et me give you a boost," Tas said helpfully.

"I . . . no! Wait!" Flint yelled. But it did no good. The energetic
kender had already grabbed hold of the dwarf's boot and heaved,
propelling Flint head first right into the hard-muscled body of
the young bronze dragon. Hands flailing wildly, Flint caught
hold of the harness on the dragon's neck and hung on for dear
life, revolving slowly in the air like a sack on a hook.

"What are you doing?" Tas asked in disgust, gazing up at
Flint. "This is no time to play! Here, let me help—"

"Stop it! Let go!" roared Flint, kicking at Tasslehoff's hands.
"Get back! Get back, I say!"

"Get up yourself, then," Tas said, hurt, backing up.

Puffing and red-faced, the dwarf dropped to the ground. "I'll
get on in my own good time!" he said, glaring at the kender.
"Without help from you!"

"Well, you'd better do it quickly!" Tas shouted, waving his
arms. "Because the others are already mounted!"

The dwarf cast a glance back at the big bronze dragon and
folded his arms across his chest stubbornly. "I've got to give this
some thought—"

"Oh, come on, Flint!" Tas begged. "You're only stalling. I want to *fly!* Please, Flint, hurry!" The kender brightened. "I could go by myself. . . ."

"You'll do no such thing!" The dwarf snorted. "The war's finally turning in our favor. Send a kender up on a dragon and that'd be the end. We could just hand the Highlord the keys to the city. Laurana said the only way you'd fly is with me—"

"Then get on!" Tas yelled shrilly. "Or the war will be over! I'll be a grandfather before you move from that spot!"

"You a grandfather," Flint grumbled, glancing once more at the dragon, who was staring at him with a very unfriendly eye, or so the dwarf imagined. "Why, the day you're a grandfather is the day my beard will fall out—"

Khirsah, the dragon, gazed down at the two with amused impatience. A young dragon, as dragons count their time on Krynn, Khirsah agreed with the kender: it was time to fly, time to fight. He had been one of the first to answer the Call that went out to all the gold and silver, bronze and brass dragons. The fire of battle burned hot within him.

Yet, young as he was, the bronze dragon held a great reverence and respect for the elders of the world. Though vastly older than the dwarf in years, Khirsah saw in Flint one who had led a long, full, rich life; one worthy of respect. But, Khirsah thought with a sigh, if I don't do something, the kender's right—the battle *will* be over!

"Pardon me, Respected Sire," Khirsah interrupted, using a term of high respect among dwarves, "may I be of assistance?"

Startled, Flint whirled around to see who spoke.

The dragon bowed its great head. "Honored and Respected Sire," Khirsah said again, in dwarven.

Amazed, Flint stumbled backward, tripping over Tasslehoff and sending the kender tumbling to the ground in a heap.

The dragon snaked forth his huge head and, gently taking hold of the kender's fur vest in his great teeth, lifted him to his feet like a newborn kitten.

"Well, I—I don't know," stammered Flint, flushing in pleased embarrassment at being thus addressed by a dragon. "You might . . . and then again you might not." Recovering his dignity, the dwarf was determined not to act overawed. "I've done this a lot, mind you. Riding dragons is nothing new to me. It's just, well, just that I've—"

"You've never ridden a dragon before in your life!" Tasslehoff said indignantly. "And—ouch!"

"Just that I've had more important things on my mind lately," Flint said loudly, punching Tas in the ribs, "and it may take me a while to get the hang of it again."

"Certainly, Sire," Khirsah said without the ghost of a smile. "May I call you Flint?"

"You may," said the dwarf gruffly.

"And I'm Tasslehoff Burrfoot," said the kender, extending his small hand. "Flint never goes anywhere without me. Oh, I guess you haven't any hand to shake with. Never mind. What's your name?"

"My name to mortals is Fireflash." The dragon gracefully bowed his head. "And now, Sir Flint, if you will instruct your squire, the kender—"

"*Squire!*" Tas repeated, shocked. But the dragon ignored him.

"Instruct your squire to come up here; I will help him prepare the saddle and the lance for you."

Flint stroked his beard thoughtfully. Then, he made a grand gesture.

"You, squire," he said to Tas, who was staring at him with his mouth open, "get up there and do as you're told."

"I—you—we—" Tas stuttered. But the kender never finished what he had been about to say because the dragon had lifted him off the ground again. Teeth clamped firmly in the kender's fur vest, Khirsah raised him up and plopped him back onto the saddle that was strapped to the dragon's bronze body.

So enchanted was Tas with the idea of actually being atop a dragon that he hushed up, which is just what Khirsah had intended.

"Now, Tasslehoff Burrfoot," said the dragon, "you were trying to boost your master up into the saddle backward. The correct position is the one you are in now. The metal lance mounting must be on the front right side of the rider, sitting squarely forward of my right wing joint and above my right fore-shoulder. Do you see?"

"Yes, I see!" called Tas in high excitement.

"The shield, which you see on the ground, will protect you from most forms of dragonbreath—"

"Whoah!" shouted the dwarf, crossing his arms and looking stubborn once more. "What do you mean *most* forms? And how am I supposed to fly and hold a lance and a shield all at the same time? Not to mention the fact that the blasted shield's bigger than me and the kender put together—"

"I thought you had done this before, *Sir Flint!*" Tas yelled.

The dwarf's face went red with rage and he let out a bellow, but Khirsah cut in smoothly.

"Sir Flint probably isn't accustomed to this newer model, Squire Burrfoot. The shield fits over the lance. The lance itself fits through that hole and the shield rests on the saddle and slides from side to side on the track. When attacked, you simply duck behind it."

"Hand me the shield, Sir Flint!" the kender yelled.

Grumbling, the dwarf stumped over to where the huge shield lay on the ground. Groaning with the weight, he managed to lift it up and haul it over to the dragon's side. With the dragon's help, the dwarf and the kender between them managed to get the shield mounted. Then Flint went back for the dragonlance. Lugging it back, he thrust the tip of the lance up to Tas, who caught hold of it and, after nearly losing his balance and tumbling overboard, pushed the lance through the hole in the shield. When the pivot locked into position, the lance was counterbalanced and swung lightly and easily, guided by the kender's small hand.

"This is great!" Tas said, experimenting. "Wham! There goes one dragon! Wham! There goes another. I—oh!" Tas stood up on the dragon's back, balanced lightly as the lance itself. "Flint! Hurry! They're getting ready to leave. I can see Laurana! She's riding that big silver dragon and she's flying this way, checking the line. They're going to be signaling in a minute! Hurry, Flint!" Tas began jumping up and down in excitement.

"First, Sir Flint," said Khirsah, "you must put on the padded vest. There . . . that's right. Put the strap through that buckle. No, not that one. The other—there, you have it."

"You look like a woolly mammoth I saw once." Tas giggled. "Did I ever tell you that story? I—"

"Confound it!" Flint roared, barely able to walk, engulfed in the heavy, fur-lined vest. "This is no time for any of your hare-brained stories." The dwarf came nose-tip to nose-tip with the dragon. "Very well, beast! How do I get up? And mind you, don't you dare lay a tooth on me!"

"Certainly not, Sire," Khirsah said in deep respect. Bowing his head, the dragon extended one bronze wing full length upon the ground.

"Well, that's more like it!" Flint said. Smoothing his beard with pride, he shot a smug glance at the stunned kender. Then, solemnly mounting the dragon's wing, Flint ascended, regally taking his place at the front of the saddle.

"There's the signal!" Tas shrieked, leaping back into the saddle behind Flint. Kicking his heels against the dragon's flanks, he yelled, "Let's go! Let's go!"

"Not so fast," said Flint, coolly testing the workings of the dragonlance. "Hey! How do I steer?"

"You indicate which direction you want me to turn by pulling on the reins," Khirsah said, watching for the signal. There it was.

"Ah, I see," said Flint, reaching down. "After all, I am in charge—ulp!"

"Certainly, Sire!" Khirsah leaped into the air, spreading his great wings to catch the rising currents of air that floated up the face of the small cliff they stood upon.

"Wait, the reins—" Flint cried, grasping at them as they slid out of his reach.

Smiling to himself, Khirsah pretended not to hear.

The good dragons and the knights who rode them were gathered on the rolling foothills east of the Vingaard Mountains. Here, the chill winter winds had given way to warm breezes from the north, melting the frost from the ground. The rich smell of growth and renewal perfumed the air as the dragons rose in flashing arcs to take their places in formation.

It was a sight that took the breath away. Tasslehoff knew he would remember it forever—and maybe even beyond that. Bronze and silver, brass and copper wings flared in the morning light. The Greater Dragonlances, mounted on the saddles, glittered in the sun. The knights' armor shone brilliantly. The Kingfisher flag with its golden thread sparkled against the blue sky.

The past few weeks had been glorious. As Flint said, it seemed the tide of war was finally flowing in their direction.

The Golden General, as Laurana came to be called by her troops, had forged an army seemingly out of nothing. The Palanthians, caught up in the excitement, rallied to her cause. She won the respect of the Knights of Solamnia with her bold ideas and firm, decisive actions. Laurana's ground forces surged out of Palanthas, flowing across the plain, pressing the unorganized armies of the Dragon Highlord, known as the Dark Lady, into panic-stricken flight.

Now, with victory after victory behind them and the dragon-armies fleeing before them, the men considered the war as good as won.

But Laurana knew better. They had yet to fight the dragons of the Highlord. Where these were and why they had not fought before was something Laurana and her officers couldn't figure out. Day after day, she held the knights and their mounts in readiness, prepared to take to the air.

And now that day had come. The dragons had been sighted— flights of blues and reds reportedly heading westward to stop the insolent general and her rag-tag army.

In a shimmering chain of silver and bronze, the Dragons of Whitestone, as they were called, soared across the Solamnic Plain. Although all the dragon-mounted knights had been trained in flight as much as time allowed (with the exception of the dwarf who steadfastly refused), this world of wispy, low-hanging clouds and rushing air was still new and foreign to them.

Their banners whipped about wildly. The foot soldiers beneath them seemed no more than bugs crawling across the grasslands. To some of the knights, flying was an exhilarating experience. To others, it was a test of every bit of courage they possessed.

But always before them, leading them in spirit and by example, flew Laurana upon the great silver dragon her brother had ridden from the Dragon Isles. The sunlight itself was not more golden than the hair that streamed out from beneath her helm. She had become a symbol to them like the dragonlance itself—slender and delicate, fair and deadly. They would have followed her to the Gates of the Abyss itself.

Tasslehoff, peering over Flint's shoulder, could see Laurana ahead of them. She rode at the head of the line, sometimes looking back to make certain everyone was keeping up, sometimes bending down to consult with her silver mount. She seemed to have things well under control, so Tas decided he could relax and enjoy the ride. It was truly one of the most wondrous experiences of his life. Tears streaked his wind-blown face as he stared down in absolute joy.

The map-loving kender had found the perfect map.

Below him was spread, in tiny, perfect detail, rivers and trees, hills and valleys, towns and farms. More than anything in the world, Tas wished he could capture the sight and keep it forever.

Why not? he wondered suddenly. Clinging to the saddle with his knees and thighs, the kender let go of Flint and began rummaging around in his pouches. Dragging out a sheet of parchment, he rested it firmly against the dwarf's back and began to draw on it with a piece of charcoal.

"Quit wiggling!" he shouted at Flint, who was still trying to grab the reins.

"What're you doing, you doorknob?" the dwarf yelled, pawing frantically at Tas behind his back like an itch he couldn't scratch.

"I'm making a map!" Tas yelled in ecstasy. "The *perfect* map! I'll be famous. Look! There are our own troops, like little ants. And there's Vingaard Keep! Stop moving! You made me mess up."

Groaning, Flint gave up trying to either grasp the reins or brush away the kender. He decided he had better concentrate on keeping a firm grip on both the dragon and his breakfast. He had made the mistake of looking down. Now he stared straight ahead, shivering, his body rigid. The hair from the mane of a griffon that decorated his helm whipped about his face wildly in the rushing wind. Birds wheeled in the skies *beneath* him. Flint decided then and there that dragons were going on his list with boats and horses as Things to Avoid at All Costs.

"Oh!" Tas gasped in excitement. "There are the dragonarmies! It's a battle! And I can see the whole thing!" The kender leaned over in the saddle, peering down. Now and again, through the rushing eddies of air, he thought he could hear the clash of armor and cries and shouts. "Say, could we fly a bit closer? I—whoops! Oh, no! My map!"

Khirsah had made a sudden, swooping dive. The force ripped the parchment from Tas's hands. Forlornly he watched it flutter away from him like a leaf. But he hadn't time to feel sad, for suddenly he felt Flint's body go even more rigid than before.

"What? What is it?" Tas yelled.

Flint was shouting something and pointing. Tas tried desperately to see and hear, but at that moment they flew into a low-hanging cloud and the kender couldn't see his nose in front of his face, as the gully dwarves said.

Then Khirsah emerged from the cloud bank and Tas saw.

"Oh my!" said the kender in awe. Below them, bearing down on the small antlike troops of men, flew line after line of dragons. Their red and blue leathery wings spread like evil banners as they dove down upon the helpless armies of the Golden General.

Tasslehoff could see the solid lines of men waver and break as the terrible dragonfear swept over them. But there was nowhere to run, nowhere to hide on the broad grasslands. This is why the dragons had waited, Tas realized, sick with the thought of the fire and lightning breath exploding among the unprotected troops.

"We've got to stop them—oof!"

Khirsah wheeled so suddenly that Tas nearly swallowed his tongue. The sky flipped over on its side and for an instant the kender had the most interesting sensation of falling *up*. More by instinct than conscious thought, Tas grabbed hold of Flint's belt, remembering suddenly that he was supposed to have strapped himself in as Flint had done. Well, he would do so next time.

If there was a next time. The wind roared around him, the ground spun below him as the dragon spiraled downward. Kenders were fond of new experiences, and this was certainly one of the most exciting, but Tas *did* wish the ground wasn't rushing up to meet them quite so *fast!*

"I didn't mean we had to stop them *right now!*" Tas shouted to Flint. Glancing up—or was it down?—he could see the other dragons far above them, no, below them. Things were getting all muddled. Now the dragons were *behind* them! They were out here in front! Alone! What was Flint doing?

"Not so fast! Slow this thing down!" he yelled at Flint. "You've gotten ahead of everybody! Even Laurana!"

The dwarf would have liked nothing better than to slow the dragon down. That last swoop had tossed the reins within his reach and now he was tugging with all his might, shouting "Whoah, beast, whoah!" which he dimly remembered was supposed to work with horses. But it wasn't working with the dragon.

It was no comfort to the terrified dwarf to notice that he wasn't the only one having trouble managing the dragons. Behind him, the delicate line of bronze and silver broke as if by some silent signal, as the dragons veered off into small groups—flights—of twos and threes.

Frantically the knights jerked on the reins, endeavoring to pull the dragons back into straight and orderly cavalry rows. But the dragons knew better, the sky was their domain. Fighting in the air was far different from fighting on the ground. They would show these horse riders how to fight on dragonback.

Spinning gracefully, Khirsah dove into another cloud, and Tas instantly lost all sense of up or down as the thick fog enveloped him. Then the sunlit sky exploded before his eyes as the dragon burst out. Now he knew which way was up and which was down. *Down* was, in fact, getting uncomfortably close!

Then Flint roared. Startled, Tas looked up and saw that they were heading straight into a flight of blue dragons who, intent upon pursuing a group of panic-stricken foot soldiers, hadn't seen them yet.

"The lance! The lance!" Tas shouted.

Flint grappled with the lance, but he didn't have time to adjust it or set it properly against his shoulder. Not that it mattered. The blue dragons still hadn't seen them. Gliding out of the cloud, Khirsah fell in behind them. Then, like a bronze flame, the young dragon flashed over the group of blues, aiming for their leader, a big blue dragon with a blue-helmed rider. Diving swiftly and silently, Khirsah struck the lead dragon with all four murderously sharp talons.

The force of the impact threw Flint forward in his harness. Tas landed on top of him, flattening the dwarf. Frantically, Flint struggled to sit up, but Tas had one arm wrapped around him tightly. Beating the dwarf on the helm with the other, Tas was shouting encouragement to the dragon.

"That was great! Hit him again!" shrieked the kender, wild with excitement, pounding Flint on the head.

Swearing loudly in dwarven, Flint flung Tas off him. At that moment, Khirsah soared upward, darting into another cloud before the flight of blues could react to his attack.

Khirsah waited for an instant, perhaps to give his shaken riders time to pull themselves together. Flint sat up and Tas clasped his arms around the dwarf tightly. He thought Flint looked strange, sort of gray-colored and oddly preoccupied. But then this certainly wasn't a normal experience, Tas reminded himself. Before he could ask Flint if he felt all right, Khirsah dove out of the cloud once more.

Tas could see the blue dragons below them. The lead dragon had pulled up in mid-air, hovering on his great wings. The blue was shaken and wounded slightly; there was blood on the rear flanks where Khirsah's sharp talons had punctured the dragon's tough, scaly hide. The dragon and his blue-helmed rider were both scanning the skies, searching for their attacker. Suddenly the rider pointed.

Risking a quick glance behind him, Tas caught his breath. The sight was magnificent. Bronze and silver flashed in the sun as the Whitestone Dragons broke out of the cloud cover and descended screaming upon the flight of blues. Instantly the flight broke as the blues fought to gain altitude and keep their pursuers from attacking them from behind. Here and there battles broke out. Lightning cracked and flared, nearly blinding the kender, as a great bronze dragon to his right screamed in pain and fell from the air, its head blackened and burning. Tas saw its rider helplessly grasping the reins, his mouth opened in a scream the kender could see but not hear as dragon and rider plunged to the ground below.

Tas stared at the ground rushing closer and closer and wondered in a dreamlike haze what it would be like to smash into the grass. But he didn't have time to wonder long, because suddenly Khirsah let out a roar.

The blue leader spotted Khirsah and heard his ringing challenge. Ignoring the other dragons fighting in the skies around him, the blue leader and his rider flew up to continue their duel with the bronze.

"Now it is your turn, dwarf! Set the lance!" Khirsah yelled. Lifting his great wings, the bronze soared up and up, gaining altitude for maneuvering and also giving the dwarf time to prepare.

"I'll hold the reins!" Tas shouted.

But the kender couldn't tell if Flint heard him or not. The dwarf's face was rigid and he was moving slowly and mechanically. Wild with impatience, Tas could do nothing but hang onto the reins and watch while Flint fumbled with gray fingers until he finally managed to fix the hilt of the lance beneath his shoulder and brace it as he had been taught. Then he just stared straight ahead, his face empty of all expression.

Khirsah continued rising, then leveled off, and Tas looked around, wondering where their enemies were. He had completely lost sight of the blue and its rider. Then Khirsah suddenly leaped upward and Tas gasped. *There* was their enemy, right ahead of them!

He saw the blue open his hideous fanged mouth. Remembering the lightning, Tas ducked behind the shield. Then he saw that Flint was still sitting straight-backed, staring grimly out over the shield at the approaching dragon! Reaching around Flint's waist, Tas grabbed hold of the dwarf's beard and yanked his head downward, behind the shield.

Lightning flared and crackled around them. The instant booming thunder nearly knocked both kender and dwarf senseless. Khirsah roared in pain but held true upon his course.

The dragons struck, head-on, and the dragonlance speared its victim.

For an instant all Tas could see were blurs of blue and red. The world spun round and round. Once a dragon's hideous, fiery eyes stared at him balefully. Claws flashed. Khirsah shrieked, the blue screamed. Wings beat upon the air. The ground spiraled round and round as the struggling dragons fell.

Why doesn't Fireflash let go? Tas thought frantically. Then he could see,

We're locked together! Tasslehoff realized numbly.

The dragonlance had missed its mark. Striking the wingbone joint of the blue dragon, the lance had bent into his shoulder and was now lodged tight. Desperately the blue fought to free himself, but Khirsah, now filled with battle rage, lashed out at the blue with his sharp fangs and ripping taloned front feet.

Intent upon their own battle, both dragons had completely forgotten their riders. Tas had forgotten the other rider, too, until, glancing up helplessly, he saw the blue-helmed dragon officer clinging precariously to his saddle only a few feet away.

Then sky and ground became a blur once more as the dragons whirled and fought. Tas watched in a haze as the blue helm of the officer fell from his head, and the officer's blonde hair whipped in the wind. His eyes were cold and bright and not the least afraid. He stared straight into Tasslehoff's eyes.

He looks familiar, thought Tas with an odd sort of detachment, as if this were happening to some other kender while he watched. Where could I have seen him before? Thoughts of Sturm came to his mind.

The dragon officer freed himself from his harness and stood up in the stirrups. One arm—his right arm—hung limply at his side, but his other hand was reaching forward—

Everything became very clear to Tas suddenly. He knew exactly what the officer intended to do. It was as if the man spoke to him, telling him his plans.

"Flint!" cried Tas frantically. "Release the lance! Release it!"

But the dwarf held onto the lance fast, that strange faraway look on his face. The dragons fought and clawed and bit in mid-air; the blue twisting, trying to free himself from the lance as well as fend off its attacker. Tas saw the blue's rider shout something, and the blue broke off its attack for an instant, holding himself steady in the air.

With remarkable agility, the officer leaped from one dragon to the other. Grasping Khirsah around the neck with his good arm, the dragon officer pulled himself upright, his strong legs and thighs clamping themselves firmly onto the struggling dragon's neck.

Khirsah paid the human no attention. His thoughts were fixed totally on his enemy.

The officer cast one quick glance back at the kender and the dwarf behind him and saw that neither was likely to be a threat, strapped, as they must be, into place. Coolly the officer drew his longsword and, leaning down, began to slash at the bronze dragon's harness straps where they crossed across the beast's chest, ahead of the great wings.

"Flint!" pleaded Tas. "Release the lance! Look!" The kender shook the dwarf. "If that officer cuts through the harness, our saddle will fall off! The lance will fall off! *We'll* fall off!"

Flint turned his head slowly, suddenly understanding. Still moving with agonizing slowness, his shaking hand fumbled at the mechanism that would release the lance and free the dragons from their deadly embrace. But would it be in time?

Tas saw the longsword flash in the air. He saw one of the harness straps sag and flutter free. There wasn't time to think or plan. While Flint grappled with the release, Tas, rising up precariously, wrapped the reins around his waist. Then, hanging onto the edge of the saddle, the kender crawled around the dwarf until he was in front of him. Here he lay down flat along the dragon's neck and, wrapping his legs around the dragon's spiny mane, he wormed his way forward and came up silently behind the officer.

The man wasn't paying any attention to the riders behind him, assuming both were safely locked in their harnesses. Intent upon his work—the harness was nearly free—he never knew what hit him.

Rising up, Tasslehoff leaped onto the officer's back. Startled, scrabbling wildly to keep himself balanced, the officer let his sword fall as he clung desperately to the dragon's neck.

Snarling in rage, the officer tried to see what had struck him when suddenly everything went dark! Small arms wrapped themselves around his head, blinding him. Frantically the officer let go of his hold on the dragon in an effort to free himself of what seemed to his enraged mind to be a creature with six legs and arms, all of them clinging to him with a buglike tenacity. But he felt himself start to slide off the dragon and was forced to grab hold of the mane.

"Flint! Release the lance! Flint . . ." Tas didn't even know what he was saying anymore. The ground was rushing up to meet him as the weakened dragons toppled from the skies. He couldn't think. White flashes of light burst in his head as he clung with all his strength to the officer, who was still struggling beneath him.

Then a great metallic bang sounded.

The lance released. The dragons were freed.

Spreading his wings, Khirsah pulled out of his spinning dive and leveled off. The sky and ground resumed their proper, correct positions. Tears streamed down Tas's cheeks. He hadn't been frightened, he told himself, sobbing. But nothing had ever looked so beautiful as that blue, blue sky, back up where it should be!

"Are you all right, Fireflash?" Tas yelled.

The bronze nodded wearily.

"I've got a prisoner," Tas called, suddenly realizing that fact himself. Slowly he let go of the man, who shook his head dizzily, half-choked.

"I guess you're not going anywhere," Tas muttered. Sliding off the man's back, the kender crawled down the mane toward the dragon's shoulders. Tas saw the officer look up into the skies, and clench his fist in bitter rage as he watched his dragons being slowly driven from the skies by Laurana and her forces. In particular, the officer's gaze fixed on Laurana, and suddenly Tas knew where he had seen him before.

The kender caught his breath. "You better take us down to the ground, Fireflash!" he cried, his hands shaking. "Hurry!"

The dragon arched his head to look around at his riders, and Tas saw that one eye was swollen shut. There were scorch and burn marks all along one side of the bronze head, and blood dripped from a torn nostril. Tas glanced around for the blue. He was nowhere to be seen.

Looking back at the officer, Tas suddenly felt wonderful. It occurred to him what he had done.

"Hey!" he yelled in elation, turning around to Flint. "We *did* it! We fought a dragon and *I* captured a prisoner! Single-handed!"

Flint nodded slowly. Turning back, Tas watched as the ground rose up to meet him, and the kender thought it had never looked so . . . so wonderfully groundlike before!

Khirsah landed. The foot-soldiers gathered around them, yelling and cheering. Someone led the officer away, Tas was not sorry to see him go, noticing that the officer gave him a sharp, penetrating look before he was led off. But then the kender forgot him as he glanced up at Flint.

The dwarf was slumped over the saddle, his face old and tired-looking, his lips blue.

"What's the matter?"

"Nothing."

"But you're holding your chest. Are you wounded?"

"No, I'm not."

"Then why are you holding your chest?"

Flint scowled. "I suppose I'll have no peace until I answer you. Well, if you must know, it's that confounded lance! And whoever designed this stupid vest was a bigger ninny than you are! The shaft of the lance drove right into my collarbone. I'll be black and blue for a week. And as for your prisoner, it's a wonder you weren't both killed, you rattlebrain! Captured, humpf! More like an accident, if you ask me. And I'll tell you something else! I'm never getting on another one of those great beasts as long as I live!"

Flint shut his lips with an angry snap, glaring at the kender so fiercely that Tas turned around and walked quickly away, knowing that when Flint was in *that* kind of mood, it was best to leave him alone to cool off. He'd feel better after lunch.

It wasn't until that night, when Tasslehoff was curled up next to Khirsah, resting comfortably against the dragon's great bronze flank, that he remembered Flint had been clutching the left side of his chest.

The lance had been on the old dwarf's right.

SPRING DAWNING.

10

As the day dawned, pink and golden light spreading across the land, the citizens of Kalaman woke to the sound of bells. Leaping out of bed, children invaded parental bedrooms, demanding that mother and father arise so that this special day could get underway. Though some grumbled and feigned to pull the blankets over their heads, most parents laughingly climbed out of bed, not less eager than their children.

Today was a memorable day in the history of Kalaman. Not only was it the annual Spring Dawning festival, it was also a victory celebration for the armies of the Knights of Solamnia. Camped on the plains outside the walled city, the army, led by its now-legendary general, an elfwoman, would be making a triumphal entry into the city at noon.

As the sun peeped over the walls, the sky above Kalaman was filled with the smoke of cooking fires, and soon smells of sizzling ham and warm muffins, frying bacon and exotic coffees rousted even the sleepiest from warm beds. They would have been roused soon enough anyway, for almost immediately the streets were filled with children. All discipline was relaxed on the occasion of Spring Dawning. After a long winter of being cooped up indoors, children were allowed to "run wild" for a day.

By nightfall there would be bruised heads, skinned knees, and stomach aches from too many sweets. But all would remember it as a glorious day.

By mid-morning the festival was in full swing. Vendors hawked their wares in gaily colored booths. The gullible lost their money on games of chance. Dancing bears capered in the streets, and illusionists drew gasps of amazement from young and old.

Then at noon the bells rang out again. The streets cleared. People lined the sidewalks. The city gates were flung open, and the Knights of Solamnia prepared to enter Kalaman.

An expectant hush came over the crowd. Peering ahead eagerly, they jostled to get a good view of the Knights, particularly the elfwoman of whom they had heard so many stories. She rode in first, alone, mounted on a pure white horse. The crowd, prepared to cheer, found themselves unable to speak, so awed were they by the woman's beauty and majesty. Dressed in flashing silver armor decorated with beaten gold work, Laurana guided her steed through the city gates and into the streets. A delegation of children had been carefully rehearsed to strew flowers in Laurana's path, but so overcome were the children at the sight of the lovely woman in the glittering armor that they clutched their flowers and never threw a single one.

Behind the golden-haired elfmaiden rode two who caused not a few in the crowd to point in wonder—a kender and a dwarf, mounted together on a shaggy pony with a back as broad as a barrel. The kender seemed to be having a wonderful time, yelling and waving to the crowds. But the dwarf, sitting behind him, grasping him around the waist with a deathlike grip, was sneezing so badly he seemed likely to sneeze himself right off the back of the animal.

Following the dwarf and kender rode an elflord, so like the elfmaiden that no one in the crowd needed his neighbor to tell him they were brother and sister. Beside the elflord rode another elfmaid with strange silver hair and deep blue eyes, who seemed shy and nervous among the crowd. Then came the the Knights of Solamnia, perhaps seventy-five strong, resplendent in gleaming armor. The crowd began to cheer, waving flags in the air.

A few of the Knights exchanged grim glances at this, all of them thinking that if they had ridden into Kalaman only a month before, they would have received a far different reception. But now they were heroes. Three hundred years of hatred and bitterness and unjust accusations were wiped from the minds of the public as they cheered those who had saved them from the terrors of the dragonarmies.

Marching after the Knights were several thousand footmen. And then, to the great delight of the crowd, the sky above the city filled with dragons—not the dreaded flights of red and blue the people had feared all winter. Instead, the sun flashed off wings of silver and bronze and gold as the awesome creatures circled and dove and pivoted in their well-organized flights. Knights sat in the dragonsaddles, the barbed blades of the dragonlances sparkling in the morning light.

After the parade, the citizens gathered to hear their Lord speak a few words in honor of the heroes. Laurana blushed to hear it told that she alone was responsible for the discovery of the dragonlances, the return of the good dragons, and the tremendous victories of the armies. Stammering, she tried to deny this, gesturing to her brother and to the Knights. But the yells and cheers of the crowd drowned her out. Helplessly Laurana looked at Lord Michael, Grand Master Gunthar Uth Wistan's representative, who had lately arrived from Sancrist. Michael only grinned.

"Let them have their hero," he said to her above the shouting. "Or heroine, I should say. They deserve it. All winter they lived in fear, waiting for the day the dragons would appear in the skies. Now they have a beautiful heroine who rides out of children's tales to save them."

"But it's not true!" Laurana protested, edging nearer Michael to make herself heard. Her arms were filled with winter roses. Their fragrance was cloying, but she dared not offend anyone by setting them aside. "I didn't ride out of a children's story. I rode out of fire and darkness and blood. Putting me in command was a political stratagem of Lord Gunthar's, we both know that. And if my brother and Silvara hadn't risked their lives to bring the good dragons, we'd be parading down these streets in chains behind the Dark Lady."

"Bah! This is good for them. Good for us, too," Michael added, glancing at Laurana out of the corner of his eye as he waved to the crowd. "A few weeks ago we couldn't have begged the Lord to give us a crust of stale bread. Now, because of the Golden General, he's agreed to garrison the army in the town, provide us with supplies, horses, anything we want. Young men are flocking to join up. Our ranks will be swelled by a thousand or more before we leave for Dargaard. And you've lifted the morale of our own troops. You saw the Knights as they were in the High Clerist's Tower—look at them now."

Yes, thought Laurana bitterly. I saw them. Split by dissension among their own ranks, fallen into dishonor, bickering and plotting among themselves. It took the death of a fine and noble man to bring them to their senses. Laurana closed her eyes. The noise, the smell of the roses, which always brought Sturm to her mind, the exhaustion of battle, the heat of the noonday sun, all crashed over her in a stifling wave. She grew dizzy and feared she might faint. The thought was mildly amusing. How would that look—for the Golden General to keel over like a wilted flower?

Then she felt a strong arm around her.

"Steady, Laurana," said Gilthanas, supporting her. Silvara was beside her, taking the roses from her arms. Sighing, Laurana opened her eyes and smiled weakly at the Lord, who was just concluding his second speech of the morning to thunderous applause.

I'm trapped, Laurana realized. She would have to sit here the rest of the afternoon, smiling and waving and enduring speech after speech praising her heroism when all she wanted was to lie down in some dark, cool place and sleep. And it was all a lie, all a sham. If only they knew the truth. What if she stood up and told them she was so frightened during the battles that she could remember details only in her nightmares? Told them that she was nothing but a game piece for the Knights? Told them that she was here only because she had run away from her home, a spoiled little girl chasing after a half-elven man who didn't love her. What would they say?

"And now"—the Lord of Kalaman's voice rang out above the noise of the crowd—"it is my honor and my very great privilege to present to you the woman who has turned the tide of this war, the woman who has sent the dragonarmies fleeing for their lives over the plains, the woman who has driven the evil dragons from the sky, the woman whose armies captured the evil Bakaris, commander of the Dragon Highlord's armies, the woman whose name is even now being coupled with the great Huma's as the most valiant warrior on Krynn. Within a week, she will be riding to Dargaard Keep to demand the surrender of the Dragon Highlord known as the Dark Lady. . . ."

The Lord's voice was drowned in cheering. He paused dramatically, then, reaching behind him, caught hold of Laurana and nearly dragged her forward.

"Lauralanthalasa of the Royal House of Qualinesti!"

The noise was deafening. It reverberated off the tall stone buildings. Laurana looked out over the sea of open mouths and wildly waving flags. They don't want to hear about my fear, she realized wearily. They've fears enough of their own. They don't want to hear about darkness and death. They want children's tales about love and rebirth and silver dragons.

Don't we all.

With a sigh, Laurana turned to Silvara. Taking the roses back, she held them up into the air, waving to the jubilant crowd. Then she began her speech.

Tasslehoff Burrfoot was having a splendid time. It had been an easy task to evade Flint's watchful gaze and slip off the platform where he had been told to stand with the rest of the dignitaries. Melting into the crowd, he was now free to explore this interesting city again. Long ago, he'd come to Kalaman with his parents and he cherished fond memories of the open-air bazaar, the seaport where the white-winged ships lay at anchor, and a hundred other wonders.

Idly he wandered among the festive crowd, his keen eyes seeing everything, his hands busy stuffing objects into his pouches. Really, Tas thought, the people of Kalaman were extremely careless! Purses had the most uncanny habit of falling from people's belts into Tas's hands. The streets might be paved with jewels the way he discovered rings and other fascinating trinkets.

Then the kender was transported into realms of delight when he came across a cartographer's stall. And, as fortune would have it, the cartographer had gone to watch the parade. The stall was locked and shuttered, with a large "CLOSED" sign hanging on a hook.

"What a pity," thought Tas. "But I'm sure he wouldn't mind if I just looked at his maps." Reaching out, he gave the lock an expert twitch, then smiled happily. A few more "twitches" and it would open easily. "He mustn't really mean for people to keep out if he puts on such a simple-minded lock. I'll just pop in and copy a few of his maps to update my collection."

Suddenly Tas felt a hand on his shoulder. Irritated that someone should bother him at a time like this, the kender glanced around to see a strange figure that seemed vaguely familiar. It was dressed in heavy cloaks and robes, though the spring day was warming rapidly. Even its hands were wrapped in cloth, like bandages. Bother—a cleric, thought the kender, annoyed and preoccupied.

"I beg your pardon," said Tas to the cleric who had hold of him, "I don't mean to be rude, but I was just—"

"Burrfoot?" interrupted the cleric in a cold, lisping voice. "The kender who rides with the Golden General?"

"Why, yes," Tas said, flattered that someone had recognized him. "That's me. I've ridden with Laura—the, er—Golden General—for a long time now. Let's see, I think it was in the late fall. Yes, we met her in Qualinesti right after we escaped from the hobgoblins' prison wagons which was a short time after we killed a black dragon in Xak Tsaroth. That's the most wonderful story—" Tas forgot about the maps. "You see we were in this old, old city that had fallen into a cavern and it was filled with gully dwarves. We met one named Bupu, who had been charmed by Raistlin—"

"Shut up!" The cleric's wrapped hand went from Tasslehoff's shoulder to the collar of his shirt. Gripping it expertly, the cleric twisted it with a sudden jerk of its hand and lifted the kender off his feet. Although kender are generally immune to the emotion of fear, Tas found that being unable to breathe was an extremely uncomfortable sensation.

"Listen to me carefully," the cleric hissed, shaking the frantically struggling kender as a wolf shakes a bird to break its neck. "That's right. Hold still and it hurts less. I've got a message for the Golden General." Its voice was soft and lethal. "It's here—" Tas felt a rough hand stuffing something into his vest pocket. "See that you deliver it some time tonight when she's alone. Understand?"

Choked by the cleric's hand, Tas couldn't speak or even nod, but he blinked his eyes twice. The cloaked head nodded, dropped the kender back to the ground, and walked rapidly off down the street.

Gasping for breath, the shaken kender stared at the figure as it walked away, its long robes fluttering in the wind. Tas absently patted the scroll that had been thrust into his pocket. The sound of that voice brought back very unpleasant memories: the ambush on the road from Solace, heavily cloaked figures like clerics . . . only they weren't clerics! Tas shuddered. A draconian! Here! In Kalaman!

Shaking his head, Tas turned back to the cartographer's stall. But the pleasure had gone out of the day. He couldn't even feel excited when the lock fell open into his small hand.

"Hey, you!" shrieked a voice. "Kender! Get away from there!"

A man was running up to him, puffing and red in the face. Probably the cartographer himself.

"You shouldn't have run," Tas said listlessly. "You needn't bother opening up for me."

"Opening!" The man's jaw sagged. "Why, you little thief! I got here just in time—"

"Thanks all the same." Tas dropped the lock into the man's hand and walked off, absent-mindedly evading the enraged cartographer's effort to grab him. "I'll be going now. I'm not feeling very well. Oh, by the way, did you know that lock's broken? Worthless. You should be more careful. You never know who could sneak in. No, don't thank me. I haven't got time. Good-bye."

Tasslehoff wandered off. Cries of "Thief! Thief!" rang out behind him. A town guardsman appeared, forcing Tas to duck into a butcher's shop to avoid being run over. Shaking his head over the corruption of the world, the kender glanced about, hoping for a glimpse of the culprit. Seeing no one interesting in sight, he kept going, and suddenly wondered irritably how Flint had managed to lose him again.

Laurana shut the door, turned the key in the lock, and leaned thankfully against it, reveling in the peace and quiet and welcome solitude of her room. Tossing the key on a table, she walked wearily over to her bed, not even bothering to light a candle. The rays of the silver moon streamed in through the leaded glass panes of the long, narrow window.

Downstairs, in the lower rooms of the castle, she could still hear the sounds of merrymaking she had just left. It was nearly midnight. She had been trying for two hours to escape. It finally took Lord Michael's intercession on her behalf, pleading her exhaustion from the battles, that induced the lords and ladies of the city of Kalaman to part with her.

Her head ached from the stuffy atmosphere, the smell of strong perfume, and too much wine. She shouldn't have drunk so much, she knew. She had a weak head for wine and, anyway, she didn't really like it. But the pain in her head was easier to bear than the pain in her heart.

Throwing herself down on the bed, she thought hazily about getting up and closing the shutters, but the moon's light was comforting. Laurana detested lying in the darkness. Things lurked in the shadows, ready to spring out at her. I should get undressed, she thought, I'll wrinkle this dress . . . and it's borrowed. . . .

There was a knock at her door.

Laurana woke with a start, trembling. Then she remembered where she was. Sighing, she lay very still, closing her eyes again. Surely they'd realize she was asleep and go away.

There was another knock, more insistent than the first.

"Laurana . . ."

"Tell me in the morning, Tas," Laurana said, trying to keep the irritation from her voice.

"It's important, Laurana," Tas called. "Flint's with me."

Laurana heard a scuffling sound outside the door.

"Come on, tell her—"

"I will not! This was your doing!"

"But he said it was important and I—"

"All right, I'm coming!" Laurana sighed. Stumbling out of bed, she fumbled for the key on the table, unlocked the door, and flung it open.

"Hi, Laurana!" Tas said brightly, walking inside. "Wasn't that a wonderful party? I've never eaten roast peacock before—"

"What is it, Tas?" Laurana sighed, shutting the door behind them.

Seeing her pale, drawn face, Flint poked the kender in the back. Giving the dwarf a reproachful look, Tas reached into the pocket of his fleecy vest and drew forth a rolled scroll of parchment, tied with a blue ribbon.

"A-a cleric—sort of—said to give this to you, Laurana," Tas said.

"Is that all?" Laurana asked impatiently, snatching the scroll from the kender's hand. "It's probably a marriage proposal. I've had twenty in the last week. Not to mention proposals of a more unique nature."

"Oh, no," said Tas, suddenly serious. "It's not anything like that, Laurana. It's from . . ." He stopped.

"How do you know who it's from?" Laurana fixed the kender with a piercing gaze.

"I—uh—guess I—sort of—glanced at it—" Tas admitted. Then he brightened. "But it was only because I didn't want to bother you with anything that wasn't important."

Flint snorted.

"Thank you," Laurana said. Unrolling the scroll, she walked over to stand by the window where the moonlight was bright enough to read by.

"We'll leave you alone," Flint said gruffly, herding the protesting kender toward the door.

"No! Wait!" Laurana choked. Flint turned, staring at her in alarm.

"Are you all right?" he said, hurrying over to her as she sank down into a nearby chair. "Tas—get Silvara!"

"No, no. Don't bring anyone. I'm . . . all right. Do you know what this says?" she asked in a whisper.

"I tried to tell him," Tasslehoff said in an injured voice, "but he wouldn't let me."

Her hand shaking, Laurana handed the scroll to Flint.

The dwarf opened it and read aloud.

"Tanis Half-Elven received a wound in the battle of Vingaard Keep. Although at first he believed it was slight, it has worsened so that he is past even the help of the dark clerics. I ordered that he be brought to Dargaard Keep, where I could care for him. Tanis knows the gravity of his injury. He asks that he be allowed to be with you when he dies, that he may explain matters to you and so rest with an easy spirit.

"I make you this offer. You have as your captive my officer, Bakaris, who was captured near Vingaard Keep. I will exchange Tanis Half-Elven for Bakaris. The exchange will take place at dawn tomorrow in a grove of trees beyond the city walls. Bring Bakaris with you. If you are mistrustful, you may also bring Tanis's friends, Flint Fireforge and Tasslehoff Burrfoot. But no one else! The bearer of this note waits outside the city gate. Meet him tomorrow at sunrise. If he deems all is well, he will escort you to the half-elf. If not, you will never see Tanis alive.

"I do this only because we are two women who understand each other.

"Kitiara"

There was an uneasy silence, then, "Humpf," Flint snorted, and rolled up the scroll.

"How can you be so calm!" Laurana gasped, snatching the scroll from the dwarf's hand. "And you"—her gaze switched angrily to Tasslehoff—"why didn't you tell me before now? How long have you known? You *read* he was dying, and you're so—so—"

MARGARET WEIS & TRACY HICKMAN

Laurana put her head in her hands.

Tas stared at her, his mouth open. "Laurana," he said after a moment, "surely you don't think Tanis—"

Laurana's head snapped up. Her dark, stricken eyes went to Flint, then to Tas. "You don't believe this message is real, do you?" she asked incredulously.

"Of course not!" Flint said.

"No," scoffed Tas. "It's a trick! A *draconian* gave it to me! Besides Kitiara's a Dragon Highlord now. What would Tanis be doing with her—"

Laurana turned her face away abruptly. Tasslehoff stopped and glanced at Flint, whose own face suddenly seemed to age.

"So that's it," the dwarf said softly. "We saw you talking to Kitiara on the wall of the High Clerist's Tower. You were discussing more than Sturm's death, weren't you?"

Laurana nodded, wordlessly, staring at her hands in her lap.

"I never told you," she murmured in a voice barely audible, "I couldn't . . . I kept hoping. . . . Kitiara said . . . said she'd left Tanis in—some place called Flotsam . . . to look after things while she was gone."

"Liar!" said Tas promptly.

"No." Laurana shook her head. "When she says we are two women who understand each other, she's right. She wasn't lying. She was telling the truth, I know. And at the Tower she mentioned the dream." Laurana lifted her head. "Do you remember the dream?"

Flint nodded uncomfortably. Tasslehoff shuffled his feet.

"Only Tanis could have told her about the dream we all shared," Laurana continued, swallowing a choking feeling in her throat. "I saw him with her in the dream, just as I saw Sturm's death. The dream's coming true. . . ."

"Now wait a minute," Flint said gruffly, grabbing hold of reality as a drowning man grabs a piece of wood. "You said yourself you saw your own death in the dream, right after Sturm's. And you didn't die. And nothing hacked up Sturm's body, either."

"I haven't died yet, like I did in the dream," Tas said helpfully. "And I've picked lots of locks, well, not lots, but a few here and there, and none were poisoned. Besides, Laurana, Tanis wouldn't —"

Flint shot Tas a warning glance. The kender lapsed into silence. But Laurana had seen the glance and understood. Her lips tightened.

"Yes, he would. You both know it. He loves her." Laurana was quiet a moment, then, "I'm going. I'll exchange Bakaris."

Flint heaved a sigh. He had seen this coming. "Laurana—"

"Wait a minute, Flint," she interrupted. "If Tanis received a message saying you were dying, what would he do?"

"That's not the point," Flint mumbled.

"If he had to go into the Abyss itself, past a thousand dragons, he'd come to you—"

"Perhaps and perhaps not," said Flint gruffly. "Not if he was leader of an army. Not if he had responsibilities, people depending on him. He'd know I'd understand—"

Laurana's face might have been carved of marble, so impassive and pure and cold was her expression. "I never asked for these responsibilities. I never wanted them. We can make it look as if Bakaris escaped—"

"Don't do it, Laurana!" Tas begged. "He's the officer who brought back Derek and Lord Alfred's body at the High Clerist's Tower, the officer you shot in the arm with the arrow. He hates you, Laurana! I—I saw the way he looked at you the day we captured him!"

Flint's brows drew together. "The lords and your brother are still below. We'll discuss the best way to handle this—"

"I'm not discussing anything," Laurana stated, lifting her chin in the old imperious gesture the dwarf knew so well. "*I'm* the general. It's my decision."

"Maybe you should ask someone's advice—"

Laurana regarded the dwarf with bitter amusement. "Whose?" she asked. "Gilthanas's? What would I say? That Kitiara and I want to exchange lovers? No, we'll tell no one. What would the knights have done with Bakaris anyway? Execute him according to knightly ritual. They owe me something for all I've done. I'll take Bakaris as payment."

"Laurana"—Flint tried desperately to think of some way to penetrate her frozen mask—"there is a protocol that must be followed in prisoner exchange. You're right. You are the general, and you must know how important this is! You were in your father's court long enough—" *That* was a mistake. The dwarf knew it as soon as he opened his mouth and he groaned inwardly.

"I am no longer in my father's court!" Laurana flashed. "And to the Abyss with protocol!" Rising to her feet, she regarded Flint coldly, as if he were someone she had just met. The dwarf was, in fact, strongly reminded of her as he had seen her in Qualinesti, the evening she had run away from her home to follow after Tanis in childish infatuation.

"Thank you for bringing this message. I have a great deal to do before morning. If you have any regard for Tanis, please return to your rooms and say nothing to anyone."

Tasslehoff cast Flint an alarmed glance. Flushing, the dwarf tried hastily to undo the damage.

"Now, Laurana," he said gruffly, "don't take my words to heart. If you've made your decision, I'll support you. I'm just being an old crotchety grandfather, that's all. I worry about you, even if you are a general. And you should take me with you—like the note says—"

"Me, too!" cried Tas indignantly.

Flint glared at him, but Laurana didn't notice. Her expression softened. "Thank you, Flint. You too, Tas," she said wearily. "I'm sorry I snapped at you. But I really believe I should go alone."

"No," Flint said stubbornly. "I care about Tanis as much as you. If there's any chance he is dy—" The dwarf choked and wiped his hand across his eyes. Then he swallowed the lump in his throat. "I want to be with him."

"Me, too," mumbled Tas, subdued.

"Very well." Laurana smiled sadly. "I can't blame you. And I'm sure he'd want you to be there."

She sounded so certain, so positive she would see Tanis. The dwarf saw it in her eyes. He made one final effort. "Laurana, what if it's a trap? An ambush—"

Laurana's expression froze again. Her eyes narrowed angrily. Flint's protest was lost in his beard. He glanced at Tas. The kender shook his head.

The old dwarf sighed.

11

There it is, sir," said the dragon, a huge red monster with glistening black eyes and a wing span that was like the shadows of night. "Dargaard Keep. Wait, you can see it clearly in the moonlight . . . when the clouds part."

"I see it," replied a deep voice. The dragon, hearing the dagger-edged anger in the man's tone, began his descent swiftly, spiraling round and round as he tested the shifting air currents among the mountains. Nervously eyeing the keep surrounded by the rocky crags of the jagged mountains, the dragon looked for a place to make a smooth and easy landing. It would never do to jounce Lord Ariakas.

At the far northern end of the Dargaard Mountains stood their destination—Dargaard Keep, as dark and dismal as its legends. Once—when the world was young—Dargaard Keep had graced the mountain peaks, its rose-colored walls rising in graceful sweeping beauty up from the rock in the very likeness of a rose itself. But now, thought Ariakas grimly, the rose has died. The Highlord was not a poetic man, nor was he much given to flights of fancy. But the fire-blackened, crumbling castle atop the rock looked so much like a decayed rose upon a withering bush that the image struck him forcibly. Black latticework,

149

stretching from broken tower to broken tower, no longer formed the petals of the rose. Instead, mused Ariakas, it is the web of the insect whose poison had killed it.

The great red dragon wheeled a final time. The southern wall surrounding the courtyard had fallen a thousand feet to the base of the cliff during the Cataclysm, leaving a clear passage to the gates of the keep itself. Breathing a heartfelt sigh of relief, the red saw smooth tiled pavement beyond, broken only here and there by rents in the stonework, suitable for a smooth landing. Even dragons—who feared few things on Krynn—found it healthier to avoid Lord Ariakas's displeasure.

In the courtyard below, there was a sudden fever of activity, looking like an anthill disturbed by the approach of a wasp. Draconians shrieked and pointed. The captain of the night watch came hurrying to the battlements, looking over the edge into the courtyard. The draconians were right. A flight of red dragons were indeed landing in the courtyard, one of them bearing an officer, too, by the armor. The captain watched uneasily as the man leaped from the dragonsaddle before his mount had come to halt. The dragon's wings beat furiously to avoid striking the officer, sending dust billowing about him in moonlit clouds as he strode purposefully across the stones of the courtyard toward the door. His black boots rang on the pavement, sounding like a death knell.

And, with that thought, the captain gasped, suddenly recognizing the officer. Turning, nearly stumbling over the draconian in his haste, he cursed the soldier and ran through the keep in search of Acting Commander Garibanus.

Lord Ariakas's mailed fist fell upon the wooden door with a thunderous blow that sent splinters flying. Draconians scrambled to open it, then shrank back abjectly as the Dragon Highlord stalked inside, accompanied by a blast of cold wind that extinguished the candles and caused torch flames to waver.

Casting a swift glance from behind the gleaming mask of the dragonhelm as he entered, Ariakas saw a large circular hallway spanned by a vaulted, domed ceiling. Two giant curved staircases rose from either side of the entryway, leading up to a balcony on the second level. As Ariakas looked around, ignoring the groveling draconians, he saw Garibanus emerge from a doorway near the top of the stairs, hastily buttoning his trousers and pulling a shirt over his head. The captain of the watch stood, quaking, next to Garibanus, pointing down at the Dragon Highlord.

Ariakas guessed in a moment whose company the acting commander had been enjoying. Apparently he was filling in for the missing Bakaris in more ways than one!

"So *that's* where she is!" Lord Ariakas thought in satisfaction. He strode across the hallway and up the stairs, taking them two at a time. Draconians scuttled out of his path like rats. The captain of the guard disappeared. Ariakas was fully halfway up the stairs before Garibanus had collected himself enough to address him.

"L-Lord Ariakas," he stammered, stuffing his shirt into his pants and hurrying down the stairs. "This is an—er—unexpected honor."

"Not *unexpected*, I believe?" Arkiakas said smoothly, his voice sounding strangely metallic coming from the depths of the dragonhelm.

"Well, perhaps not," Garibanus said with a weak laugh.

Ariakas continued climbing, his eyes fixed on a doorway above him. Realizing the Lord's intended destination, Garibanus interposed himself between Ariakas and the door.

"My lord," he began apologetically, "Kitiara is dressing. She—"

Without a word, without even pausing in his stride, Lord Ariakas swung his gloved hand. The blow caught Garibanus in the ribcage. There was a whooshing sound, like a bellows deflating, and the sound of bones cracking, then a wet soggy splatter as the force of the blow sent the young man's body into the wall opposite the stairs some ten yards distant. The limp body slid to the floor below, but Ariakas never noticed. Without a backward glance, he resumed his climb, his eyes on the door at the top of the stairs.

Lord Ariakas, commander-in-chief of the dragonarmies, reporting directly to the Dark Queen herself, was a brilliant man, a military genius. Ariakas had nearly held the rulership of the Ansalon continent in his grasp. Already he was styling himself "Emperor." His Queen was truly pleased with him, his rewards from her were many and lavish.

But now he saw his beautiful dream slipping through his fingers like smoke from autumn fires. He had received reports of his troops fleeing wildly across the Solamnic plains, falling back from Palanthas, withdrawing from Vingaard Keep, abandoning plans for the siege of Kalaman. The elves had allied with human forces in Northern and Southern Ergoth. The mountain dwarves had emerged from their subterranean home of Thorbardin and, it was reported, allied with their ancient enemies, the hill dwarves and a group of human refugees in an attempt to drive the dragonarmies from Abanasinia. Silvanesti had been freed. A Dragon Highlord had been killed in Ice Wall. And, if rumor was to be believed, a group of gully dwarves held Pax Tharkas!

Thinking of this as he swept up the stairs, Ariakas worked himself into a fury. Few survived Lord Ariakas's displeasure. None survived his furies.

Ariakas inherited his position of authority from his father, who had been a cleric in high standing with the Queen of Darkness. Although only forty, Ariakas had held his position almost twenty years—his father having met an untimely death at the hands of his own son. When Ariakas was two, he had watched his father brutally murder his mother, who had been attempting to flee with her little son before the child became as perverted with evil as his father.

Though Ariakas always treated his father with outward shows of respect, he never forgot his mother's murder. He worked hard and excelled in his studies, making his father inordinately proud. Many wondered whether that pride was with the father as he felt the first thrusts of the knife-blade his nineteen-year-old son plunged into his body in revenge for his mother's death—and with an eye to the throne of Dragon Highlord.

Certainly it was no great tragedy to the Queen of Darkness, who quickly found young Ariakas more than made up for the loss of her favorite cleric. The young man had no clerical talents himself, but his considerable skills as a magic-user won him the Black Robes and the commendations of the evil wizards who instructed him. Although he passed the dreadful Tests in the Tower of High Sorcery, magic was not his love. He practiced it infrequently, and never wore the Black Robes that marked his standing as a wizard of evil powers.

Ariakas's true passion was war. It was he who had devised the strategy that had enabled the Dragon Highlords and their armies to subjugate almost all of the continent of Ansalon. It was he who had insured that they met with almost no resistance, for it had been Ariakas's brilliant strategy to move swiftly, striking the divided human, elf, and dwarven races before they had time to unite, and snap them up piecemeal. By summer, Ariakas's plan called for him to rule Ansalon unchallenged. Other Dragon Highlords on other continents of Krynn were looking to him with undisguised envy, and fear. For one continent could never satisfy Ariakas. Already his eyes were turning westward, across the Sirrion Sea.

But now—disaster.

Reaching the door of Kitiara's bedchamber, Ariakas found it locked. Coldly he spoke one word in the language of magic and the heavy wooden door blew apart. Ariakas strode through the shower of sparks and blue flame that engulfed the door into Kitiara's chamber, his hand on his sword.

Kit was in bed. At the sight of Ariakas she rose, her hand clutching a silken dressing gown around her lithe body. Even through his raging fury, Ariakas was still forced to admire the woman who, of all his commanders, he had come to rely on most. Though his arrival must have caught her offguard, though she must know she had forfeited her life by allowing herself to be defeated, she faced him coolly and calmly. Not a spark of fear lit her brown eyes, not a murmur escaped her lips.

This only served to enrage Ariakas further, reminding him of his extreme disappointment in her. Without speaking, he yanked off the dragonhelm and hurled it across the room where it slammed into an ornately carved wooden chest, shattering it like glass.

At the sight of Ariakas's face, Kitiara momentarily lost control and shrank back in her bed, her hand nervously clasping the ribbons of her gown.

Few there were who could look up Ariakas's face without blenching. It was a face devoid of any human emotion. Even his anger showed only in the twitching of a muscle along his jaw. Long black hair swept down around his pallid features. A day's growth of beard appeared blue on his smooth-shaven skin. His eyes were black and cold as an ice-bound lake.

Ariakas reached the side of the bed in a bound. Ripping down the curtains that hung around it, he reached out and grabbed hold of Kitiara's short, curly hair. Dragging her from her bed, he hurled her to the stone floor.

Kitiara fell heavily, an exclamation of pain escaping her. But she recovered quickly, and was already starting to twist to her feet like a cat when Ariakas's voice froze her.

"Stay on your knees, Kitiara," he said. Slowly and deliberately he removed his long, shining sword from its scabbard. "Stay on your knees and bow your head, as the condemned do when they come to the block. For I am your executioner, Kitiara. Thus do my commanders pay for their failure!"

154

Kitiara remained kneeling, but she looked up at him. Seeing the flame of hatred in her brown eyes, Ariakas felt a moment's thankfulness that he held his sword in his hand. Once more he was compelled to admire her. Even facing imminent death, there was no fear in her eyes. Only defiance.

He raised his blade, but the blow did not fall.

Bone-cold fingers wrapped around the wrist of his swordarm.

"I believe you should hear the Highlord's explanation," said a hollow voice.

Lord Ariakas was a strong man. He could hurl a spear with force enough to drive it completely through the body of a horse. He could break a man's neck with one twist of his hand. Yet he found he could not wrench himself loose from the chill grasp that was slowly crushing his wrist. Finally, in agony, Ariakas dropped the sword. It fell to the floor with a clatter.

Somewhat shaken, Kitiara rose to her feet. Making a gesture, she commanded her minion to release Ariakas. The Lord whirled around, raising a hand to call forth the magic that would reduce this creature to cinders.

Then he stopped. Sucking in his breath, Ariakas stumbled backward, the magic spell he had been prepared to cast slipping from his mind.

Before him stood a figure no taller than himself, clad in armor so old it predated the Cataclysm. The armor was that of a Knight of Solamnia. The symbol of the Order of the Rose was traced upon the front, barely visible and worn with age. The armored figure wore no helm, it carried no weapon. Yet Ariakas—staring at it—fell back another step. For the figure he stared at was not the figure of a living man.

The being's face was transparent. Ariakas could see right through it to the wall beyond. A pale light flickered in the cavernous eyes. It stared straight ahead, as if it, too, could see right through Ariakas.

"A death knight!" he whispered in awe.

The Lord rubbed his aching wrist, numb with the cold of those who dwell in realms far removed from the warmth of living flesh. More frightened than he dared admit, Ariakas bent down to retrieve his sword, muttering a charm to ward off the aftereffects of such a deadly touch. Rising, he cast a bitter glance at Kitiara, who was regarding him with a crooked smile.

"This—this creature serves you?" he asked hoarsely.

Kitiara shrugged. "Let us say, we agree to serve each other."

Ariakas regarded her in grudging admiration. Casting a sidelong glance at the death knight, he sheathed his sword.

"Does he always frequent your bedroom?" he sneered. His wrist ached abominably.

"He comes and goes as he chooses," Kitiara replied. She gathered the folds of the gown casually around her body, reacting apparently more from the chill in the early spring air than out of a desire for modesty. Shivering, she ran her hand through her curly hair and shrugged. "It's *his* castle, after all."

Ariakas paused, a faraway look in his eyes, his mind running back over ancient legends.

"Lord Soth!" he said suddenly, turning to the figure. "Knight of the Black Rose."

The knight bowed in acknowledgment.

"I had forgotten the ancient story of Dargaard Keep," Ariakas murmured, regarding Kitiara thoughtfully. "You have more nerve than even *I* gave you credit for, lady, taking up residence in this accursed dwelling! According to legend, Lord Soth commands a troop of skeletal warriors—"

"An effective force in a battle," Kitiara replied, yawning. Walking over to a small table near a fireplace, she picked up a cut-glass carafe. "Their touch alone"—she regarded Ariakas with smile—"well, you know what their touch is like to those who lack the magic skills to defend against it. Some wine?"

"Very well," Ariakas replied, his eyes still on the transparent face of Lord Soth. "What about the dark elves, the banshee women who reputedly follow him?"

"They're here . . . somewhere." Kit shivered again, then lifted her wine glass. "You'll probably hear them before long. Lord Soth doesn't sleep, of course. The ladies help him pass the long hours in the night."

For an instant, Kitiara paled, holding the wine glass to her lips. Then she set it down untouched, her hand shaking slightly. "It is not pleasant," she said briefly. Glancing around, she asked, "What have you done with Garibanus?"

Tossing off the glass of wine, Ariakas gestured negligently. "I left him . . . at the bottom of the stairs."

"Dead?" Kitiara questioned, pouring the Highlord another glass.

Ariakas scowled. "Perhaps. He got in my way. Does it matter?"

"I found him . . . entertaining," Kitiara said. "He filled Bakaris's place in more than one respect."

"Bakaris, yes." Lord Ariakas drank another glass. "So your commander managed to get himself captured as your armies went down to defeat!"

"He was an imbecile," Kitiara said coldly. "He tried riding dragonback, even though he is still crippled."

"I heard. What happened to his arm?"

"The elfwoman shot him with an arrow at the High Clerist's Tower. It was his own fault, and he now has paid for it. I had removed him from command, making him my bodyguard. But he insisted on trying to redeem himself."

"You don't appear to be mourning his loss," Ariakas said, eyeing Kitiara. The dressing gown, tied together only by two ribbons at the neck, did little to cover her lithe body.

Kit smiled. "No, Garibanus is . . . quite a good replacement. I hope you haven't killed him. It will be a bother getting someone else to go to Kalaman tomorrow."

"What are you doing at Kalaman—preparing to surrender to the elfwoman and the knights?" Lord Ariakas asked bitterly, his anger returning with the wine.

"No," Kitiara said. Sitting down in a chair opposite Ariakas, she regarded him coolly. "I'm preparing to accept *their* surrender."

"Ha!" Ariakas snorted. "They're not insane. They know they're winning. And they're right!" His face flushed. Picking up the carafe, he emptied it into his glass.

"You owe your death knight your life, Kitiara. Tonight at least. But he won't be around you forever."

"My plans are succeeding much better than I had hoped," Kitiara replied smoothly, not in the least disconcerted by Ariakas's flickering eyes. "If I fooled you, my lord, I have no doubt that I have fooled the enemy."

"And how have you fooled me, Kitiara?" Ariakas asked with lethal calm. "Do you mean to say that you are *not* losing on all fronts? That you are *not* being driven from Solamnia? That the dragonlances and the good dragons have *not* brought about ignominious defeat?" His voice rose with each word.

"They have not!" Kitiara snapped, her brown eyes flashing. Leaning across the table, she caught hold of Ariakas's hand as he was about to raise the wine glass to his lips. "As for the good dragons, my lord, my spies tell me their return was due to an elflord and a silver dragon breaking into the temple at Sanction where they discovered what was happening to the good dragon eggs. Whose fault was that? Who slipped up there? Guarding that temple was *your* responsibility—"

Furiously, Ariakas wrenched his hand free of Kitiara's grip. Hurling the wine glass across the room, he stood and faced her.

"By the gods, you go too far!" he shouted, breathing heavily.

"Quit posturing," Kitiara said. Coolly rising to her feet, she turned and walked across the room. "Follow me to my war room, and I will explain my plans."

Ariakas stared down at the map of northern Ansalon. "It might work," he admitted.

"Of course, it will work," Kit said, yawning and stretching languidly. "My troops have run before them like frightened rabbits. Too bad the knights weren't astute enough to notice that we always drifted southward, and they never wondered why my forces just seemed to melt away and vanish. Even as we speak, my armies are gathering in a sheltered valley south of these mountains. Within a week, an army several thousand strong will be ready to march on Kalaman. The loss of their 'Golden General' will destroy their morale. The city will probably capitulate without a fight. From there, I regain all the land we appear to have lost. Give me command of that fool Toede's armies to the south, send the flying citadels I've asked for, and Solamnia will think it's been hit by another Cataclysm!"

"But the elfwoman—"

."Need not concern us," Kitiara said.

Ariakas shook his head. "This seems the weak link in your plans, Kitiara. What about Half-Elven? Can you be certain he won't interfere?"

"It doesn't matter about him. *She* is the one who counts and she is a woman in love." Kitiara shrugged. "She trusts me, Ariakas. You scoff, but it's true. She trusts me too much and Tanis Half-Elven too little. But that's always the way of lovers. The ones we love most are those we trust least. It proved quite fortunate Bakaris fell into their hands."

Hearing a change in her voice, Ariakas glanced at Kitiara sharply, but she had turned from him, keeping her face averted. Immediately he realized she was not as confident as she seemed, and then he knew she had lied to him. The half-elf! What about him? Where *was* he, for that matter. Ariakas had heard a great deal about him, but had never met him. The Dragon Highlord considered pressing her on this point, then abruptly changed his mind. Much better to have in his possession the knowledge that she had lied. It gave him a power over this dangerous woman. Let her relax in her supposed complacency.

Yawning elaborately, Ariakas feigned indifference. "What will you do with the elfwoman?" he asked as she would expect him to ask. Ariakas's passion for delicate blonde women was well-known.

Kitiara raised her eyebrows, giving him a playful look. "Too bad, my lord," she said mockingly, "but Her Dark Highness has asked for the lady. Perhaps you could have her when the Dark Queen is finished."

Ariakas shivered. "Bah, she'll be of no use to me then. Give her to your friend, Lord Soth. He liked elfwomen once upon a time, if I remember correctly."

"You do," murmured Kitiara. Her eyes narrowed. She held up her hand. "Listen," she said softly.

Ariakas fell silent. At first he heard nothing, then he gradually became aware of a strange sound—a wailing keen, as if a hundred women mourned their dead. As he listened, it grew louder and louder, piercing the stillness of the night.

The Dragon Highlord set down his wine glass, startled to see his hand trembling. Looking at Kitiara, he saw her face pale beneath its tan. Her large eyes were wide. Feeling his eyes upon her, Kitiara swallowed and licked her dry lips.

"Awful, isn't it?" she asked, her voice cracking.

"I faced horrors in the Towers of High Sorcery," said Ariakas softly, "but that was nothing compared to this. What is it?"

"Come," Kit said, standing up.

"If you have the nerve, I'll show you."

Together, the two left the war room, Kitiara leading Ariakas through the winding corridors of the castle until they came back to Kit's bedroom above the circular entryway with the vaulted ceiling.

"Stay in the shadows," Kitiara warned.

An unnecessary warning, Ariakas thought as they crept softly out onto the balcony overlooking the circular room. Looking down over the edge of the balcony, Ariakas was overcome with sheer horror at the sight below him. Sweating, he drew back swiftly in the shadows of Kitiara's bedroom.

"How can you stand that?" he asked her as she entered and shut the door softly behind her. "Does that go on every night?"

"Yes," she said, trembling. She drew a deep breath and closed her eyes. Within a moment she was back in control. "Sometimes I think I'm used to it, then I make the mistake of looking down there. The song isn't so bad. . . ."

"It's ghastly!" Ariakas muttered, wiping cold sweat from his face. "So Lord Soth sits down there on his throne every night, surrounded by his skeletal warriors, and the dark hags sing that horrible lullaby!"

"And it is the same song, always," Kitiara murmured. Shivering, she absently picked up the empty wine carafe, then set it back down on the table. "Though the past tortures him, he cannot escape it. Always he ponders, wondering what he might have done to avoid the fate that dooms him to walk forever upon the land without rest. The dark elven women, who were part of his downfall, are forced to relive his story with him. Nightly they must repeat it. Nightly he must hear it."

"What are the words?"

"I know them, now, almost as well as he does." Kitiara laughed, then shuddered. "Call for another carafe of wine and I'll tell you his tale, if you have the time."

"I have time," Ariakas said, settling back in his chair. "Though I must leave in the morning if I am to send the citadels."

Kitiara smiled at him, the charming, crooked smile that so many had found so captivating.

"Thank you, my lord," she said. "I will not fail you again."

"No," said Ariakas coolly, ringing a small silver bell, "I can promise you that, Kitiara. If you do, you will find *his* fate"—he motioned downstairs where the wailing had reached a shivering pitch—"a pleasant one compared to your own."

The Knight
of the Black Rose.

12

"As you know," began Kitiara, "Lord Soth was a true and noble knight of Solamnia. But he was an intensely passionate man, lacking in self-discipline, and this was his downfall.

"Soth fell in love with a beautiful elfmaid, a disciple of the Kingpriest of Istar. He was married at the time, but thoughts of his wife vanished at the sight of the elfmaid's beauty. Forsaking both his sacred marriage vows and his knightly vows, Soth gave in to his passion. Lying to the girl, he seduced her and brought her to live at Dargaard Keep, promising to marry her. His wife disappeared under sinister circumstances."

Kitiara shrugged, then continued:

"According to what I've heard of the song, the elfmaid remained true to the knight, even after she discovered his terrible misdeeds. She prayed to the Goddess Mishakal that the knight be allowed to redeem himself and, apparently, her prayers were answered. Lord Soth was given the power to prevent the Cataclysm, though it would mean sacrificing his own life.

"Strengthened by the love of the girl he had wronged, Lord Soth left for Istar, fully intending to stop the Kingpriest and restore his shattered honor.

"But the knight was halted in his journey by elven women,

163

disciples of the Kingpriest, who knew of Lord Soth's crime and threatened to ruin him. To weaken the effects of the elfmaid's love, they intimated that she had been unfaithful to him in his absence.

"Soth's passions took hold of him, destroying his reason. In a jealous rage he rode back to Dargaard Keep. Entering his door, he accused the innocent girl of betraying him. Then the Cataclysm struck. The great chandelier in the entryway fell to the floor, consuming the elfmaid and her child in flames. As she died, she called down a curse upon the knight, condeming him to eternal, dreadful life. Soth and his followers perished in the fire, only to be reborn in hideous form."

"So this is what he hears," Ariakas murmured, listening.

> And in the climate of dreams
> When you recall her, when the world of the dream
> expands, wavers in light,
> when you stand at the edge of blessedness and sun,
>
> Then we shall make you remember,
> shall make you live again
> through the long denial of body
>
> For you were first dark in the light's hollow,
>   expanding like a stain, a cancer
>
> For you were the shark in the slowed water
>   beginning to move
>
> For you were the notched head of a snake,
>   sensing forever warmth and form
>
> For you were inexplicable death in the crib,
>   the long house in betrayal

And you were more terrible than this
    in a loud alley of visions,
      for you passed through unharmed, unchanging

As the women screamed, unraveling silence,
    halving the door of the world,
      bringing forth monsters

As a child opened in parabolas of fire
    There at the borders
      of two lands burning

As the world split, wanting to swallow you back
    willing to give up everything
      to lose you in darkness.

You passed through these unharmed, unchanging,
but now you see them
strung on our words—on your own conceiving
as you pass from night—to awareness of night
to know that hatred is the calm of philosophers
that its price is forever
that it draws you through meteors
through winter's transfixion
through the blasted rose
through the sharks' water
through the black compression of oceans
through rock—through magma
to yourself—to an abscess of nothing
that you will recognize as nothing
that you will know is coming again and again
under the same rules.

The trap . . .

13

Bakaris slept fitfully in his jail cell. Though haughty and insolent during the day, his nights were tortured by dreams of Kitiara and of his execution at the hands of the Knights of Solamnia. Or perhaps it was his execution at Kitiara's hands. He was never certain, when he woke in a cold sweat, which it had been. Lying in his cold cell in the still hours of the night when he could not sleep, Bakaris cursed the elven woman who had been the cause of his downfall. Over and over he plotted his revenge upon her —if only she would fall into his hands.

Bakaris was thinking of this, hovering between sleep and wakefulness, when the sound of a key in the lock of his cell door brought him to his feet. It was near dawn, near the hour of execution! Perhaps the knights were coming for him!

"Who is it?" Bakaris called harshly.

"Hush!" commanded a voice. "You are in no danger, if you keep quiet and do as you are told."

Bakaris sat back down on his bed in astonishment. He recognized the voice. How not? Night after night it had spoken in his vengeful thoughts. The elfwoman! And the commander could see two other figures in the shadows, small figures. The dwarf and the kender, most likely. They always hung around the elfwoman.

167

The cell door opened. The elfwoman glided inside. She was heavily cloaked and carried another cloak in her hand.

"Hurry," she ordered coldly. "Put this on."

"Not until I know what this is about," Bakaris said suspiciously, though his soul sang for joy.

"We are exchanging you for . . . for another prisoner," Laurana replied.

Bakaris frowned. He mustn't seem too eager.

"I don't believe you," he stated, lying back down on his bed. "It's a trap—"

"I don't care what you believe!" Laurana snapped impatiently. "You're coming if I have to knock you senseless! It won't matter whether you are conscious or not, just so long as I'm able to exhibit you to Kiti—the one wants you!"

Kitiara! So that was it. What was she up to? What game was she playing? Bakaris hesitated. He didn't trust Kit any more than she trusted him. She was quite capable of using him to further her own ends, which is undoubtedly what she was doing now. But perhaps he could use her in return. If only he knew what was going on! But looking at Laurana's pale, rigid face, Bakaris knew that she was quite prepared to carry out her threat. He would have to bide his time.

"It seems I have no choice," he said. Moonlight filtered through a barred window into the filthy cell, shining on Bakaris's face. He'd been in prison for weeks. How long he didn't know, he'd lost count. As he reached for the cloak, he caught Laurana's cold green eyes, which were fixed on him intently, narrow slightly in disgust.

Self-consciously, Bakaris raised his good hand and scratched the new growth of beard.

"Pardon, your ladyship," he said sarcastically, "but the servants in your establishment have not thought fit to bring me a razor. I know how the sight of facial hair disgusts you elves!"

To his surprise, Bakaris saw his words draw blood. Laurana's face turned pale, her lips chalk-white. Only by a supreme effort did she control herself. "Move!" she said in a strangled voice.

At the sound, the dwarf entered the room, hand on his battle-axe. "You heard the general," Flint snarled. "Get going. Why your miserable carcass is worth trading for Tanis—"

"Flint!" said Laurana tersely.

Suddenly Bakaris understood!

Kitiara's plan began to take shape in his mind.

"So—Tanis! He's the one I'm being exchanged for." He watched Laurana's face closely. No reaction. He might have been speaking of a stranger instead of a man Kitiara had told him was this woman's lover. He tried again, testing his theory. "I wouldn't call him a prisoner, however, unless you speak of a prisoner of love. Kit must have tired of him. Ah, well. Poor man. I'll miss him. He and I have much in common—"

Now there was a reaction. He saw the delicate jaws clench, the shoulders tremble beneath the cloak. Without a word, Laurana turned and stalked out of the cell. So he was right. This had something to do with the bearded half-elf. But what? Tanis had left Kit in Flotsam. Had she found him again? Had he returned to her? Bakaris fell silent, wrapping the cloak around him. Not that it mattered, not to him. He would be able to use this new information for his own revenge. Recalling Laurana's strained and rigid face in the moonlight, Bakaris thanked the Dark Queen for her favors as the dwarf shoved him out the cell door.

The sun had not risen yet, although a faint pink line on the eastern horizon foretold that dawn was an hour or so away. It was still dark in the city of Kalaman—dark and silent as the town slept soundly following its day and night of revelry. Even the guards yawned at their posts or, in some cases, snored as

169

they slept soundly. It was an easy task for the four heavily cloaked figures to flit silently through the streets until they came to a small locked door in the city wall.

"This used to lead to some stairs that led up to the top of the wall, across it, then back down to the other side," whispered Tasslehoff, fumbling in one of his pouches until he found his lock-picking tools.

"How do you know?" Flint muttered, peering around nervously.

"I used to come to Kalaman when I was little," Tas said. Finding the slender piece of wire, his small, skilled hands slipped it inside the lock. "My parents brought me. We always came in and out this way."

"Why didn't you use the front gate, or would that have been too simple?" Flint growled.

"Hurry up!" ordered Laurana impatiently.

"We would have used the front gate," Tas said, manipulating the wire. "Ah, there." Removing the wire, he put it carefully back into his pouch, then quietly swung the old door open. "Where was I? Oh, yes. We would have used the front gate, but kender weren't allowed in the city."

"And your parents came in anyway!" Flint snorted, following Tas through the door and up a narrow flight of stone stairs. The dwarf was only half-listening to the kender. He kept his eye on Bakaris, who was, in Flint's view, behaving himself just a bit too well. Laurana had withdrawn completely within herself. Her only words were sharp commands to hurry.

"Well, of course," Tas said, prattling away cheerfully. "They always considered it an oversight. I mean, why should we be on the same list as goblins? Someone must have put us there accidentally. But my parents didn't consider it polite to argue, so we just came in and out by the side door. Easier for everyone all around. Here we are. Open that door—it's not usually locked. Oops, careful. There's a guard. Wait until he's gone."

170

Pressing themselves against the wall, they hid in the shadows until the guard had stumbled wearily past, nearly asleep on his feet. Then they silently crossed the wall, entered another door, ran down another flight of stairs, and were outside the city walls.

They were alone. Flint, looking around, could see no sign of anybody or anything in the half-light before dawn. Shivering, he huddled in his cloak, feeling apprehension creep over him. What if Kitiara was telling the truth? What if Tanis was with her? What if he was dying?

Angrily Flint forced himself to stop thinking about that. He almost hoped it was a trap! Suddenly his mind was wrenched from its dark thoughts by a harsh voice, speaking so near that he started in terror.

"Is that you, Bakaris?"

"Yes. Good to see you again, Gakhan."

Shaking, Flint turned to see a dark figure emerge from the shadows of the wall. It was heavily cloaked and swathed in cloth. He remembered Tas's description of the draconian.

"Are they carrying any other weapons?" Gakhan demanded, his eyes on Flint's battle-axe.

"No," Laurana answered sharply.

"Search them," Gakhan ordered Bakaris.

"You have my word of honor," Laurana said angrily. "I am a princess of the Qualinesti—"

Bakaris took a step toward her. "Elves have their own code of honor," he sneered. "Or so you said the night you shot me with your cursed arrow."

Laurana's face flushed, but she made no answer nor did she fall back before his advance.

Coming to stand in front of her, Bakaris lifted his right arm with his left hand, then let it fall. "You destroyed my career, my life."

Laurana, holding herself rigid, watched him without moving. "I said I carry no weapons."

"You can search me, if you like," offered Tasslehoff, interposing himself—accidentally—between Bakaris and Laurana. "Here!" He dumped the contents of a pouch onto Bakaris's foot.

"Damn you!" Bakaris swore, cuffing the kender on the side of the head.

"Flint!" Laurana cautioned warningly through clenched teeth. She could see the dwarf's face red with rage. At her command, the dwarf choked back his anger.

"I'm s-sorry, truly!" Tas snuffled, fumbling around the ground after his things.

"If you delay much longer, we won't have to alert the guard," Laurana said coldly, determined not to tremble at the man's foul touch. "The sun will be up and they will see us clearly."

"The elfwoman is right, Bakaris," Gakhan said, an edge in his reptilian voice. "Take the dwarf's battle-axe and let's get out of here."

Looking at the brightening horizon—and at the cloaked and hooded draconian—Bakaris gave Laurana a vicious glance, then snatched the battle-axe away from the dwarf.

"He's no threat! What's an old man like him going to do, anyway?" Bakaris muttered.

"Get moving," Gakhan ordered Laurana, ignoring Bakaris. "Head for that grove of trees. Keep hidden and don't try alerting the guard. I am a magic-user and my spells are deadly. The Dark Lady said to bring you safely, 'general.' I have no instructions regarding your two friends."

They followed Gakhan across the flat, open ground outside the city gates to a large grove of trees, keeping in the shadows as much as possible. Bakaris walked beside Laurana. Holding her head high, she resolutely refused to even acknowledge his existence. Reaching the trees, Gakhan pointed.

"Here are our mounts," he said.

"We're not going anywhere!" Laurana said angrily, staring at the creatures in alarm.

At first Flint thought they were small dragons, but as he drew nearer, the dwarf caught his breath.

"Wyvern!" he breathed.

Distantly related to dragons, wyvern are smaller and lighter and were often used by the Highlords to relay messages, as the griffons were used by the elven lords. Not nearly as intelligent as dragons, the wyvern are noted for their cruel and chaotic natures. The animals in the grove peered at the companions with red eyes, their scorpionlike tails curled menacingly. Tipped with poison, the tail could sting an enemy to death within seconds.

"Where is Tanis?" Laurana demanded.

"He grew worse," Gakhan answered. "If you want to see him, you must come to Dargaard Keep."

"No," Laurana drew back, only to feel Bakaris's hand close over her arm in a firm grip.

"Don't call for help," he said pleasantly, "or one of your friends will die. Well, it seems we're taking a little trip to Dargaard Keep. Tanis is a *dear* friend. I'd hate for him to miss seeing you." Bakaris turned to the draconian. "Gakhan, go back to Kalaman. Let us know the reaction of the people when they discover their 'general' missing."

Gakhan hesitated, his dark reptilian eyes regarding Bakaris warily. Kitiara had warned him something like this might occur. He guessed what Bakaris had in mind—his own private revenge. Gakhan could stop Bakaris, that was no problem. But there was the chance that—during the unpleasantness—one of the prisoners might escape and go for help. They were too near the city walls for comfort. Blast Bakaris anyway! Gakhan scowled, then realized there was nothing he could do but hope Kitiara had provided for this contingency. Shrugging, Gakhan comforted himself with the thought of Bakaris's fate when he returned to the Dark Lady.

"Certainly, Commander," the draconian replied smoothly. Bowing, Gakhan faded back into the shadows. They could see his cloaked figure darting from tree to tree, heading for Kalaman. Bakaris's face grew eager, the cruel lines around the bearded mouth deepened.

"Come on, General." Bakaris shoved Laurana toward the wyvern.

But instead of advancing, Laurana whirled to face the man.

"Tell me one thing," she said through pale lips. "Is it true? Is Tanis with . . . with Kitiara? Th-the note said he was wounded at Vingaard Keep . . . dying!"

Seeing the anguish in her eyes—anguish not for herself, but for the half-elf—Bakaris smiled. He had never dreamed revenge could be so satisfying. "How should I know? I've been locked in your stinking prison. But I find it difficult to believe he'd be wounded. Kit never allowed him near a fight! The only battles he wages are those of love. . . ."

Laurana's head drooped. Bakaris laid a hand on her arm in mocking sympathy. Angrily Laurana shook free, turning to keep her face hidden.

"I don't believe you!" Flint growled. "Tanis would never allow Kitiara to do this—"

"Oh, you're right there, dwarf," Bakaris said, realizing quickly just how far his lies would be believed. "He knows nothing of this. The Dark Lady sent him to Neraka weeks ago, to prepare for our audience with the Queen."

"You know, Flint," Tas said solemnly. "Tanis was really fond of Kitiara. Do you remember that party at the Inn of the Last Home? It was Tanis's Day of Life Gift party. He'd just 'come of age' by elven standards and, boy! Was that some party! Do you remember? Caramon got a tankard of ale dumped over his head when he grabbed Dezra. And Raistlin drank too much wine and one of his spells misfired and burned up Otik's apron, and Kit and Tanis were together in that corner next to the firepit, and they were—"

Bakaris glanced at Tas in annoyance. The commander disliked being reminded of how close Kitiara really was to the half-elf.

"Tell the kender to keep quiet, General," Bakaris growled, "or I'll let the wyvern have him. Two hostages would suit the Dark Lady just as well as three."

"So it is a trap," Laurana said softly, looking around in a daze. "Tanis isn't dying . . . he's not even there! I've been a fool—"

"We're not going anywhere with you!" Flint stated, planting his feet on the ground firmly.

Bakaris regarded him coolly. "Have you ever seen a wyvern sting anyone to death?"

"No," said Tas with interest, "but I saw a scorpion once. Is it like that? Not that I'd want to try it, mind you," the kender faltered, seeing Bakaris's face darken.

"The guards on the walls of the city might well hear your screams," Bakaris said to Laurana, who stared at him as if he were speaking a language she didn't comprehend. "But, by then, it would be too late."

"I've been a fool," Laurana repeated softly.

"Say the word, Laurana!" Flint said stubbornly. "We'll fight—"

"No," she said in a small voice, like a child's. "No. I won't risk your lives, not you and Tas. It was my folly. I will pay. Bakaris, take me. Let my friends go—"

"Enough of this!" Bakaris said impatiently. "I'm not letting anyone go!" Climbing onto the back of a wyvern, he extended his hand to Laurana. "There's only two, so we'll have to double up."

Her face expressionless, Laurana accepted Bakaris's help and climbed onto the wyvern. Putting his good arm around her, he held her close, grinning.

At his touch, Laurana's face regained some of its color. Angrily, she tried to free herself from his grip.

"You are much safer this way, General," Bakaris said harshly in her ear. "I would not want you to fall."

Laurana bit her lip and stared straight ahead, forcing herself not to cry.

"Do these creatures *always* smell so awful," Tas said, regarding the wyvern with disgust as he helped Flint mount. "I think you should convince them to bathe—"

"Watch the tail," Bakaris said coldly. "The wyvern will generally not kill unless I give them the command, but they are high-strung. Little things upset them."

"Oh." Tas gulped. "I'm sure I didn't mean to be insulting. Actually, I suppose one could get used to the smell, after a bit—"

At a signal from Bakaris, the wyvern spread their leathery wings and soared into the air, flying slowly under the unaccustomed burden. Flint gripped Tasslehoff tightly and kept his eyes on Laurana, flying ahead of them with Bakaris. Occasionally the dwarf saw Bakaris lean close to Laurana and he saw Laurana pull away from him. The dwarf's face grew grim.

"That Bakaris is up to no good!" the dwarf muttered to Tas.

"What?" said Tas, turning around.

"I said that Bakaris is up to no good!" the dwarf shouted. "And I'll wager he's acting on his own and not following orders, either. That Gakhan-character wasn't at all pleased about being ordered off."

"What?" Tas yelled. "I can't hear! All this wind—"

"Oh, never mind!" The dwarf felt dizzy all of a sudden. He was finding it hard to breathe. Trying to take his mind off himself, he stared gloomily down at the tree tops emerging from the shadows as the sun began to rise.

After flying for about an hour, Bakaris made a motion with his hand and the wyvern began slowly circling, searching for a clear place to land on the heavily forested mountainside. Pointing at a small clearing just barely visible among the trees, Bakaris shouted instructions to the lead beast. The wyvern landed as ordered and Bakaris climbed down.

Flint glanced around, his fears growing. There was no sign of any fortress. No sign of life of any kind. They were in a small

M ARGARET W EIS & T RACY H ICKMAN

cleared area, surrounded by tall pine trees whose ancient limbs were so thick and tangled that they effectively shut out most of the sun's light. Around them, the forest was dark and filled with moving shadows. At one end of the clearing Flint saw a small cave, carved out of the cliff face.

"Where are we?" Laurana asked sternly. "This can't possibly be Dargaard Keep. Why are we stopping?"

"Astute observation, General," Bakaris said pleasantly. "Dargaard Keep is about a mile farther up the mountain. They're not expecting us yet. The Dark Lady probably hasn't even had her breakfast. We wouldn't want to be impolite and disturb her, would we?" He glanced over at Tas and Flint. "You two—stay put," he instructed as the kender seemed about to jump down. Tas froze.

Moving to stand near Laurana, Bakaris placed his hand on the neck of the wyvern. The beast's lidless eyes followed his every move as expectantly as a dog waiting to be fed.

"You get down, Lady Laurana," Bakaris said with lethal softness, coming quite near her as she sat upon the wyvern's back, regarding him scornfully. "We've time for a little . . . breakfast ourselves. . . ."

Laurana's eyes flashed. Her hand moved to her sword with such conviction she almost convinced herself it was there. "Stand away from me!" she commanded with such presence that, for a moment, Bakaris halted. Then, grinning, he reached up and grabbed hold of her wrist.

"No, lady. I wouldn't struggle. Remember the wyvern—and your friends over there. One word from me, and they will die very nasty deaths!"

Cringing, Laurana looked over to see the wyvern's scorpion tail poised above Flint's back. The beast quivered with anticipation of the kill.

"No! Laurana, " Flint began in agony, but she cast a sharp glance at him, reminding him that she was still the general. Her face drained of life, she allowed Bakaris to help her down.

"There, I thought you looked hungry," Bakaris said, grinning.

"Let them go!" Laurana demanded. "It's me you want—"

"You're right there," Bakaris said, grabbing hold of her around her waist. "But their presence seems to insure your good behavior."

"Don't you worry about us, Laurana!" Flint roared.

"Shut up, dwarf!" Bakaris cried in a rage. Shoving Laurana back against the body of the wyvern, he turned to stare at the dwarf and the kender. Flint's blood chilled as he saw the wild madness in the man's eyes.

"I—I think we'd better do as he says, Flint," Tas said, swallowing. "He'll hurt Laurana—"

"Hurt her? Oh, not much," Bakaris said, laughing. "She will still be useful to Kitiara for whatever purpose she may have in mind. But don't move, dwarf. I may forget myself!" Bakaris warned, hearing Flint choke in anger. He turned back to Laurana. "As it is, Kitiara won't mind if I have a little fun with the lady first. No, don't faint—"

It was an old elven self-defense technique. Flint had seen it done often and he tensed, ready to act as Laurana's eyes rolled up, her body sagged, and her knees seemed to give way.

Instinctively, Bakaris reached to catch her.

"No, you don't! I like my women lively—oof!"

Laurana's fist slammed into his stomach, knocking the breath from his body. Doubling over in pain, he fell forward. Bringing her knee up, Laurana caught him directly under the chin. As Bakaris pitched into the dirt, Flint grabbed the startled kender and slid off the wyvern.

"Run, Flint! Quickly!" Laurana gasped, leaping away from the wyvern and the man groaning on the ground. "Get into the woods!"

But Bakaris, his face twisted with rage, reached out his hand and grabbed Laurana's ankle. She stumbled and fell flat, kicking

MARGARET WEIS & TRACY HICKMAN

frantically at him. Wielding a tree limb, Flint leaped at Bakaris
as the commander was struggling to his feet. Hearing Flint's
roar, Bakaris spun around and struck the dwarf in the face
with the back of his hand. In the same motion, he caught hold
of Laurana's arm and dragged her to her feet. Then, turning, he
glared at Tas, who had run up beside the unconscious dwarf.

"The lady and I are going into the cave . . . " Bakaris said,
breathing heavily. He gave Laurana's arm a wrench, causing her
to cry out in pain. "Make one move, kender, and I'll break her
arm. Once we get into the cave, I don't want to be disturbed.
There's a dagger in my belt. I'll be holding it to the lady's throat.
Do you understand, little fool?"

"Yes, s-sir," stammered Tasslehoff. "I—I wouldn't dream of
interfering. I—I'll just stay here with—with Flint."

"Don't go into the woods." Bakaris began to drag Laurana
toward the cave. "Draconians guard the forest."

"N-no, sir," stuttered Tas, kneeling down beside Flint, his
eyes wide.

Satisfied, Bakaris glared once more at the cowering kender,
then shoved Laurana toward the entrance to the cave.

Blinded by tears, Laurana stumbled forward. As if to remind
her she was trapped, Bakaris twisted her arm again. The pain
was excruciating. There was no way to break free of the man's
powerful grip. Cursing herself for falling into this trap, Laurana
tried to battle her fear and think clearly. It was hard, the man's
hand was strong, and his smell—the human smell—reminded
her of Tanis in a horrifying way.

As if guessing her thoughts, Bakaris clutched her close to
him, rubbing his bearded face against her smooth cheek.

"You will be one more woman the half-elf and I have shared—"
he whispered hoarsely, then his voice broke off in a bubble of
agony.

For an instant, Bakaris's grip on Laurana's arm tightened
almost past endurance. Then it loosened. His hand slipped from

her arm. Laurana tore free of his grip, then spun around to face him.

Blood oozed between Bakaris's fingers as he clutched at his side where Tasslehoff's little knife still protruded from the wound. Drawing his own dagger, the man lunged at the defiant kender.

Something snapped in Laurana, letting loose a wild fury and hatred she had not guessed lurked inside her. No longer feeling any fear, no longer caring if she lived or died, Laurana had one thought in mind—she would kill this human male.

With a savage shriek, she flung herself at him, knocking him to the ground. He gave a grunt, then lay still beneath her. Desperately Laurana fought, trying to grab his knife. Then she realized his body was not moving. Slowly she rose to her feet, shaking in reaction.

For a moment she could see nothing through the red mist before her eyes. When it cleared, she saw Tasslehoff roll the body over. Bakaris lay dead. His eyes stared up at the sky, a look of profound shock and surprise on his face. His hand still clutched the dagger he had driven into his own gut.

"What happened?" Laurana whispered, quivering with anger and revulsion.

"You knocked him down and he fell on his knife," Tas said calmly.

"But before that—"

"Oh, I stuck him," Tas said. Plucking his knife from the man's side, he looked at it proudly. "And Caramon told me it wouldn't be of any use unless I met a vicious rabbit! Wait until I tell him!

"You know, Laurana," he continued, somewhat sadly, "everyone always underestimates us kender. Bakaris really should have searched my pouches. Say, that was a neat fainting trick you pulled. Did you—"

"How's Flint?" Laurana interrupted, not wanting to remember those last few horrible moments. Without quite knowing what she was doing or why, she pulled her cape from her shoulders and threw it down over the bearded face. "We've got to get out of here."

"He'll be all right," Tas said, glancing over at the dwarf, who was groaning and shaking his head. "What about the wyvern? Do you think they'll attack us?"

"I don't know," Laurana said, eyeing the animals. The wyvern stared around uneasily, uncertain as to what had happened to their master. "I've heard they're not very smart. They generally won't act on their own. Maybe—if we don't make any sudden moves—we can escape into the forest before they figure out what's happened. Help Flint."

"Come on, Flint," Tas said urgently, tugging at the dwarf. "We've got to esc—"

The kender's voice was cut off by a wild cry, a cry of such fear and terror that it made Tas's hair stand on end. Looking up, he saw Laurana staring at a figure that had—apparently—emerged from the cave. At the sight of the figure, Tasslehoff felt the most terrible sensation sweep over his body. His heart raced, his hands went cold, he couldn't breathe.

"Flint!" he managed to gasp before his throat closed completely.

The dwarf, hearing a tone in the kender's voice he'd never heard before, struggled to sit up. "What—"

Tas could only point.

Flint focused his bleary vision in the direction Tas indicated.

"In the name of Reorx," the dwarf said, his voice breaking, "what is that?"

The figure moved relentlessly toward Laurana, who—held spellbound at its command—could do nothing but stare at it. Dressed in antique armor, it might have been a Knight of Solamnia. But the armor was blackened as if it had been burned by fire. An orange light flared beneath its helm, while the helm itself seemed perched on empty air.

The figure reached out an armored arm. Flint choked in horror. The armored arm did not end in a hand. The knight seemingly grasped hold of Laurana with nothing but air. But she screamed in pain, falling to her knees in front of the ghastly vision. Her head slumped forward, she collapsed, senseless from the chill touch. The knight released his grip, letting the inert body slip to the ground. Bending down, the knight lifted her in his arms.

Tas started to move, but the knight turned his flaring orange gaze upon him and the kender was held fast, gazing into the orange flame of the creature's eyes. Neither he nor Flint could look away, though the horror was so great that the dwarf feared he might lose his reason. Only his love and concern for Laurana kept him clinging to consciousness. Over and over he told himself he must do something, he must save her. But he couldn't make his trembling body obey. The knight's flickering gaze swept over the two.

"Go back to Kalaman," said a hollow voice. "Tell them we have the elfwoman. The Dark Lady will arrive tomorrow at noon, to discuss terms of surrender."

Turning, the knight walked over Bakaris's body, the figure's shimmering armor passing right through the corpse as if it no longer existed. Then the knight vanished into the dark shadows of the woods, carrying Laurana in his arms.

With the knight's departure, the spell was lifted. Tas, feeling weak and sick, began to shiver uncontrollably. Flint struggled to his feet.

"I'm going after it—" the dwarf muttered, though his hands shook so he could barely lift his helm from the dirt.

"N-no," stammered Tasslehoff, his face strained and white as he stared after the knight. "Whatever that thing was, we can't fight it. I—I was scared, Flint!" The kender shook his head in misery. "I—I'm sorry, but I can't face that, that thing again! We've got to go back to Kalaman. Maybe we can get help—"

Tas started off into the woods at a run. For a moment Flint stood angry and irresolute, staring after Laurana. Then his face crumpled in agony. "He's right," he mumbled. "I can't go after that thing either. Whatever it was, it wasn't of this world."

Turning away, Flint caught a glimpse of Bakaris, lying beneath Laurana's cloak. Swift pain cramped the dwarf's heart. Ignoring it, Flint said to himself with sudden certainty, "He was lying about Tanis. And so was Kitiara. He's not with her, I know it!" The dwarf clenched his fist. "I don't know where Tanis is, but someday I'll have to face him and I'll have to tell him . . . I let him down. He trusted me to keep her safe, and I failed!" The dwarf closed his eyes. Then he heard Tas shout. Sighing, he stumbled blindly after the kender, rubbing his left arm as he ran. "How will I ever tell him?" he moaned. "How?"

A PEACEFUL INTERLUDE.

14

"All right," said Tanis, glaring at the man who sat so calmly in front of him. "I want answers. You deliberately took us into the maelstrom! Why? Did you know this place was here? Where are we? Where are the others?"

Berem sat before Tanis in a wooden chair. It was ornately carved with figures of birds and animals in a style popular among the elves. In fact, it reminded Tanis strongly of Lorac's throne in the doomed elven kingdom of Silvanesti. The likeness did nothing to calm Tanis's spirits, and Berem flinched under the half-elf's angry stare. The hands that were too young for the middle-aged man's body plucked at his shabby trousers. He shifted his gaze to glance nervously around their strange surroundings.

"Answer me!" Tanis raved. Flinging himself at Berem, he gripped the man's shirt and yanked him up from his chair. Then his clenching hands moved to the man's throat.

"Tanis!" Swiftly Goldmoon rose and laid a restraining hand on Tanis's arm. But the half-elf was beyond reason. His face was so twisted with fear and anger that she didn't recognize him. Frantically she tore at the hands that gripped Berem. "Riverwind, make him stop!"

The big Plainsman grasped Tanis by the wrists and wrenched him away from Berem, holding the half-elf in his strong arms.

"Leave him alone, Tanis!"

For a moment, Tanis struggled, then went limp, drawing a deep, shuddering breath.

"He's a mute," Riverwind said sternly. "Even if he wanted to tell you, he couldn't. He can't talk—"

"Yes, I can."

The three stopped, startled, staring at Berem.

"I can talk," he said calmly, speaking Common. Absently he rubbed his throat where the marks of Tanis's fingers stood out red against his tan skin.

"Then why pretend you can't?" Tanis asked, breathing heavily.

Berem rubbed his neck, his eyes on Tanis. "People don't ask questions of a man who can't talk. . . ."

Tanis forced himself to calm down, to think about this a moment. Glancing at Riverwind and Goldmoon, he saw Riverwind scowl and shake his head. Goldmoon shrugged slightly. Finally Tanis dragged another wooden chair over to sit in front of Berem. Noticing that the back of the chair was split and cracked, he sat down carefully. "Berem," Tanis spoke slowly, curbing his impatience, "you're talking to us. Does that mean you'll answer our questions?"

Berem stared at Tanis, then nodded his head, once.

"Why?" Tanis asked.

Berem licked his lips, glancing around. "I—You must help me—get out of here—I—I can't stay here—"

Tanis felt chilled, despite the warm stuffiness of the room. "Are you in danger? Are we in danger? What is this place?"

"I don't know!" Berem looked around helplessly. "I don't know where we are. I only know I cannot stay here. I must get back!"

"Why? The Dragon Highlords are hunting for you. One of th-the Highlords—" Tanis coughed, then spoke huskily. "One of them told me that you were the key to complete victory for the Dark Queen. Why, Berem? What do you have that they want?"

"I don't know!" Berem cried, clenching his fist. "I only know that they have been chasing me . . . I have been fleeing them for, for years! No peace . . . no rest!"

"How long, Berem?" Tanis asked softly. "How long have they been chasing you?"

"Years!" Berem said in a strangled voice. "Years . . . I don't know how long." Sighing, he seemed to sink back into his calm complacency. "I am three hundred and twenty-two years old. Twenty-three? Twenty-four?" He shrugged. "For most of those years, the Queen has been seeking me."

"Three hundred and twenty-two!" Goldmoon said in astonishment. "But—but you're human! That's not possible!"

"Yes, I am human," Berem said, his blue eyes focusing on Goldmoon. "I know it is impossible. I have died. Many times." His gaze switched to Tanis. "You saw me die. It was in Pax Tharkas. I recognized you when you first came on the ship."

"You *did* die when the rocks fell on you!" Tanis exclaimed. "But we saw you *alive* at the wedding feast, Sturm and I—"

"Yes. I saw you, too. That's why I fled. I knew . . . there would be more questions." Berem shook his head. "How could I explain my survival to you? I do not know myself how I survive! All I know is that I die and then I'm alive again. Again and again." His head sank into his hands. "All I want is peace!"

Tanis was completely mystified. Scratching his beard, he stared at the man. That he was lying was almost certain. Oh, not about dying and coming back to life. Tanis had seen that himself. But he knew for a fact that the Queen of Darkness was exerting almost all the forces she could spare from the war to search for this man. Surely he must know why!

"Berem, how did the green gemstone get, uh, into your flesh?"

"I don't know," Berem answered in such a low voice they could barely hear him. Self-consciously, his hand clutched his breast as if it pained him. "It is part of my body, like my bones and my blood. I—I think it is what brings me back to life."

"Can you remove it?" Goldmoon asked gently, sinking down onto a cushion next to Berem, her hand on his arm.

Berem shook his head violently, his gray hair falling over his eyes. "I've tried!" he muttered, "Many times I've tried to rip it out! I might as well try to tear out my own heart!"

Tanis shivered, then sighed in exasperation. This was no help! He still had no idea where they were. He'd hoped Berem could tell them. . . .

Once more, Tanis looked around their strange surroundings. They were in a room of an obviously ancient building, lit with a soft eerie light that seemed to come from the moss that covered the walls like tapestry. The furniture was as old as the building and in battered, shabby condition, though it must have been rich once. There were no windows. Nothing could be heard outside. They had no idea how long they'd been here. Time had grown confused, broken only by eating some of the strange plants and sleeping fitfully.

Tanis and Riverwind had explored the building but could find no exit and no other signs of life. Tanis wondered, in fact, if some magical spell had not been laid over the whole thing, a spell designed to keep them inside. For every time they ventured forth, the narrow, dimly lit hallways always led them inexplicably back to this room.

They remembered little about what happened after the ship sank into the maelstrom. Tanis recalled hearing the wooden planks shattering. He remembered seeing the mast fall, the sails rip. He heard screams. He saw Caramon washed overboard by a gigantic wave. He remembered seeing Tika's red curls swirling in the water, then she, too, was gone. There had been the dragon . . . and Kitiara . . . The scratches of the dragon's talons remained on his arm. Then there was another wave . . . he remembered holding his breath until he knew he would die from the pain in his lungs. He remembered thinking that death would be easy and welcome, even as he fought to grab hold of a piece of wood. He remembered surfacing in the rushing water, only to be sucked down again and knowing it was the end. . . .

And then he had awakened in this strange place, his clothes wet with sea water, to find Riverwind and Goldmoon and Berem here with him.

At first Berem had seemed terrified of them, crouching in a corner, refusing to let them come near. Patiently Goldmoon spoke to him and brought him food. Gradually, her gentle ministrations won him over. That and—Tanis recognized now—his intense desire to leave this place.

Tanis had supposed, when he first began to question Berem, that the man had steered the ship into the maelstrom because he knew this place existed, that he had brought them here on purpose.

But now the half-elf wasn't so certain. It was apparent from the confused and frightened look on Berem's face that he had no idea where they were either. The mere fact that he was even talking to them gave an indication that what he said was true. He was desperate. He wanted out of here. Why?

"Berem . . ." Tanis began, getting up and pacing about the room. He felt Berem's gaze follow him. "If you are running from the Queen of Darkness, this seems like it might be an ideal place to hide—"

"No!" Berem shouted, half-rising.

Tanis spun around. "Why not? Why are you so determined to get out of here? Why do you want to go back to where she will find you?"

Berem cringed, huddling back down in his chair. "I—I don't know anything about this place! I swear it! I—I m—must get back. . . . There's someplace I must go . . . I'm hunting for something. . . . Until I find it, there'll be no rest."

"Find it! Find what?" Tanis shouted. He felt Goldmoon's hand on his arm and he knew he was raving like a maniac, but it was so frustrating! To have what the Queen of Darkness would give the world to acquire and not know why!

"I can't tell you!" Berem whimpered.

Tanis sucked in his breath, closing his eyes, trying to calm himself. His head throbbed. He felt as if he might fly into a thousand pieces. Goldmoon rose to her feet. Putting both her hands on his shoulders, she whispered soothing words he could not comprehend, except for the name of Mishakal. Slowly the terrible feeling passed, leaving him drained and exhausted.

"All right, Berem." Tanis sighed. "It's all right. I'm sorry. We won't talk about it anymore. Tell me about yourself. Where are you from?"

Berem hesitated a moment, his eyes narrowed and he grew tense. Tanis was struck by Berem's peculiar manner. "I'm from Solace. Where are you from?" he repeated casually.

Berem regarded him warily. "You, you would never have heard of it. A —A small village outside of . . . outside of . . ." He swallowed, then cleared his throat. "Neraka."

"Neraka?" Tanis looked at Riverwind.

The Plainsman shook his head. "He's right. I have never heard of it."

"Nor I," Tanis muttered. "Too bad Tasslehoff and his maps aren't here. . . . Berem, why—"

"Tanis!" Goldmoon cried.

The half-elf rose at the sound of her voice, his hand going reflexively to the sword that wasn't there. Dimly he remembered struggling with it in the water, its weight dragging him down. Cursing himself for not setting Riverwind to guard the door,

189

he could do nothing now but stare at the red-robed man who stood framed in its opening.

"Hello," the man said pleasantly, speaking Common.

The red robes brought Raistlin's image back to Tanis with such force that the half-elf's vision blurred. For a moment he thought it was Raistlin. Then he saw clearly. This mage was older, much older, and his face was kind.

"Where are we?" Tanis demanded harshly. "Who are you? Why were we brought here?"

"*KreeaQUEKH,*" the man said in disgust. Turning, he walked away.

"Damn!" Tanis jumped forward, intent on grabbing the man and dragging him back. But he felt a firm hand on his shoulder.

"Wait," Riverwind counseled. "Calm down, Tanis. He's a magic-user. You couldn't fight him even if you had a sword. We'll follow him, see where he goes. If he laid a spell on this place, perhaps he'll have to lift it to get out himself."

Tanis drew a deep breath. "You're right, of course." He gasped for air. "I'm sorry. I don't know what's wrong with me. I feel tight and stretched, like the skin over a drum. We'll follow him. Goldmoon, you stay here with Berem—"

"No!" Berem shouted. Throwing himself out of the chair, he clutched at Tanis with such force he nearly knocked him down. "Don't leave me here! Don't!"

"We're not going to leave you!" Tanis said, trying to extricate himself from Berem's deathlike grip. "Oh, all right. Maybe we'd all better stay together anyway."

Hurrying out into the narrow corridor, they started down the bleak, deserted hallway.

"There he goes!" Riverwind pointed.

In the dim light, they could just see a bit of red robe whisking around a corner. Walking softly, they followed after it. The hallway led down another hallway with other rooms branching off it.

"This was never here before!" Riverwind exclaimed. "There was always solid wall."

"Solid illusion," Tanis muttered.

Stepping into the hallway, they looked around curiously. Rooms filled with the same ancient, mismatched furniture as in their room opened from the empty corridor. These rooms, too, were empty, but all lit with the same strange glowing lights. Perhaps it was an inn. If so, they appeared to be its only customers and might have been its only customers for a hundred years.

They made their way through broken corridors and vast pillared halls. There wasn't time to investigate their surroundings, not while trailing the red-robed man, who was proving remarkably quick and elusive. Twice they thought they had lost him, only to catch a glimpse of the red robes floating down a circular stairway beneath them, or flitting through an adjacent hallway.

It was at one such juncture that they stood for a moment, glancing down two divergent hallways, feeling lost and frustrated.

"Split up," Tanis said after a moment. "But don't go far. We'll meet back here. If you see any sign of him, Riverwind, whistle once. I'll do the same."

Nodding, the Plainsman and Goldmoon slipped down one hallway while Tanis—with Berem practically tripping on his heels—searched the other one.

He found nothing. The hallway led to a large room, eerily lit as was everything else in this strange place. Should he look in it or turn back? After hesitating a moment, Tanis decided to take a quick glance inside. The room was empty, except for a huge round table. And on the table, he saw as he drew closer, was a remarkable map!

Tanis bent quickly over the map, hoping for a clue as to where and what this mysterious place was. The map was a miniature replica of the city! Protected by a dome of clear crystal, it was so exact in detail that Tanis had the strange feeling the city beneath the crystal was more real than the one where he stood.

"Too bad Tas isn't here," he thought to himself wistfully, picturing the kender's delight.

The buildings were constructed in the ancient style; delicate spires rose into the crystal sky, light sparkled off the white domes. Stone archways spanned garden boulevards. The streets were laid out like a great spider web, leading directly into the heart of the city itself.

Tanis felt Berem pluck nervously at his sleeve, gesturing that they should leave. Even though he could talk, it was obvious that the man had grown accustomed to, and perhaps even preferred, silence.

"Yes, just a moment," Tanis said, reluctant to go. He had heard nothing from Riverwind and there was every possibility this map might lead them out of this place.

Bending over the glass, he stared at the miniature more closely. Around the center of the city stood great pavilions and columned palaces. Domes made of glass cradled summer flowers amid the winter snows. In the exact center of the city itself rose a building that seemed familiar to Tanis, though he knew he had never been in this city in his life. Still, he recognized it. Even as he studied it, searching his memory, the hair prickled on the back of his neck.

It seemed to be a temple to the gods. And it was the most beautiful structure he had ever seen, more beautiful than the Towers of the Sun and the Stars in the elven kingdoms. Seven towers rose to the heavens as if praising the gods for their creation. The center tower soared into the skies far above the rest, as if it did not praise the gods, but rivaled them. Confused memories of his elven teachers came back to him, telling him stories of the Cataclysm, stories of the Kingpriest—

Tanis drew back from the miniature, his breath catching in his throat. Berem stared at him in alarm, the man's face going white.

"What is it?" he croaked in fear, clutching at Tanis.

The half-elf shook his head. He could not speak. The terrible implications of where they were and what was going on were breaking over him like red waters of the Blood Sea.

In confusion, Berem looked at the center of the map. The man's eyes widened, then he shrieked, a scream unlike any Tanis had heard before. Suddenly Berem threw himself bodily upon the crystal dome, beating at it as if he would tear it apart.

"The City of Damnation!" Berem moaned. "The City of Damnation."

Tanis started forward to calm him, then he heard Riverwind's shrill whistle. Grabbing Berem, Tanis hauled him away from the crystal. "I know," he said. "Come on, we've got to get out of here."

But how? How did you get out of a city that was supposed to have been blasted off the face of Krynn? How did you get out of a city that must lie at the very bottom of the Blood Sea? How did you get out of—

As he shoved Berem through the door of the map room, Tanis glanced above the doorway. Words were carved in its crumbling marble. Words that had once spoken of one of the wonders of the world. Words whose letters were now cracked and covered with moss. But he could read them.

Welcome, O noble visitor, to our beautiful city.
Welcome to the city beloved of the gods.
Welcome, honored guest, to
Istar.

15

I 've seen what you're doing to him! You're trying to murder him!" Caramon shouted at Par-Salian. Head of the Tower of High Sorcery, the last Tower of High Sorcery located in the weird, alien forests of Wayreth, Par-Salian was the highest ranking in the Order of magic-users currently living on Krynn.

To the twenty-year-old warrior, the withered old man in the snowy white robes was a thing he might have broken with his bare hands. The young warrior had put up with a good deal the last two days, but now his patience had run out.

"We are not in the business of murder," Par-Salian said in his soft voice. "Your brother knew what he faced when he agreed to undergo these Trials. He knew death was the penalty for failure."

"He didn't, not really," Caramon mumbled, brushing his hand across his eyes. "Or if he did, he didn't care. Sometimes his . . . his love for his magic clouds his thinking."

"Love? No." Par-Salian smiled sadly. "I do not think we could call it love."

"Well, whatever," Caramon muttered. "He didn't realize what you were going to do to him! It's all so damn serious—"

"Of course," Par-Salian said mildly "What would happen to you, warrior, if you went into battle without knowing how to use your sword?"

Caramon scowled. "Don't try to weasel out—"

"What would happen?" Par-Salian persisted.

"I'd be killed," Caramon said with the elaborate patience one uses when speaking to an elderly person who is growing a bit childish. "Now—"

"Not only would you die," Par-Salian continued, "but your comrades, those who depend on you, might they also die because of your incompetence?"

"Yes," Caramon said impatiently, starting to continue his tirade. Then, pausing, he fell silent.

"You see my point," Par-Salian said gently. "We do not require this Test of all who would use magic. There are many with the gift who go through life content with using the first elementary spells taught by the schools. These are enough to help them in their day-to-day lives, and that is all they want. But sometimes there comes a person like your brother. To him, the gift is more than a tool to help him through life. To him, the gift is life. He aspires higher. He seeks knowledge and power that can be dangerous, not only to the user but to those around him as well. Therefore we force all magic-users who would enter into those realms where true power can be attained to take the Test, to submit themselves to the Trials. Thus we weed out the incompetent. . . ."

"You've done your best to weed out Raistlin!" Caramon snarled. "He's not incompetent, but he's frail and now he's hurt, maybe dying!"

"No, he isn't incompetent. Quite the contrary. Your brother has done very well, warrior. He has defeated all of his enemies. He has handled himself like a true professional. Almost too professional." Par-Salian appeared thoughtful. "I wonder if someone hasn't taken an interest in your brother."

"I wouldn't know." Caramon's voice hardened with resolve. "And I don't care. All I know is that I am putting a stop to it. Right now."

"You cannot. You will not be permitted. He isn't dying—"

"You can't stop me!" Caramon stated coldly. "Magic! Tricks to keep kids amused! True power! Bah! It's not worth getting killed over—"

"*Your brother believes it is,*" *Par-Salian said softly.* "*Shall I show you how much he believes in his magic? Shall I show you true power?*"

Ignoring Par-Salian, Caramon took a step forward, determined to end his brother's suffering. That step was his last, at least for some time. He found himself immobilized, frozen in place as surely as if his feet were encased in ice. Fear gripped Caramon. It was the first time he had ever been spellbound, and the helpless feeling of being totally under another's control was more terrifying than facing six axe-wielding goblins.

"*Watch.*" *Par-Salian began to chant strange words.* "*I am going to show you a vision of what might have been. . . .*"

Suddenly Caramon saw himself entering the Tower of High Sorcery! He blinked in astonishment. He was walking through the doors and down the eerie corridors! The image was so real that Caramon looked down at his own body in alarm, half-afraid he might find he wasn't really there. But he was. He seemed to be in two places at the same time. True power: The warrior began to sweat, then shivered with a chill.

Caramon—the Caramon in the Tower—was searching for his brother. Up and down empty corridors he wandered, calling Raistlin's name. And finally he found him.

The young mage lay on the cold stone floor. Blood trickled from his mouth. Near him was the body of a dark elf, dead, by Raistlin's magic. But the cost had been terrible. The young mage himself seemed near death.

Caramon ran to his brother and lifted the frail body in his strong arms. Ignoring Raistlin's frantic pleas to leave him alone, the warrior began to carry his twin from this evil Tower. He would take Raistlin from this place if it was the last thing he did.

But, just as they came near the door that led out of the Tower, a wraith appeared before them. Another test, Caramon thought grimly. Well, this will be one test Raistlin won't have to handle. Gently laying his brother down, the warrior turned to meet this final challenge.

What happened then made no sense. The watching Caramon blinked in astonishment. He saw himself cast a magic spell! Dropping his sword, he held strange objects in his hands and began to speak words he didn't understand! Lightning bolts shot from his hands! The wraith vanished with a shriek.

The real Caramon looked wildly at Par-Salian, but the mage only shook his head and—wordlessly—pointed back to the image that wavered before Caramon's eyes. Frightened and confused, Caramon turned back to watch.

He saw Raistlin rise slowly

"How did you do that?" Raistlin asked, propping himself up against the wall.

Caramon didn't know. How could he do something that took his brother years of study! But the warrior saw himself rattling off a glib explanation. Caramon also saw the look of pain and anguish on his brother's face.

"No, Raistlin!" the real Caramon cried. "It's a trick! A trick of this old man's! I can't do that! I'd never steal your magic from you! Never!"

But the image Caramon, swaggering and brash, went over to "rescue" his "little" brother, to save him from himself.

Raising his hands, Raistlin held them out toward his brother. But not to embrace him. No. The young mage, sick and injured and totally consumed with jealousy, began to speak the words of the one spell, the last spell he had strength to cast.

Flames flared from Raistlin's hands. The magical fire billowed forth, and engulfed his brother.

Caramon watched in horror, too stunned to speak, as his own image was consumed in fire. . . . He watched as his brother collapsed onto the cold stone floor.

"No! Raist—"

Cool, gentle hands touched his face. He could hear voices, but their words were meaningless. He could understand, if he chose. But he didn't want to understand. His eyes were closed.

He could open them, but he refused. Opening his eyes, hearing those words, would only make the pain real.

"I must rest," Caramon heard himself say, and he sank back into darkness.

He was approaching another Tower, a different Tower. The Tower of the Stars in Silvanesti. Once more Raistlin was with him, only now his brother wore the Black Robes. And now it was Raistlin's turn to help Caramon. The big warrior was wounded. Blood pulsed steadily from a spear-wound that had nearly taken off his arm.

"I must rest," *Caramon said again.*

Gently Raistlin laid him down, making him comfortable, his back propped up against the cold stone of the Tower. And then Raistlin started to leave.

"Raist! Don't," *Caramon cried.* "You can't leave me here!"

Looking around, the injured, defenseless warrior saw hordes of the undead elves who had attacked them in Silvanesti waiting to leap upon him. Only one thing held them back, his brother's magical power.

"Raist! Don't leave me!" *he screamed.*

"How does it feel to be weak and alone?" *Raistlin asked him softly.*

"Raist! My brother . . ."

"I killed him once, Tanis. I can do it again!"

"Raist! No! Raist!"

"Caramon, please . . ." Another voice. This one gentle. Soft hands touched him.

"Caramon, please! Wake up! Come back, Caramon. Come back to me. I need you."

No! Caramon pushed away that voice. He pushed away the soft hands. No, I don't want to come back. I won't. I'm tired. I hurt. I want to rest.

But the hands, the voice, wouldn't let him rest. They grabbed him, pulling him from the depths where he longed to sink.

And now he was falling, falling into a horrible red darkness. Skeletal fingers clutched at him, eyeless heads whirled past him, their mouths gaping in silent cries. He drew a breath, then sank into blood.

Struggling, smothering, he finally fought his way back to the surface and gasped for air once more. Raistlin! But no, he's gone. His friends. Tanis. Gone, too. He saw him swept away. The ship. Gone. Cracked in half. Sailors cut apart, their blood mingling with the blood-red sea.

Tika! She was near him. He pulled her close. She was gasping for air. But he could not hold onto her. The swirling water tore her from his arms and swept him under. This time he could not find the surface. His lungs were on fire, bursting. Death . . . rest . . . sweet, warm. . . .

But always those hands! Dragging him back to the gruesome surface. Making him breathe the burning air. No, let me go!

And then other hands, rising up from the blood-red water. Firm hands, they took him down from the surface. He fell down . . . down . . . into merciful darkness. Whispered words of magic soothed him, he breathed. . . breathed water. . . and his eyes closed . . . the water was warm and comforting . . . He was a child once more.

But not complete. His twin was missing.

No! Waking was agony Let him float in that dark dream forever. Better than the sharp, bitter pain.

But the hands tugged at him. The voice called to him.

"Caramon, I need you . . ."

Tika.

"I'm no cleric, but I believe he'll be all right now. Let him sleep awhile."

Tika brushed away her tears quickly, trying to appear strong and in control.

"What . . . what was wrong?" she made herself ask calmly, though she was unable to restrain a shudder. "Was he hurt when the ship . . . went into th-the whirlpool? He's been like this for days! Ever since you found us."

"No, I don't think so. If he had been injured, the sea elves would have healed him. This was something within himself. Who is this 'Raist' he talks about?"

"His twin brother," Tika said hesitantly.

"What happened? Did he die?"

"No—no. I—I'm not quite sure what happened. Caramon loved his brother very much and he . . . Raistlin betrayed him."

"I see." The man nodded solemnly. "It happens, up there. And you wonder why I choose to live down here."

"You saved his life!" Tika said. "And I don't know you . . . your name."

"Zebulah," the man answered, smiling. "And I didn't save his life. He came back for love of you."

Tika lowered her head, her red curls hid her face. "I hope so," she whispered. "I love him so much. I would die myself, if it would save him."

Now that she was certain Caramon would be all right, Tika focused her attention on this strange man. She saw he was middle-aged, clean-shaven, his eyes as wide and frank as his smile. Human, he was dressed in red robes. Pouches dangled from his belt.

"You're a magic-user," Tika said suddenly. "Like Raistlin!"

"Ah, that explains it." Zebulah smiled. "Seeing me, in his semiconscious state, made this young man think of his brother."

"But what are you doing here?" Tika glanced around at her strange surroundings, seeing them for the first time.

She had seen them, of course, when the man brought her here, but she hadn't noticed them in her worry. Now she realized she was in a chamber of a ruined, crumbling building. The air was warm and stifling. Plants grew lushly in the moist air.

There was some furniture, but it was as ancient and ruined as the room in which it was haphazardly placed. Caramon lay on a three-legged bed, the fourth corner being held up by a stack of old, mosscovered books. Thin rivulets of water, like small, glistening snakes, trickled down a stone wall that gleamed with moisture. Everything gleamed with moisture, in fact, reflecting the pale, eerie, green light that glowed from the moss growing on the wall. The moss was everywhere, of every different color and variety. Deep green, golden yellow, coral red, it climbed the walls and crawled across the domed ceiling.

"What am I doing here?" she murmured. "And where is here?"

"Here is—Well, I suppose you could say here," Zebulah answered pleasantly. "The sea elves saved you from drowning and I brought you here."

"Sea elves? I never heard of sea elves," Tika said, glancing around curiously, as if she might see one hiding in a closet. "And I don't remember elves saving me. All I remember is some sort of huge, gentle fish. . . ."

"Oh, you needn't look around for the sea elves. You won't see them. They fear and distrust KreeaQUEKH—'air-breathers' in their language. And those fish were the sea elves, in the only shape they let KreeaQUEKH see them. Dolphins, you call them."

Caramon stirred and moaned in his sleep. Laying her hand upon his forehead, Tika brushed back his damp hair, soothing him.

"Why did they save our lives, then?" she asked.

"Do you know any elves, land elves?" Zebulah asked

"Yes," Tika answered softly, thinking of Laurana.

"Then you know that to all elves, life is sacred."

"I understand." Tika nodded. "And like the land elves, they renounce the world rather than help it."

"They are doing what they can to help," Zebulah rebuked her severely. "Do not criticize what you do not understand, young woman."

"I'm sorry," Tika said, flushing. She changed the subject. "But you, you're human. Why—"

"Why am I here? I have neither the time nor the inclination to relate my story to you, for it is obvious you would not understand me either. None of the others do."

Tika caught her breath. "There are others? Have you seen any more from our ship . . . our friends?"

Zebulah shrugged. "There are *always* others down here. The ruins are vast, and many hold small pockets of air. We take those we rescue to the nearest dwellings. As for your friends, I couldn't say. If they were on the ship with you, they were most likely lost. The sea elves have given the dead the proper rituals and sent their souls upon their way." Zebulah stood up. "I'm glad your young man survived. There's lots of food around here. Most of the plants you see are edible. Wander about the ruins if you like. I've laid a magic spell on them so you can't get into the sea and drown. Fix the place up. You'll find more furniture—"

"But wait!" Tika cried. "We can't stay here! We must return to the surface. Surely there must be some way out?"

"They all ask me that," Zebulah said with a touch of impatience. "And, frankly, I agree. There *must* be some way out. People seem to find it on occasion. Then, there are those who simply decide that—like me—they don't want to leave. I have several old friends who have been around for years. But, see for yourself. Look around. Just be careful you stay in the parts of the ruins we've arranged." He turned toward the door.

"Wait! Don't go!" Jumping up, tipping over the rickety chair she sat upon, Tika ran after the red-robed magic-user. "You might see my friends. You could tell them—"

"Oh, I doubt it," Zebulah replied. "To tell you the truth—and no offense, young woman—I'm fed up with your conversation. The longer I live here, the more *KreeaQUEKH* like you irritate me. Always in a hurry. Never satisfied to stay in one place. You and your young man would be much happier down here in this world than up there in that one. But no, you'll kill yourselves trying to find your way back. And what do you face up there? Betrayal!" He glanced back at Caramon.

"There is a war up there!" Tika cried passionately. "People are suffering. Don't you care about that?"

"People are always suffering up there," Zebulah said. "Nothing I can do about it. No, I don't care. After all, where does caring get you? Where did it get him?" With a angry gesture at Caramon, Zebulah turned and left, slamming the ramshackle door behind him.

Tika stared after the man uncertainly, wondering if she shouldn't run out and and grab him and hang onto him. He was apparently their only link to the world *up there*. Wherever *down here* was . . .

"Tika . . ."

"Caramon!" Forgetting Zebulah, Tika ran to the warrior, who was struggling to sit up.

"Where in the name of the Abyss are we?" he asked, looking around with wide eyes. "What happened? The ship—"

"I'm—I'm not sure," Tika faltered. "Do you feel well enough to sit? Perhaps you should lie down. . . ."

"I'm all right," Caramon snapped. Then, feeling her flinch at his harshness, he reached out and pulled her in his arms. "I'm sorry, Tika. Forgive me. It's just . . . I . . ." He shook his head.

"I understand," Tika said softly. Resting her head on his chest, she told him about Zebulah and the sea elves. Caramon listened, blinking in confusion as he slowly absorbed all he heard. Scowling, he looked at the door.

"I wish I'd been conscious," he muttered. "That Zebulah character knows the way out, more than likely. I'd have made him show us."

"I'm not so sure," Tika said dubiously. "He's a magic-user like—" She broke off hurriedly. Seeing the pain in Caramon's face, she nestled closer to him, reaching up to stroke his face.

"Do you know, Caramon," she said softly, "he's right in a way. We *could* be happy here. Do you realize, this is the first time we've ever been alone? I mean really and truly alone together? And it's so still and peaceful and beautiful in a way. The glowing light from the moss is so soft and eerie, not harsh and glaring like sunlight. And listen to the water murmuring, it's singing to us. Then there's this old, old furniture, and this funny bed . . ."

Tika stopped talking. She felt Caramon's arms tighten around her. His lips brushed her hair. Her love for him surged through her, making her heart stand still with pain and longing. Swiftly she put her arms around him, holding him close, feeling his heart beat against hers.

"Oh, Caramon!" she whispered breathlessly. "Let's be happy! Please! I—I know that—that sometime we'll have to leave. We'll have to find the others and return to the world above. But for now, let's be alone, together!"

"Tika!" Caramon clasped her, crushing her to him as if he would mold their bodies into one, single, living being. "Tika, I love you! I—I told you once that I couldn't make you mine until I could commit myself to you completely. I can't do that—not yet."

"Yes, you can!" Tika said fiercely. Pushing away from him, she looked into his eyes. "Raistlin's gone, Caramon! You can make your own life!"

Caramon shook his head gently. "Raistlin's still a part of me. He always will be, just as I'll always be a part of him. Can you understand?"

No, she couldn't, but she nodded anyway, her head drooping.

Smiling, Caramon drew a quivering breath. Then he put his hand beneath her chin and raised her head. Her eyes were beautiful, he thought. Green with flecks of brown. They shimmered now with tears. Her skin was tan from living outdoors and more freckled than ever. Those freckles embarrassed her. Tika would have given seven years of her life for creamy skin like Laurana's. But Caramon loved every freckle, he loved the crisp, curling red hair that clung to his hands.

Tika saw the love in his eyes. She caught her breath. He drew her near. His heart beating faster, he whispered, "I'll give you what I can of myself, Tika, if you'll settle for that. I wish, for your sake, it was more."

"I love you!" was all she said, clasping him around the neck.

He wanted to be certain she understood. "Tika—" he began.

"Hush, Caramon . . ."

APOLETTA.

16

After a long chase through the streets of a city whose crumbling beauty seemed a horror to Tanis, they entered one of the lovely palaces in the center. Running through a dead garden and into a hall, they rounded a corner and came to a halt. The red-robed man was nowhere to be seen.

"Stairs!" Riverwind said suddenly. His own eyes growing accustomed to the strange light, Tanis saw they were standing at the top of a flight of marble stairs that descended so steeply they had lost sight of their quarry. Hurrying to the landing, they could once more see the red robes fluttering down them.

"Keep in the shadows near the wall," Riverwind cautioned, motioning them to the side of the stairway that was big enough for fifty men to walk down it abreast.

Faded and cracked murals on the walls were still so exquisite and life-like that Tanis had the fevered impression the people portrayed there were more alive than he was. Perhaps some of them had been standing in this very spot when the fiery mountain struck the Temple of the Kingpriest. . . . Putting the thought out of his mind, Tanis kept going.

After running down about twenty steps, they came to a broad landing, decorated with life-size statues of silver and gold. From

206

here, the stairs continued down, leading to another landing, leading to more steps, and so on until they were all exhausted and breathless. Still the red robes fluttered ahead of them.

Suddenly Tanis noticed a change in the air. It was becoming more humid, the smell of the sea was strong. Listening, he could hear the faint sounds of water lapping against stone. He felt Riverwind touch his arm, pulling him back into the shadows. They were near the bottom of the steps. The red-robed man was in front of them, standing at the very bottom, peering into a pool of dark water that stretched out before him into a vast, shadowy cavern.

The red-robed man knelt by the side of the water. And then Tanis was aware of another figure; this one in the water! He could see hair shining in the torchlight—it had a faint greenish cast. Two slender white arms rested on the stone steps, the rest of the figure was submerged. The figure's head lay cradled on its arms, in a state of complete relaxation. The red-robed man reached out a hand and gently touched the figure in the water. The figure raised its head.

"I have been waiting," a woman's voice said, sounding reproachful.

Tanis gasped. The woman spoke elven! Now he could see her face, the large, luminous eyes, pointed ears, delicate features. . . .

A sea elf!

Confused tales from his childhood came back to Tanis as he tried to follow the conversation of the red-robed man and the elven woman, who was smiling at him fondly.

"I'm sorry, beloved," the red-robed man said soothingly, in elven, sitting down beside her. "I went to see how the young man you were concerned about was doing. He'll be all right, now. It was a close one, though. You were correct. He was certainly intent on dying. Something about his brother—a magic-user— betraying him."

"Caramon!" Tanis murmured. Riverwind looked at him questioningly. The Plainsman could not, of course, follow the elven conversation. Tanis shook his head, not wanting to miss what else was said.

"*QueaKI' ICHKeecx,*" said the woman in scorn. Tanis was puzzled, that word was certainly not elven!

"Yes!" The man frowned. "After I made sure those two were safe, I went to see some of the others. One of them, a bearded fellow, a half-elf, leaped at me as if he would swallow me whole! The others we managed to save are doing well."

"We laid out the dead with ceremony," said the woman, and Tanis could hear the ages-old sorrow in her voice, the sorrow of the elves for the loss of life.

"I would have liked to ask them what they were doing in the Blood Sea of Istar. I've never known a ship's captain foolish enough to dare the maelstrom. The girl told me there's war going on above. Maybe they had no choice."

The elven woman playfully splashed water on the red-robed man. "There's *always* war going on above! You are too curious, my beloved. Sometimes I think you might leave me and return to your world. Especially after you talk with these *KreeaQUEKH.*"

Tanis heard a note of true concern in the woman's voice, though she was still playfully splashing the man.

The red-robed man leaned down and kissed her on the wet, greenish hair shining in the light of the sputtering torch on the wall above them. "No, Apoletta. Let them have their wars and their brothers who betray brothers. Let them have their impetuous half-elves and their foolish sea captains. As long as my magic serves me, I will live below the waves—"

"Speaking of impetuous half-elves," Tanis interrupted in elven as he strode rapidly down the stairs. Riverwind, Goldmoon, and Berem followed, though they had no idea what was being said.

The man turned his head in alarm. The elven woman disappeared into the water so swiftly that Tanis wondered for a moment if he might have imagined her existence. Not a ripple on the dark surface betrayed where she had been. Reaching the bottom of the steps, Tanis caught hold of the magic-user's hand just as he was about to follow the sea elf into the water.

"Wait! I'm *not* going to swallow you!" Tanis pleaded. "I'm sorry I acted the way I did back there. I know this looks bad, sneaking around after you like this. But we had no choice! I know I can't stop you if you're going to cast a spell or something. I know you could engulf me in flames or put me to sleep or wrap me in cobweb or a hundred other things. I've been around magic-users. But won't you please listen to us? Please help us. I heard you talking about two of our friends—a big man and a pretty red-haired girl. You said the man nearly died—his brother betrayed him. We want to find them. Won't you tell us where they are?"

The man hesitated.

Tanis went on hurriedly, losing coherence in his efforts to keep hold of this man who might be able to help them. "I saw the woman here with you. I heard her speak. I know who she is. A sea elf, isn't she? You are right. I am half-elven. But I was raised among the elves, and I've heard their legends. I thought that's all they were, legends. But then I thought dragons were legends, too. There *is* a war being fought in the world above. And you're right. There always seems to be a war being fought somewhere. But this war won't stay up above. If the Queen of Darkness conquers, you can be certain she'll find out the sea elves are down here. I don't know if there are dragons below the ocean, but—"

"There are sea dragons, half-elf," said a voice, and the elven woman reappeared in the water once more. Moving with a flash of silver and green, she glided through the dark sea until she reached the stone steps. Then, resting her arms on them, she

209

gazed up at him with brilliant green eyes. "And we have heard rumors of their return. We did not believe them, though. We did not know the dragons had awakened. Whose fault was that?"

"Does it matter?" asked Tanis wearily. "They have destroyed the ancient homeland. Silvanesti is a land of nightmares now. The Qualinesti were driven from their homes. The dragons are killing, burning. Nothing, no one is safe. The Dark Queen has one purpose—to gain dominance over every living being. Will you be safe? Even down here? For I presume we are below the sea?"

"You are right, half-elf," said the red-robed man, sighing. "You are below the sea, in the ruins of the city of Istar. The sea elves saved you and brought you here, as they bring all those whose ships are wrecked. I know where your friends are and I can take you there. Beyond that, I don't see what more I can do for you."

"Get us out of here," Riverwind said flatly, understanding the conversation for the first time. Zebulah had spoken in Common. "Who is this woman, Tanis? She looks elven."

"She is a sea elf. Her name is . . ." Tanis stopped.

"Apoletta," said the elven woman, smiling. "Forgive me for not extending a formal greeting, but we do not clothe our bodies as do you *KreeaQUEKH*. Even after all these years, I cannot persuade my husband to quit covering his body in those ridiculous robes when he goes onto the land. Modesty, he calls it. So I will not embarrass either you or him by getting out of the water to greet you as is proper."

Flushing, Tanis translated the elven woman's words to his friends. Goldmoon's eyes widened. Berem did not seem to hear, he was lost in some sort of inner dream, only vaguely aware of what was happening around him. Riverwind's expression did not change. Apparently nothing he heard about elves could surprise him anymore.

"Anyway, the sea elves are the ones who rescued us," Tanis went on. "Like all elves, they consider life sacred and will help anyone lost at sea or drowning. This man, her husband—"

"Zebulah," he said, extending his hand.

"I am Tanis Half-Elven, Riverwind and Goldmoon of the Que-shu tribe, and Berem, uh—" Tanis faltered and fell silent, not quite knowing where to go from here.

Apoletta smiled politely, but her smile quickly faded. "Zebulah," she said, "find the friends the half-elf speaks of and bring them back here."

"We should go with you," Tanis offered. "If you thought I was going to swallow you, there's no telling what Caramon might do—"

"No," said Apoletta, shaking her head. The water glistened on her hair and sparkled on her smooth green-tinged skin. "Send the barbarians, half-elf. You stay here. I would talk with you and learn more of this war you say could endanger us. It saddens me to hear the dragons have awakened. If that is true, I fear you might be right. Our world will no longer be safe."

"I will be back soon, beloved," Zebulah said.

Apoletta reached out her hand to her husband. Taking it, he raised it to his lips, kissing it gently. Then he left. Tanis quickly translated for Riverwind and Goldmoon, who readily agreed to go in search of Caramon and Tika.

As they followed Zebulah back through the eerie, broken streets, he told them tales of the fall of Istar, pointing out various landmarks as they went along.

"You see," he explained, "when the gods hurled the fiery mountain onto Krynn, it struck Istar, forming a giant crater in the land. The sea water rushed in to fill up the void, creating what came to be known as the Blood Sea. Many of the buildings in Istar were destroyed, but some survived and, here and there, retained small pockets of air. The sea elves discovered that this was an excellent place to bring mariners they rescued from capsized ships. Most of them soon feel quite at home."

The mage spoke with a hint of pride which Goldmoon found amusing, though she kindly did not allow her amusement to show. It was the pride of ownership, as if the ruins belonged to Zebulah and he had arranged to display them for the public's enjoyment.

"But you are human. You are not a sea elf. How did you come to live here?" Goldmoon asked.

The magic-user smiled, his eyes looking back across the years. "I was young and greedy," he said softly, "always in hopes of finding a quick way to make my fortune. My magic arts took me down into the depths of the ocean, searching for the lost wealth of Istar. I found riches all right, but not gold or silver.

"One evening I saw Apoletta, swimming among the sea forests. I saw her before she saw me, before she could change her shape. I fell in love with her . . . and long I worked to make her mine. She could not live up above and, after I had existed so long in the peace and tranquil beauty down here, I knew I no longer had a life in the world above either. But I enjoy talking to your kind occasionally, so I wander among the ruins now and then, to see who the elves have brought in."

Goldmoon looked around the ruins as Zebulah paused to catch his breath between stories.

"Where is the fabled temple of the Kingpriest?" she asked.

A shadow passed over the mage's face. The look of pleasure he had worn was replaced by an expression of deep sorrow tinged with anger.

"I'm sorry," Goldmoon said quickly. "I did not mean to cause you pain. . . ."

"No, it's all right," Zebulah said with a brief, sad smile. "In fact, it is good for me to remember the darkness of that dreadful time. I tend to forget—in my daily ramblings here—that this used to be a city of laughing, crying, living, and breathing beings. Children played in these streets—they were playing that terrible evening when the gods cast the fiery mountain down."

He was silent for a moment then, with a sigh, continued.

"You ask where the temple stands. It stands no longer. In the place where the Kingpriest stood, shouting his arrogant demands to the gods, there is a dark pit. Although it is filled with sea water, nothing lives within it. None know its depth, for the sea elves will not venture near it. I have looked into its dark, still waters as long as I could bear the terror, and I do not believe there is an end to its darkness. It is as deep as the heart of evil itself."

Zebulah stopped in one of the sea-dark streets and peered at Goldmoon intently. "The guilty were punished. But why the innocent? Why did they have to suffer? You wear the medallion of Mishakal the Healer. Do you understand? Did the goddess explain it to you?"

Goldmoon hesitated, startled by the question, searching within her soul for the answer. Riverwind stood beside her, stern and silent as always, his thoughts hidden.

"Often I myself have questioned," Goldmoon faltered. Moving nearer Riverwind, she touched his arm with her hand as though to reassure herself he was near. "In a dream, once, I was punished for my questioning, for my lack of faith. Punished by losing the one I love." Riverwind put his strong arm around her and held her close. "But whenever I feel ashamed of my questioning, I am reminded that it was my questioning that led me to find the ancient gods."

She was silent a moment. Riverwind stroked her silver-gold hair and she glanced up at him with a smile. "No," she said softly to Zebulah, "I do not have the answer to this great riddle. I still question. I still burn with anger when I see the innocent suffer and the guilty rewarded. But I know now that my anger can be as a forging fire. In its heat, the raw lump of iron that is my spirit is tempered and shaped to form the shining rod of steel that is my faith. That rod supports my weak flesh."

Zebulah studied Goldmoon silently as she stood amid the ruins of Istar, her silver-golden hair shining like the sunlight that would never touch the crushed buildings. The classic beauty of her face was marked by the effects of the dark roads she had traveled. Far from marring that beauty, the lines of suffering and despair had refined it. There was wisdom in her eyes, enhanced now by the great joy that came from the knowledge of the new life she carried within her body.

The mage's gaze went to the man who held the woman so tenderly. His face, too, bore the marks of the long, tortuous path he had walked.

Although stern and stoic that face would always be, his deep love for this woman showed clearly in the man's dark eyes and the gentleness of his touch.

Perhaps I have made a mistake staying beneath the waters so long, Zebulah thought, suddenly feeling very old and sad. Perhaps I could have helped, if I had stayed above and used my anger as these two used theirs, to help them find answers. Instead, I let my anger gnaw at my soul until it seemed easiest to hide it down here.

"We should delay no longer," said Riverwind abruptly. "Caramon will soon get it into his head to come looking for us, if he has not already."

"Yes," said Zebulah, clearing his throat. "We should go, although I do not think the young man and woman will have left. He was very weak—"

"Was he injured?" Goldmoon asked in concern.

"Not in body," Zebulah replied as they entered a tumble-down building on a crumbling side-street. "But he has been injured in his soul. I could see that even before the girl told me about his twin brother."

A dark line appeared between Goldmoon's finely drawn brows, her lips tightened.

"Pardon me, Lady of the Plains," Zebulah said with a slight smile, "but I see that the forging fire you spoke of blazes in your eyes."

Goldmoon flushed. "I told you I was still weak. I should be able to accept Raistlin and what he did to his brother without questioning. I should have faith that it is all part of the greater good I cannot envision. But I'm afraid I can't. All I can do is pray that the gods keep him out of my path."

"Not me," said Riverwind suddenly, his voice harsh. "Not me," he repeated grimly.

Caramon lay staring into the darkness. Tika, cradled in his arms, was fast asleep. He could feel her heart beating, he could hear her soft breathing. He started to run his hand through the tangle of red curls that lay upon his shoulder, but Tika stirred at his touch and he stopped, fearful of waking her. She should rest. The gods alone knew how long she had been awake, watching over him. She would never tell him, he knew that. When he had asked, she had only laughed and teased him about his snoring.

But there had been a tremor in her laughter, and she had been unable to look into his eyes.

Caramon patted her shoulder reassuringly and she nestled close. He felt comforted as he realized she slept soundly, and then he sighed. Only a few weeks ago, he had vowed to Tika that he would never take her love unless he could commit himself to her body and soul. He could still hear his words, "My first commitment is to my brother. I am his strength."

Now Raistlin was gone, he had found his own strength. As he had told Caramon, "I need you no longer."

I should be glad, Caramon told himself, staring into the darkness. I love Tika and I have her love in return. And now we are free to express that love. I can make that commitment to her.

She can come first in all my thoughts now. She is loving, giving. She deserves to be loved.

Raistlin never did. At least that's what they all believe. How often have I heard Tanis ask Sturm when he thought I couldn't hear why I put up with the sarcasm, the bitter recriminations, the imperious commands. I've seen them look at me with pity. I know they think I'm slow-thinking sometimes and I am—compared to Raistlin. I am the ox, lumbering along, bearing the burden without complaint. That's what they think of me.

They don't understand. They don't *need* me. Even Tika doesn't *need* me, not like Raist needed me. They never heard him wake screaming in the night when he was little. We were left alone so much, he and I. There was no one there in the darkness to hear him and comfort him but me. He could never remember those dreams, but they were awful. His thin body shook with fear. His eyes were wild with the sight of terrors only he could see. He clutched at me, sobbing. And I'd tell him stories or make funny shadow-pictures on the wall to drive away the horror.

"Look, Raist," I'd say, "bunnies . . ." and I'd hold up two fingers and wiggle them like a rabbit's ears.

After a while, he'd stop trembling. He wouldn't smile or laugh. He never did either, much, even when he was little. But he would relax.

"I must sleep. I am so tired," he'd whisper, holding my hand fast. "But you stay awake, Caramon. Guard my sleep. Keep them away. Don't let them get me."

"I'll stay awake. I won't let anything hurt you, Raist!" I'd promise.

Then he would smile—almost—and, exhausted, his eyes would close. I kept my promise. I would stay awake while he slept. And it was funny. Maybe I did keep them away, because as long as I was awake and watching, the nightmares never came to him.

Even when he was older, sometimes he'd still cry out in the night and reach out to me. And I'd be there. But what will he do now? What will he do without me when he's alone, lost, and frightened in the darkness?

What will I do without him?

Caramon shut his eyes and, softly, fearful of waking Tika, he began to cry.

17

A nd that's our story," said Tanis simply.

Apoletta had listened attentively to him, her green eyes intent upon his face. She had not interrupted. When he was finished, she remained silent. Resting her arms on the side of the steps leading into the still water, she seemed lost in thought. Tanis did not disturb her. The feeling of peace and serenity present beneath the sea soothed and comforted him. The thought of returning to the harsh, glaring world of sunlight and blaring noise seemed suddenly frightening. How easy it would be to ignore everything and stay here, beneath the sea, hidden forever in this silent world.

"What about him?" she asked finally, nodding her head at Berem.

Tanis came back to reality with a sigh.

"I don't know," he said, shrugging, glancing at Berem. The man was staring into the darkness of the cavern. His lips were moving, as if repeating a chant over and over.

"He is the key, according to the Queen of Darkness. Find him, she said, and victory is hers."

"Well," Apoletta said abruptly, "you've got him. Does that make victory yours?"

Tanis blinked. The question caught him by surprise. Scratching his beard, he pondered. It was something that had not occurred to him.

"True . . . we have got him," he murmured, "but what do we do with him? What is there about him that grants victory—to either side?"

"Doesn't he know?"

"He claims he doesn't."

Apoletta regarded Berem, frowning. "I would say he was lying," she said after a moment, "but then he is human, and I know little of the strange workings of the human mind. There is a way you can find out, however. Journey to the Temple of the Dark Queen at Neraka."

"Neraka!" repeated Tanis, startled. "But that's . . ." He was interrupted by a cry of such wild fear and terror that he nearly leaped into the water. His hand went to his empty scabbard. With a curse, he whirled around expecting nothing less than a horde of dragons.

There was only Berem, staring at him with wide eyes.

"What is it, Berem?" Tanis asked irritably. "Did you see something?"

"He didn't see anything, Half-Elf," Apoletta said, studying Berem with interest. "He reacted that way when I said Neraka—"

"Neraka!" Berem repeated, shaking his head wildly. "Evil! Great evil! No . . . no . . ."

"That's where you came from," Tanis told him, stepping nearer.

Berem shook his head firmly.

"But you told me—"

"A mistake!" Berem muttered. "I didn't mean Neraka. I m-meant . . . Takar . . . Takar! That's what I meant . . ."

"You meant Neraka. You know the Dark Queen has her great Temple there, in Neraka!" Apoletta said sternly.

"Does she?" Berem looked directly at her, his blue eyes wide and innocent. "The Dark Queen, a Temple in Neraka? No, there's nothing there but a small village. My village . . ." Suddenly he grasped his stomach and doubled over, as if in pain. "I don't feel good. Leave me alone," he mumbled like a child and slumped to the marble floor near the edge of the water. Sitting there, clutching his stomach, he stared into the darkness.

"Berem!" said Tanis in exasperation.

"Don't feel good . . ." Berem muttered sullenly.

"How old did you say he was?" Apoletta asked.

"Over three hundred years, or so he claims," Tanis said in disgust. "If you believe only half of what he says, that cuts it down to one hundred and fifty, which doesn't seem too plausible either, not for a human."

"You know," replied Apoletta thoughtfully, "the Queen's Temple at Neraka is a mystery to us. It appeared suddenly, after the Cataclysm, so far as we have been able to determine. Now we find this man who would trace his own history to that same time and place."

"It is strange . . ." said Tanis, glancing again at Berem.

"Yes. It may be nothing more than coincidence, but follow coincidence far enough and you'll find it tied to fate, so my husband says." Apoletta smiled.

"Coincidence or not, I don't see myself walking into the Temple of the Queen of Darkness and asking why she's searching the world for a man with a green gemstone buried in his chest," Tanis said wryly, sitting down near the water's edge again.

"I suppose not," Apoletta admitted. "It's hard to believe, though from what you say, that she has grown so powerful. What have the good dragons been doing all this time?"

"Good dragons!" Tanis repeated, astounded. "What good dragons?"

Now it was Apoletta's turn to look amazed. "Why, the good dragons. The silver dragons and gold dragons. Bronze dragons.

And the dragonlances. Surely the silver dragons gave you those that were in their keeping. . . ."

"I never heard of silver dragons," Tanis replied, "except in some old song about Huma. The same with dragonlances. We've been searching for them so long without a trace, I was beginning to believe they didn't exist except in children's stories."

"I don't like this." Apoletta rested her chin on her hands, her face drawn and pale. Something's wrong. Where are the good dragons? Why aren't they fighting? At first I discounted rumors of the sea dragons' return, for I knew the good dragons would never permit it. But if the good dragons have disappeared, as I must believe from talking with you, Half-Elf, then I fear my people truly are in danger." She lifted her head, listening. "Ah, good, here comes my husband with the rest of your friends." She pushed away from the edge. "He and I can go back to my people and discuss what we must do—"

"Wait!" Tanis said, hearing footsteps coming down the marble stairs. "You've got to show us the way out! We can't stay here!"

"But I don't know the way out," Apoletta said, her hands making circles in the water as she kept herself afloat. "Neither does Zebulah. It was never our concern."

"We could wander through these ruins for weeks!" Tanis cried. "Or maybe forever! You're not certain people do escape from this place, are you? Maybe they just die!"

"As I said," Apoletta repeated coldly, "it was never our concern."

"Well, make it your concern!" Tanis shouted. His voice echoed back eerily across the water. Berem looked up at him and shrank away in alarm. Apoletta's eyes narrowed in anger. Tanis drew in a deep breath, then bit his lip, suddenly ashamed.

"I'm sorry, " he began, but then Goldmoon came up to him, placing her hand on his arm.

"Tanis? What is it?" she asked.

"Nothing that can be helped." Sighing, he glanced past her. "Did you find Caramon and Tika? Are they all right?"

"Yes, we found them," Goldmoon answered, her gaze following Tanis's. Together they watched the two come slowly down the stairs behind Riverwind and Zebulah. Tika was staring around in wonder. Caramon, Tanis noticed, kept his eyes focused straight ahead. Seeing the man's face, Tanis looked back at Goldmoon.

"You didn't answer my second question?" he said softly.

"Tika's all right," Goldmoon answered. "As for Caramon," She shook her head.

Tanis looked back at Caramon and could barely restrain an exclamation of dismay. He would not have recognized the jovial, good-natured warrior in this man with the grim, tear-streaked face, the haunted, shadowed eyes.

Seeing Tanis's shocked look, Tika drew near Caramon and slipped her hand through his arm. At her touch, the warrior seemed to awaken from his dark thoughts. He smiled down at her. But there was something in Caramon's smile—a gentleness, a sorrow—that had never been there before.

Tanis sighed again. More problems. If the ancient gods had returned, what were they trying to do to them? See how heavy the burden could get before they collapsed beneath it? Did they find this amusing? Trapped beneath the sea . . . Why not just give up? Why not just stay down here? Why bother searching for a way out? Stay down here and forget everything. Forget the dragons . . . forget Raistlin . . . forget Laurana . . . Kitiara. . . .

"Tanis . . ." Goldmoon shook him gently.

They were all standing around him now. Waiting for him to tell them what to do.

Clearing his throat, he started to speak. His voice cracked and he coughed. "You needn't look at me!" he said finally, harshly. "I don't have any answers. We're trapped, apparently. There's no way out."

Still they watched him, with no dimming of the faith and trust in their eyes. Tanis glared at them angrily. "Quit looking at me to lead you! I *betrayed* you! Don't you realize that! It's my fault. Everything's my fault! Find someone else—"

Turning to hide tears he could not stop, Tanis stared out across the dark water, wrestling with himself to regain control. He did not realize, until she spoke, that Apoletta had been watching him.

"Perhaps I can help you, after all," the sea elf said slowly.

"Apoletta, what are you saying?" Zebulah said fearfully, hurrying to the edge of the water. "Consider—"

"I have considered," Apoletta replied. "The half-elf said we should be concerned about what happens in the world. He is right. The same thing could happen to us that happened to our Silvanesti cousins. They renounced the world and allowed dark and evil things to creep into their land. We have been warned in time. We can still fight the evil. Your coming here may have saved us, Half-Elf," she said earnestly. "We owe you something in return."

"Help us get back to our world," Tanis said.

Apoletta nodded gravely. "I will do so. Where would you go?"

Sighing, Tanis shook his head. He couldn't think. "I suppose one place is as good as another," he said wearily.

"Palanthas," Caramon said suddenly. His deep voice echoed across the still water.

The others glanced at him in uncomfortable silence. Riverwind frowned darkly.

"No," said Apoletta, swimming to the edge once more, "I cannot take you to Palanthas. Our borders extend only as far as Kalaman. Beyond that, we dare not venture. Especially if what you say is true, for beyond Kalaman lies the ancient home of the sea dragons."

Tanis wiped his eyes and nose, then turned back to face his friends. "Well? Any more suggestions?"

They were silent, watching him. Then Goldmoon stepped forward.

"Shall I tell you a story, Half-Elf?" she said, resting her gentle hand upon his arm. "A story of a woman and man, lost and alone and frightened. Bearing a great burden, they came to an inn. The woman sang a song, a blue crystal staff performed a miracle, a mob attacked them. One man stood up. One man took charge. One man—a stranger—said, 'We'll go out through the kitchen.' " She smiled. "Do you remember, Tanis?"

"I remember," he whispered, caught and held by her beautiful, sweet expression.

"We're waiting, Tanis," she said simply.

Tears dimmed his vision again. Tanis blinked rapidly, then glanced around. Riverwind's stern face was relaxed. Smiling a half-smile, he laid his hand on Tanis's arm. Caramon hesitated a moment, then—striding forward—embraced Tanis in one of his bearlike hugs.

"Take us to Kalaman," Tanis told Apoletta when he could breathe again. "It's where we were headed anyway."

The companions slept at the edge of the water, getting what rest they could before the journey, which Apoletta told them would be long and strenuous.

"How will we travel? By boat?" Tanis asked, watching as Zebulah stripped off his red robes and dove into the water.

Apoletta glanced at her husband, treading water easily beside her. "You will swim," she said. "Didn't you wonder how we brought you down here? Our magic arts, and those of my husband, will give you the ability to breathe water as easily as you now breathe air."

"You're going to turn us into fish?" Caramon asked, horrified.

"I suppose you could look at it that way," Apoletta replied. "We will come for you at the ebb tide."

Tika clasped Caramon's hand. He held onto her tightly, and Tanis, seeing them share a secret look between them, suddenly felt his burden lighten. Whatever turmoil surged in Caramon's soul, he had found a strong anchor to keep him from being swept out into dark waters.

"We'll never forget this beautiful place," Tika said softly.

Apoletta only smiled.

HOPE'S FLAME

225

DARK TIDINGS.

18

"Papa! Papa!"

"What is it, Little Rogar?" The fisherman, accustomed to the excited cries of his small son, who was just big enough to begin discovering the wonders of the world, did not raise his head from his work. Expecting to hear about anything from a starfish stranded on the bank to a lost shoe found stuck in the sand, the fisherman kept on restringing his net as the little boy dashed up to him.

"Papa," said the tow-haired child, eagerly grabbing his father's knee and getting himself entangled in the net in the process, "a pretty lady. Drown dead."

"Eh?" the fisherman asked absently.

"A pretty lady. Drown dead," the little boy said solemnly, pointing with a chubby finger behind him.

The fisherman stopped his work now to stare at his son. This was something new.

"A pretty lady? Drowned?"

The child nodded and pointed again, down the beach.

The fisherman squinted his eyes against the blazing noon sun and peered down the shoreline. Then he looked back at his son and his brows came together in a stern expression.

"Is this more of Little Rogar's stories?" he asked severely.

226

"Because if it is, you'll be taking yer dinner standing up."

The child shook his head, his eyes wide. "No," he said, rubbing his small bottom in memory. "I promised."

The fisherman frowned, looking out to sea. There'd been a storm last night, but he hadn't heard anything that sounded like a ship smashing up on the rocks. Perhaps some of the town's people with their fool pleasure boats had been out yesterday and been stranded after dark. Or worse, murder. This wouldn't be the first body washed up ashore with a knife in its heart.

Hailing his oldest son, who was sluicing out the bottom of the dingy, the fisherman put his work aside and stood up. He started to send the small boy in to his mother, then remembered he needed the child to guide them.

"Take us to the pretty lady," the fisherman said in a heavy voice, giving his other son a meaningful glance.

Tugging his father along eagerly, Little Rogar headed back down the beach while his parent and his older brother followed more slowly, fearing what they might find.

They had gone only a short distance before the fisherman saw a sight that caused him to break into a run, his older son pounding along behind.

"A shipwreck. No doubt!" the fisherman puffed. "Blasted landlubbers! Got no business going out in those eggshell boats."

There was not just one pretty lady lying on the beach, but two. Near them were four men. All were dressed in fine clothes. Broken timbers lay scattered around, obviously the remains of a small pleasure craft.

"Drown dead," said the little boy, bending to pat one of the pretty ladies.

"No, they're not!" grunted the fisherman, feeling for the life-beat in the woman's neck. One of the men was already beginning to stir—an older man, seemingly about fifty, he sat up and stared around in confusion. Seeing the fisherman, he started in terror and crawled over on his hands and knees to shake one of his unconscious companions.

"Tanis, Tanis!" the man cried, rousing a bearded man, who sat up suddenly.

"Don't be afraid," the fisherman said, seeing the bearded man's alarm. "We're going to help, if we can. Davey, run back and get yer ma. Tell her to bring blankets and that bottle of brandy I saved from Yuletide. Here, mistress," he said gently, helping one of the women to sit up. "Take it easy. You'll be all right. Strange sort of business," the fisherman muttered to himself, holding the woman in his arms and patting her soothingly. "For being near drowned, none of them seems to have swallowed any water. . . ."

Wrapped in blankets, the castaways were escorted back to the fisherman's small house near the beach. Here they were given doses of brandy and every other remedy the fisherman's wife could think of for drowning. Little Rogar regarded them all with pride, knowing that his "catch" would be the talk of the village for the next week.

"Thank you again for your help," Tanis said gratefully.

"Glad to be there," the man said gruffly. "Just be wary. Next time you go out in one of them small boats, head for shore the first sign of a storm."

"Er, yes, I'll—we'll do that," Tanis said in some confusion. "Now, if you could just tell us where we are. . . ."

"Yer north of the city," the fisherman said, waving a hand. "About two-three miles. Davey can give ye a lift in the cart."

"That's very kind of you," Tanis said, hesitating and glancing at the others. They returned his look, Caramon shrugging. "Uh, I know this sounds strange, but we—we were blown off course. What city are we north of?"

"Why, Kalaman, to be sure," the fisherman said, eyeing them suspiciously.

"Oh!" said Tanis. Laughing weakly, he turned to Caramon. "What did I tell you? We—uh—weren't blown as far off course as you thought."

"We weren't?" Caramon said, his eyes open wide. "Oh, we weren't," he amended hastily as Tika dug her elbow into his ribs. "Yeah, I guess I was wrong, as usual. You know me, Tanis, never could get my bearings—"

"Don't overdo it!" Riverwind muttered, and Caramon fell silent.

The fisherman gave them all a dark look. "Yer a strange bunch, no doubt," he said. "You can't remember how you came to smash up. Now you don't even know where you are. I reckon you was all drunk, but that's not my concern. If you'll take my advice, you'll none of you set foot in a boat again, drunk or sober. Davey, bring round the cart."

Giving them a final, disgusted glance, the fisherman lifted his small son on his shoulder and went back to work. His older son disappeared, presumably going to fetch the cart.

Tanis sighed, looking around at his friends.

"Do any of you know how we got here?" he asked quietly. "Or why we're dressed like this?"

One by one, they all shook their heads.

"I remember the Blood Sea and the maelstrom," Goldmoon said. "But then the rest seems like something I dreamed."

"I remember Raist . . ." Caramon said softly, his face grave. Then, feeling Tika's hand slip through his, he looked down at her. His expression softened. "And I remember—"

"Hush," Tika said, blushing, laying her cheek against his arm. Caramon kissed her red curls. "It wasn't a dream," she murmured.

"I remember a few things, too," Tanis said grimly, looking at Berem. "But it's disjointed, fragmented. None of it seems to go together right in my mind. Well, it's no good looking back. We've got to look forward. We'll go to Kalaman and find out what's been happening. I don't even know what day it is! Or month for that matter. Then—"

"Palanthas," Caramon said. "We'll go to Palanthas."

"We'll see," Tanis said, sighing. Davey was returning with the cart, drawn by a bony horse. The half-elf looked at Caramon. "Are you really certain you want to find that brother of yours?" he asked quietly.

Caramon did not answer.

The companions arrived in Kalaman about mid-morning.

"What's going on?" Tanis asked Davey as the young man drove the cart through the city streets. "Is there a festival?"

The streets were crowded with people. Most of the shops were closed and shuttered. Everyone stood around in small clumps, talking together in excited tones.

"It looks more like a funeral," Caramon said. "Someone important must have died."

"That, or war," Tanis muttered. Women were weeping, men looked sorrowful or angry, children stood about, staring fearfully at their parents.

"Can't be war, sir," Davey said, "and Spring Dawning festival was two days ago. Don't know what's the matter. Just a minute. I can find out if you want," he said, pulling the horse to a stop.

"Go ahead," Tanis said. "Just a minute, though. Why can't it be war?"

"Why, we've won the war!" Davey said, staring at Tanis in astonishment. "By the gods, sir, you musta been drunk if you don't remember. The Golden General and the good dragons—"

"Oh, yes," Tanis said hastily.

"I'll stop in here, at the fish market," Davey said, hopping down. "They'll know."

"We'll come with you." Tanis motioned the others.

"What's the news?" Davey called, running up to a knot of men and women standing before a shop redolent with the odor of fresh fish.

Several men turned immediately, all speaking at once. Coming up behind the boy, Tanis caught only parts of the excited conversation. "Golden General captured! . . . City doomed . . . people fleeing . . . evil dragons . . ."

Try as they might, the companions could make nothing out of this. The people seemed reluctant to talk around strangers—giving them dark, mistrustful glances, especially seeing their rich clothing.

The companions thanked Davey once more for the ride into town, then left him among his friends. After a brief discussion, they decided to head for the marketplace, hoping to find out more details of what had happened. The crowds grew denser as they walked until they practically had to fight their way through the packed streets. People ran here and there, asking for the latest rumors, shaking their heads in despair. Occasionally they saw some citizens, their belongings hastily packed in bundles, heading for the city gates.

"We should buy weapons," Caramon said grimly. "The news doesn't sound good. Who do you suppose this 'Golden General' is, anyway? The people seem to think a lot of him if his disappearance throws them into this much turmoil."

"Probably some Knight of Solamnia," Tanis said. "And you're right, we should buy weapons." He put his hand to his belt. "Damn! I had a purse of funny-looking old gold coins, but it's gone now! As if we didn't have enough trouble. . . ."

"Wait a minute!" Caramon grunted, feeling his belt. "Why! What the—My purse was here a second ago!" Whirling around, the big warrior caught a glimpse of small figure disappearing among the crush of people, a worn leather pouch in its hand. "Hey! You! That's mine!" Caramon roared. Scattering people like straws in the wind, he leaped after the small thief. Reaching out a huge hand, he caught hold of a fleecy vest and plucked the squirming figure up off the street. "Now give me back—" The big warrior gasped. "Tasslehoff!"

"Caramon!" Tasslehoff cried.

Caramon dropped him in astonishment. Tasslehoff stared around wildly.

"Tanis!" he shouted, seeing the half-elf coming through the crowd. "Oh, Tanis!" Running forward, Tas threw his arms around his friend. Burying his face in Tanis's belt, the kender burst into tears.

The people of Kalaman lined the walls of their city. Just a few days before they had done the same thing, only then their mood had been festive as they watched the triumphant procession of knights and silver and golden dragons. Now they were quiet, grim with despair. They looked out over the plain as the sun rose to its zenith in the sky. Nearly noon. They waited silently.

Tanis stood next to Flint, his hand on the dwarf's shoulder. The old dwarf had nearly broken down at the sight of his friend.

It was a sad reunion. In hushed and broken voices, Flint and Tasslehoff took turns telling their friends what had happened since they were parted in Tarsis months ago. One would talk until overcome, then the other would carry on the story. Thus the companions heard of the discovery of the dragonlances, the destruction of the dragon orb, and Sturm's death.

Tanis bowed his head, overwhelmed with sorrow at this news. For a moment, he couldn't imagine the world without this noble friend. Seeing Tanis's grief, Flint's gruff voice went on to tell of Sturm's great victory and the peace he had found in death.

"He is a hero in Solamnia now," Flint said. "Already they're telling stories of him, like they do of Huma. His great sacrifice saved the Knighthood, or so it is said. He would have asked for nothing more, Tanis."

The half-elf nodded wordlessly. Then, trying to smile, "Go on," he said. "Tell me what Laurana did when she arrived in Palanthas. And is she still there? If so, we were thinking about going—"

Flint and Tas exchanged glances. The dwarf's head bowed. The kender looked away, snuffling and wiping his small nose with a handkerchief.

"What is it?" Tanis asked in a voice he didn't recognize as his own. "Tell me."

Slowly, Flint related the story. "I'm sorry, Tanis," the dwarf said, wheezing. "I let her down—"

The old dwarf began to sob so pitifully that Tanis's heart ached with sorrow. Clasping his friend in his arms, he held him tightly.

"It wasn't your fault, Flint," he said, his voice harsh with tears. "It's mine, if anyone's. It was for me she risked death and worse."

"Start placing blame and you will end cursing the gods," said Riverwind, laying his hand on Tanis's shoulder. "Thus do my people say."

Tanis was not comforted.

"What time is the—the Dark Lady to come?"

"Noon," said Tas softly.

Now it was nearly noon and Tanis stood with the rest of the citizens of Kalaman, waiting for the arrival of the Dark Lady. Gilthanas stood some distance from Tanis, pointedly ignoring him. The half-elf couldn't blame him. Gilthanas knew why Laurana had left, he knew what bait Kitiara had used to snare his sister. When he asked Tanis coldly if it was true that he had been with the Dragon Highlord, Kitiara, Tanis could not deny it.

"Then I hold you responsible for whatever happens to Laurana," Gilthanas said, his voice shaking in rage. "And I will pray to the gods nightly that whatever cruel fate befalls her, you will meet the same thing—only a hundred times worse!"

"Don't you think I'd accept that if it would bring her back!" Tanis cried in anguish. But Gilthanas only turned away.

Now the people began to point and murmur. A dark shadow was visible in the sky—a blue dragon.

"That's her dragon," Tasslehoff said solemnly. "I saw it at the High Clerist's Tower."

The blue dragon circled lazily above the city in slow spirals, then landed leisurely within bow-shot of the city walls. A deathly hush fell upon the city as the dragon's rider stood up in the stirrups. Removing her helm, the Dark Lady began to speak, her voice ringing through the clear air.

"By now you have heard that I have captured the elfwoman you call the 'Golden General!'" Kitiara shouted. "In case you need proof, I have this to show you." She raised her hand. Tanis saw the flash of sunlight on a beautifully crafted silver helm. "In my other hand, though you cannot see it from where you stand, I have a lock of golden hair. I will leave both these here, on the plain, when I depart, that you may have something to remember your 'general' by."

There was a harsh murmur from the people lining the walls. Kitiara stopped speaking a moment, regarding them coldly. Watching her, Tanis dug his nails into his flesh to force himself to remain calm. He had caught himself contemplating a mad scheme to leap from the wall and attack her where she stood.

Goldmoon, seeing the wild, desperate look on his face, moved near and laid her hand on his arm. She felt his body shaking, then he stiffened at her touch, bringing himself under control. Looking down at his clenched hands, she was horrified to see blood trickling down his wrists.

"The elfmaid, Lauralanthalasa, has been taken to the Queen of Darkness at Neraka. She will remain as hostage with the Queen until the following conditions are met. First, the Queen

234

demands that a human called Berem, the Everman, be turned over to her immediately. Second, she demands that the good dragons return to Sanction, where they will give themselves up to Lord Ariakas. Finally, the elflord Gilthanas will call for the Knights of Solamnia and the elves of both the Qualinesti and Silvanesti tribes to lay down their arms. The dwarf, Flint Fireforge will require of his people that they do the same."

"This is madness!" Gilthanas called out in answer, stepping forward to the edge of the wall and staring down at the Dark Lady. "We cannot agree to these demands! We have no idea who this Berem is, or where to find him. I cannot answer for my people, nor can I answer for the good dragons. These demands are totally unreasonable!"

"The Queen is not unreasonable," Kitiara replied smoothly. "Her Dark Majesty has foreseen that these demands will need time to be acted upon. You have three weeks. If, within that time, you have not found the man Berem, whom we believe to be in the area around Flotsam, and if you have not sent away the good dragons, I will return and, this time, you will find more than a lock of your general's hair before the gates of Kalaman."

Kitiara paused.

"You will find her head."

With that, she tossed the helm down onto the ground at her dragon's feet, then, at a word, Skie lifted his wings and rose into the air.

For long moments, no one spoke or moved. The people stared down at the helm lying before the wall. The red ribbons fluttering bravely from the top of the silver helm seemed the only movement, the only color. Then someone cried out in terror, pointing.

Upon the horizon appeared an incredible sight. So awful was it that no one believed it at first, each thinking privately he must be going mad. But the object drifted closer and all were forced to admit its reality, though that did not diminish the horror.

Thus it was that the people of Krynn had their first glimpse of Lord Ariakas's most ingenious war machine, the flying citadels.

Working in the depths of the temples of Sanction, the black-robed magic-users and dark clerics ripped a castle from its foundations and set it in the skies. Now, floating upon dark gray storm clouds, lit by jagged barbs of white lightning, surrounded by a hundred flights of red and black dragons, the citadel loomed over Kalaman, blotting out the noon sun, casting its dreadful shadow over the city.

The people fled the walls in terror. Dragonfear worked its horrible spell, causing panic and despair to fall upon all who dwelt in Kalaman. But the citadel's dragons did not attack. Three weeks, their Dark Queen had ordered. They would give these wretched humans three weeks. And they would keep watch to see that, during this time, the Knights and the good dragons did not take the field.

Tanis turned to the rest of the companions who stood huddled upon the walls, staring bleakly at the citadel. Accustomed to the effects of dragonfear, they had been able to withstand it and were not fleeing in panic as were the rest of the citizens of Kalaman. Consequently they stood alone together upon the walls.

"Three weeks," Tanis said clearly, and his friends turned to him,

For the first time since they had left Flotsam, they saw that his face was free of its self-condemning madness. There was peace in his eyes, much as Flint had seen peace in Sturm's eyes after the knight's death.

"Three weeks," Tanis repeated in a calm voice that sent shivers up Flint's spine, "we have three weeks. That should be time enough. I'm going to Neraka, to the Dark Queen." His eyes went to Berem, who stood silently nearby. "You're coming with me."

Berem's eyes opened wide in stark terror. "No!" he whimpered, shrinking backward. Seeing the man about to run, Caramon's huge hand reached out and caught hold of him.

"You will go with me to Neraka," Tanis said in a soft voice, "or I will take you right now and give you to Gilthanas. The elflord loves his sister dearly. He would not hesitate to hand you over to the Queen of Darkness if he thought that would buy Laurana's freedom. You and I know differently. We know that giving you up wouldn't change matters a bit. But he doesn't. He is an elf, and he would believe she would keep her bargain."

Berem stared at Tanis warily. "You won't give me up?"

"I'm going to find out what's going on," Tanis stated coldly, avoiding the question. "At any rate, I'll need a guide, someone who knows the area. . . ."

Wrenching himself free of Caramon's grip, Berem regarded them with a hunted expression. "I'll go," he whimpered. "Don't give me to the elf . . ."

"All right," Tanis said coldly. "Quit sniveling. I'll be leaving before dark and I've got a lot to do—"

Turning abruptly, he was not surprised to feel a strong hand grip his arm. "I know what you're going to say, Caramon." Tanis did not turn around. "And the answer is no. Berem and I are going alone."

"Then you'll go to your deaths alone," Caramon said quietly, holding onto Tanis firmly.

"If so, then that's what I'll do!" Tanis tried without success to break free of the big man. "I'm not taking any of you with me."

"And you'll fail," Caramon said. "Is that what you want? Are you going just to find a way to die that will end your guilt? If so, I can offer you my sword right now. But if you truly want to free Laurana, then you're going to need help."

"The gods have reunited us," Goldmoon said gently. "They have brought us together again in our time of greatest need. It is a sign from the gods, Tanis. Don't deny it."

The half-elf bowed his head. He could not cry, there were no tears left. Tasslehoff's small hand slipped into his.

"Besides," said the kender cheerfully, "think how much trouble you'd get into without me!"

MARGARET WEIS & TRACY HICKMAN

A SINGLE CANDLE.

19

The city of Kalaman was deathly silent the night after the Dark Lady issued her ultimatum. Lord Calof declared a State of War, which meant all taverns were closed, the city gates were locked and barred, no one allowed to leave. The only people permitted to enter were families from the small farming and fishing villages near Kalaman. These refugees began arriving near sundown, telling fearful tales of draconians swarming over their land, looting and burning.

Although some of the noblemen of Kalaman had been opposed to such a drastic measure as a declared State of War, Tanis and Gilthanas—united for once—had forced the Lord to make this decision. Both of them painted vivid and horrifying pictures of the burning of the city of Tarsis. These proved extremely convincing. Lord Calof made his declaration, but then stared at the two men helplessly. It was obvious he had no idea what to do in regard to the defense of the city. The horrifying shadow of the floating citadel hovering above had completely unnerved the lord, and most of his military leaders were in little better shape. After listening to some of their wilder ideas, Tanis rose to his feet.

"I have a suggestion, my lord," he said respectfully. "You have a person here, well-qualified to take over the defense of this city—"

"You, Half-Elf?" interrupted Gilthanas with a bitter smile.

"No," said Tanis gently. "You, Gilthanas."

"An elf?" said Lord Calof in amazement.

"He was in Tarsis. He has had experience fighting the draconians and the dragons. The good dragons trust him and will follow his judgment."

"That's true!" Calof said. A look of vast relief crossed his face as he turned to Gilthanas. "We know how elves feel about humans, my lord, and—I must admit—most humans feel the same about elves. But we would be eternally grateful if you could help us in this time of peril."

Gilthanas stared at Tanis, puzzled for a moment. He could read nothing in the half-elf's bearded face. It was almost, he thought, the face of a dead man. Lord Calof repeated his question, adding something about "reward," apparently thinking Gilthanas's hesitation was due to a reluctance to accept the responsibility.

"No, my lord!" Gilthanas came out of his reverie with a start. "No reward is necessary or even wanted. If I can help save the people of this city, that will be reward enough. As for being of different races"—Gilthanas looked once more at Tanis—"perhaps I have learned enough to know that doesn't make any difference. It never did."

"Tell us what to do," Calof said eagerly.

"First, I would like a word with Tanis," Gilthanas said, seeing the half-elf preparing to depart.

"Certainly. There is a small room through the door to your right where you may talk in private." The Lord gestured.

Once inside the small, luxuriously appointed room, both men stood in uncomfortable silence for long moments, neither looking at the other directly. Gilthanas was the first to break the silence.

"I have always despised humans," the elflord said slowly, "and now I find myself preparing to take on the responsibility of protecting them." He smiled. "It is a good feeling," he added softly, looking directly at Tanis for the first time.

Tanis's eyes met Gilthanas's and his grim face relaxed for a moment, though he did not return the elflord's smile. Then his gaze fell, his grave expression returned.

"You're going to Neraka, aren't you?" Gilthanas said after another long pause.

Tanis nodded, wordlessly.

"Your friends? They're going with you?"

"Some of them," Tanis replied. "They all want to go, but—" He found he could not continue, remembering their devotion. He shook his head.

Gilthanas stared down at an ornately carved table, absently running his hand over the gleaming wood.

"I must leave," Tanis said heavily, starting for the door. "I have a lot yet to do. We plan to leave at midnight, after Solinari's set—"

"Wait." Gilthanas put his hand on the half-elf's arm. "I—I want to tell you I'm sorry . . . about what I said this morning. No, Tanis, don't leave. Hear me out. This isn't easy for me." Gilthanas paused a moment. "I've learned a great deal, Tanis—about myself. The lessons have been hard ones. I forgot them . . . when I heard about Laurana. I was angry and frightened and I wanted to hit someone. You were the closest target. What Laurana did, she did out of love for you. I'm learning about love, too, Tanis. Or I'm trying to learn." His voice was bitter. "Mostly I'm learning about pain. But that's my problem."

Tanis was watching him now. Gilthanas's hand was still on his shoulder.

"I know now, after I've had time to think," Gilthanas continued softly, "that what Laurana did was right. She *had* to go, or her love would have been meaningless. She had faith in you, believed in you enough to go to you when she heard you were dying, even though it meant going to that evil place—"

Tanis's head bowed. Gilthanas gripped him tightly, both hands on his shoulders.

"Theros Ironfeld said once that—in all the years he had lived—he had never seen anything done out of love come to evil. We have to believe that, Tanis. What Laurana did, she did out of love. What you do now, you do out of love. Surely the gods will bless that."

"Did they bless Sturm?" Tanis asked harshly. "He loved!"

"Didn't they? How do you know?"

Tanis's hand closed over Gilthanas's. He shook his head. He wanted to believe. It sounded wonderful, beautiful . . . just like tales of dragons. As a child, he'd wanted to believe in dragons, too. . . .

Sighing, he walked away from the elflord. His hand was on the doorknob when Gilthanas spoke again.

"Farewell . . . brother."

The companions met by the wall, at the secret door Tasslehoff had found that led up and over the walls, out into the plains beyond. Gilthanas could, of course, have given them permission to leave by the front gates, but the fewer people who knew of this dark journey the better as far as Tanis was concerned.

Now they were gathered inside the small room at the top of the stairs. Solinari was just sinking behind the distant mountains. Tanis, standing apart from the others, watched the moon as its last silvery rays touched the battlements of the horrible citadel hovering above them. He could see lights in the floating castle. Dark shapes moved around. Who lived in that dreadful thing? Draconians? The black-robed mages and dark clerics whose power had torn it from the soil and now kept it drifting among masses of thick gray clouds?

Behind him, he heard the others talking in soft voices—all

except for Berem. The Everman—watched over closely by Caramon—stood apart, his eyes wide and fearful.

For long moments Tanis watched them, then he sighed. He faced another parting, and this one grieved him so that he wondered if he had the strength to make it. Turning slightly, he saw the last beaming rays of Solinari's fading light touch Goldmoon's beautiful silver-gold hair. He saw her face, peaceful and serene, even though she contemplated a journey into darkness and danger. And he knew he had the strength.

With a sigh, he walked away from the window to rejoin his friends.

"Is it time?" Tasslehoff asked eagerly.

Tanis smiled, his hand reaching out fondly to stroke Tas's ridiculous topknot of hair. In a changing world, kenders remained constant.

"Yes," Tanis said, "it is time." His eyes went to Riverwind. "For *some* of us."

As the Plainsman met the half-elf's steady, unwavering gaze, the thoughts in his mind were reflected in his face, as clear to Tanis as clouds flitting across the night sky. First Riverwind was uncomprehending, perhaps he had not even heard Tanis's words. Then the Plainsman realized what had been said. Now he understood, and his stern, rigid face flushed, the brown eyes flared. Tanis said nothing. He simply shifted his gaze to Goldmoon.

Riverwind looked at his wife, who stood in a pool of silvery moonlight, waiting, her own thoughts far away. There was a sweet smile on her lips. A smile Tanis had seen only recently. Perhaps she was seeing her child playing in the sun.

Tanis looked back at Riverwind. He saw the Plainsman's inner struggle, and Tanis knew that the Que-shu warrior would offer, no, he would insist, on accompanying them, even though it meant leaving Goldmoon behind.

Walking to him, Tanis put his hands on the tall man's shoulders, looking into the Plainsman's dark eyes.

"Your work is done, my friend," Tanis said. "You have walked winter's path far enough. Here our roads separate. Ours leads into a bleak desert. Yours wends its way through green and blossoming trees. You have a responsibility to the son or daughter you are bringing into the world." He put his hand on Goldmoon's shoulder now, drawing her near, seeing her about to protest.

"The baby will be born in the autumn," Tanis said softly, "when the vallenwoods are red and golden. Don't cry, my dear." He gathered Goldmoon into his arms. "The vallenwoods will grow again. And you will take the young warrior or the young maiden into Solace, and you will tell them a story of two people who loved each other so much they brought hope into a world of dragons."

He kissed her beautiful hair. Then Tika, weeping softly, took his place, bidding Goldmoon farewell. Tanis turned to Riverwind. The Plainsman's stern mask was gone, his face showed plainly the marks of his grief. Tanis himself could barely see through his tears.

"Gilthanas will need help, planning the defense of the city." Tanis cleared his throat. "I wish to the gods this was truly the end of your dark winter, but I'm afraid it must last a little longer."

"The gods are with us, my friend, my brother," Riverwind said brokenly, embracing the half-elf. "May they be with you, as well. We will wait here for your return."

Solinari dipped behind the mountains. The only lights in the night sky were the cold and glittering stars and the hideous gleam of windows in the citadel, watching them with yellow eyes. One by one, the companions bid the Plainsmen good-bye. Then, following Tasslehoff, they silently crossed the wall, entered another door, and crept down another staircase. Tas shoved open the door at the bottom. Moving cautiously, hands on their weapons, the companions stepped out onto the plain.

For a moment, they stood huddled together, staring out across the plain where, even in the deep darkness, it seemed to them they would be visible to thousands of eyes watching from the citadel above.

Standing next to Berem, Tanis could feel the man shivering with fear and he felt glad he had assigned Caramon to watch him. Ever since Tanis had stated they were going to Neraka, the half-elf had seen a frantic, haunted look in the man's blue eyes, much like the look of a trapped animal. Tanis caught himself pitying the man, then hardened his heart. Too much was at stake. Berem was the key, the answer lay within him and within Neraka. Just how they were going to go about discovering the answer, Tanis hadn't decided yet, although the beginnings of a plan stirred in his brain.

Far away, the blaring noise of horns split the night air. An orange light flared on the horizon. Draconians, burning a village. Tanis gripped his cloak around him. Though Spring Dawning had come and past, the chill of winter was still in the air.

"Move out," he said softly.

One by one, he watched them run across the strip of open grassland, racing to reach the shelter of the grove of trees beyond. Here small, fast-flying brass dragons waited to carry them into the mountains.

This might all end tonight, Tanis though nervously, watching Tasslehoff scamper into the darkness like a mouse. If the dragons were discovered, if the watching eyes in the citadel saw them, it would be all over. Berem would fall into the hands of the Queen. Darkness would cover the land.

Tika followed Tas, running lightly and surely. Flint ran close behind, wheezing. The dwarf looked older. The thought that he was unwell crossed Tanis's mind, but he knew Flint would never agree to stay behind. Now Caramon ran through the darkness, his armor clanking. One hand was fixed firmly on Berem, tugging him along beside him.

My turn, Tanis realized, seeing the others safely sheltered within the grove. This is it. For good or for evil, the story is drawing near its end. Glancing up, he saw Goldmoon and Riverwind watching them from the small window in the tower room.

For good or for evil.

What if it does end in darkness, Tanis wondered for the first time. What will become of the world? What will become of those I'm leaving behind?

Steadily he looked up at these two people who were as dear to him as the family he'd never known. And, as he watched, he saw Goldmoon light a candle. For a brief instant the flame illuminated her face and Riverwind's. They raised their hands in parting, then extinguished the flame lest unfriendly eyes see it.

Taking a deep breath, Tanis turned and tensed himself to run.

The darkness might conquer, but it could never extinguish hope. And though one candle, or many, might flicker and die, new candles would be lit from the old.

Thus hope's flame always burns, lighting the darkness until the coming of day.

The story continues in

A DAWN OF DRAGONS

by Margaret Weis & Tracy Hickman

Available March 2004